RAW MATERIAL

RAW MATERIAL

JÖRG FAUSER

Translated from the German by
Jamie Bulloch

With an introduction by Niall Griffiths

THE CLERKENWELL PRESS

Published in Great Britain in 2014 by
CLERKENWELL PRESS
An imprint of Profile Books Ltd
Pine Street
Exmouth Market
London ECIR OJH
www.profilebooks.com

10 9 8 7 6 5 4 3 2 1

Typeset by MacGuru Ltd in Garamond
info@macguru.org.uk

Printed and bound in Great Britain by
CPI Group (UK) Ltd, Croydon, CRO 4YY

A CIP catalogue record for this book is available from the British Library.

ISBN 978 1 84668 973 4
eISBN 978 1 78283 028 3

 The translation of this work was supported by a grant from the
Goethe-Institut which is funded by the German Ministry of Foreign
Affairs.

For my parents

l Raw Material Raw Material Raw Material Raw l
terial Raw Material Raw Material Raw Material
l Raw Material Raw Material Raw Material Raw l
aterial Raw Material Raw Material Raw Material

Introduction

What do we know about Jorg Fauser? Outside Germany, not a great deal; Wikipedia has a small entry, and the website www.jorg-fauser.de offers some information: He was born in 1944 and became a drifter at a young age, a factotum in Britain, Ireland, Spain and Turkey, where he also became a junkie. He wrote poetry, novels, edited a small-press magazine, wrote a biography of Marlon Brando, kicked heroin and turned to booze. He wrote lyrics for, and performed in, various bands. His reputation as an important and respected figure in the German counter-culture survived even his commercial success as a detective novelist. His nomination for the Ingeborg Bachmann Prize aroused the ire of some leading literary notables, who publicly denounced him, not long before he was run over and killed by a truck in 1987 on the autobahn outside Munich at the age of forty-three (there is an online rumour that this was an assassination: Fauser was, at the time of his death, researching the links between the drug trade and high-ranking politicians). He is frequently mentioned in the same breath as the Beats and, especially compared to Charles Bukowski, who he travelled to LA to interview for *Playboy* in 1977 (at least, that's what the website says; I can find no other reference to this online, nor in any Bukowski biography).

Which brings us to the 'B' word. What is forgotten, or conveniently ignored, is that, when detached from his avowed project of warts-and-all running autobiography, much of Bukowski's work is mediocre. When he hits, he hits powerfully, but all too often he misses by a mile or more, and his work needs to be seen as inextricable from his lived life, the performance of it, the determination to eschew all bourgeois rules, be they social, political, literary or grammatical. Such a project, when done once, is done entirely, is exhausted; any imitation will, of necessity, not just be poor but otiose. The term 'Bukowskian' oftentimes simply equates to confessional boasting about drinking too much and tweaking tits and feeling a bit miserable while doing it (no foredoomed poet, either, destined to burn twice as bright but half as long – Bukowski was seventy-four when he died). Put simply, a comparison to Bukowski does not imply quality, or even readability; there are times, many of them, when his imitators become, unwittingly, his detractors.

So I would urge you to forget about such facile comparisons before you open *Raw Material*, because what you are about to read is, in many ways, like nothing else you will have read before. To foist a genre on it, it's a picaresque, but what a crazed, leaping, unmoored and hilarious voyage it is. It opens in the spring of 1968, a time of socio-political upheaval and an atmosphere drenched in revolutionary fervour, in Paris, Prague, Vietnam and Northern Ireland … . The Baader-Meinhof gang is active; the Red Army Faction, too. *Lady Chatterley's Lover* and *Last Exit to Brooklyn* are under scrutiny as is *Oz*. Our hero, Harry Gelb ('gelb'='yellow') is twenty-four and living on a rooftop in Istanbul with his partner in crime, Ede. Gelb is a struggling writer (struggling so hard that he's crashed through the garret roof and landed on the tiles) and a struggling junkie (is there any other kind?), a swindler, a rip-off merchant, a scammer, a thief. This is the sixties, yes, but there's no peace-and-love, release the doves, flower-power, incense-and-kaftan idealism here; Gelb is 'rapidly approaching the season of hell'. No sooner are we settled on that roof-top with Harry, though, than we're whisked away, scooting across Europe, to a commune in Berlin, to Frankfurt, Vienna, back to Berlin, squat to squat, dead-end job to dead-end job, all in the company of an intensely observant and cuttingly incisive commentator, achingly aware of the terribly transitory nature of existence, the flux and the chaos of it, a breathless whirl of drugs and drink and women and doomed enterprises. The one point of solidity in Gelb's life is his heavy old typewriter, and the masterpieces he will write on it, one of which, *Stamboul Blues*, accompanies him wherever he goes, hawking it to various hopeless publishers in superbly comedic set-pieces. He gets a job on the editorial board of *Zero* magazine, where staff members levitate to attract funding, and where a table-tennis table is an essential item of office furniture because ping-pong 'represented the defeat of capitalist heteronomy, social democratic lethargy and Russian hegemonic self-importance'. Gelb is sent to London to interview William S Burroughs, specifically about his cut-up technique, an encounter related in a perfect pen-portrait of the man: 'Burroughs was tall, gaunt and slightly stooped when he walked. He'd turned white at the temples and his mouth was a narrow, bloodless line ... Through his glasses he fixed me with his gaze. His eyes were blue and radiated the unshakeable authority of a high-court judge who's seen all manner of corruption, and even when every bribe is added together still doesn't amount to enough for him'. Burroughs witters on for a bit about cut-ups and about the apomorphine cure for heroin addiction, but that's about all we get of him; a couple of brilliantly withering sentences.

Characters appear without introduction in this book, and then vanish without fanfare or explanation. Trips are made on a whim and without any preliminary arrangements. The world just happens to Harry Gelb. Plot is a bourgeois construction, since to the materially disadvantaged, daily life is dramatic enough; there is ample conflict in renting a room from 'widowed house owners with dyed-blonde perms and eyes the colour of old family safes'. There is very little on the physiological effects of junk, and even less on the attendant bliss; the concern is more with the act of scoring and the acquisition of money and the neglect that goes with addiction. Alcohol, however, is given close study; booze puts the fun in oblivion. Junkies require nothing and talk about nothing but 'the Nirvana of the needle' but drink is an immersive, highly social drug that can often lead to new friendships and interesting sexual adventures. It also leads to weight-gain and bloat, which is not a good look for a revolutionary; love-handles signify a lack of commitment to the cause. And it is in a drinking den – the Schmale Handtuch – where Gelb unearths a sense of belonging, even meaning, where, on 'days when you simply had to drink whether you wanted to or not', he meets Ede again, who searches only for the next hit, and where he realises that the cards are stacked in this world, the game is rigged, and romantic revolutionary idealism is, really, nothing more than a passing phase: 'the lies of the revolutionaries sounded different from those of the reactionaries, but they were lies too. Revolutions were a hoax. One ruling class was replaced by another and the cultural apparatus spat out the pertinent editorials, the witty observations … If you saw through the lies, you could live in spite of them.'

Raw Material is a book of dashed dreams, then, at the last. More, it's a book about how the doomed nature of political idealism can undermine any calmness in settled compromise. The image of an accepted domesticity can be seen in the dazzle of wildness – the future faithful wife in the sexually experimental one-night-stand, for instance. Or the reward of a few convivial beers at the end of a working week foreshadowed in the chaotic marathon drinking sessions that begin and end at dawn. Both yearned for and reviled, is this idea of a comfortable life, and no happy ending can issue from this clash; it must end with a bad beating in an alleyway. At the urging of his friend Fritz, Gelb is enticed away from playing with cut-ups, which 'ignored the hurly-burly', and towards the more linear and inexorable horror of Lowry's *Under the Volcano*, wherein the protagonist's collapse is all the more terrifying for its traceability. But where Lowry's hero is chased out of the novel by a dead dog, Fauser's is introduced into something else by a solitary blade of grass; as we are told, immediately before the knuckles and the toe-caps and the blood, 'writing is different. You can't give it up like alcohol or the needle. The most that can happen is that writing gives *you* up. And it hasn't properly started with me yet.' This is the only safe anchorage in the mad world of this book, this crazed cut-up collage of wanderings and wishes and the inevitable destruction of dreams.

It's saddening to think on what the world has been deprived of by that truck on the autobahn outside Munich. But what you're now going to read – well, at least we have that. Gratitude and congratulations to the translator, Jamie Bulloch, and to Clerkenwell Press for giving us this. I'll be forever thankful.

Niall Griffiths, Cymru, August 2014

l Raw Material Raw Material Raw Material Raw l
terial Raw Material Raw Material Raw Material
l Raw Material Raw Material Raw Material Raw l
aterial Raw Material Raw Material Raw Materia

one

For most of my time in Istanbul I lived in the Cağaloğlu district, just up from the Blue Mosque. The hotel was an old, five-storey building in a side street. It stood next to a school, and in the mornings the pupils would file out into the playground and sing the 'İstiklâl marşı'. The Turkish national anthem goes on a bit and, like the song, Istanbul itself resembled a collage where the overlaps stray into infinity.

As they didn't rake in enough with their five storeys, the hotel owners had put another structure on the roof. The view was overwhelming, as were the heat in summer and cold in winter. But for around two marks a day we could enjoy the same panorama for which tourists would have to shell out twenty or fifty times as much. And we could get ours on credit.

With the arrival of winter, Ede and I moved into the same rooftop room. When the wind from Russia whistled through the cracks and the snow seeped through the unrendered roof, it was definitely more practical to share. One of us would pour spirit on the stone floor and light it, and, while the flames gave out a little heat, the other would try to find a vein. We took everything we could get our hands on. Mainly we'd cook up raw opium, Nembutal to make us comatose and all manner of amphetamines to get us up and running. When we were up and running we had to score fresh supplies of gear and get whatever else we needed – we lived predominantly off tea and sweets – and then we'd lie there, wrapped up snugly in our covers, playing with the cat and working. Ede painted and I wrote.

Ede was a powerful guy from Stuttgart, whose addiction was burning him out from the inside. His bone structure was still stable, but all tissue, fat and muscles were gradually being pared down to the bare minimum. I watched this process with fascination to begin with, but then couldn't be bothered any more. Addiction makes you retreat into yourself, and only when your metabolism sets off alarm bells do you become aware of your environment, which can easily set you into a panic. That's why you always need to have something to do besides drugs, so that the time in-between still exists when you need it (time: the thing we can never get enough of), and Ede found out that for him this meant painting. Most of the money we occasionally made went on canvases and paint. Ede had what you might call a fresh style; he plonked his colours at random on the canvas. Once he'd passed through this initial abstract phase he went over to painting figures and landscapes. They were probably rather naive canvases, but I liked them. The gloomier the winter, the more colourful Ede's pictures became. A psychiatrist would have had a field day with the two of us.

Like I said, I wrote. The Turks sold hard-wearing notebooks with oilcloth covers in all conceivable sizes, and I discovered the advantages of the Rapidograph pen – a fine stroke combined with the durability and class of real ink. What persuaded me to write from the outset was that it was a relatively cheap activity, compared to what Ede had to fork out for his materials. But I had to concede that he risked a lot for it. Maybe he was a born painter.

There was one district where virtually no foreigners dared go: Tophane. I expect there were just as many opiate addicts living there per square metre as in Harlem or Hong Kong. They said Tophane was a fairly dangerous place – and you did see the odd corpse lying on the street – but nothing bad ever happened to me apart from being fleeced when purchasing. If a large sum of money was involved and the customer who'd been ripped off came back, the place could be transformed within a few hours, as if the entire squalid area were a film set. Where a jammed teahouse had been, now the doors were barricaded up with dust on the windows; the cinema on the corner was showing a romance rather than the flick about the Huns; the hut where you'd been swindled was a carpenter's workshop; and where a corpse had lain beneath a bush on the corner, a mechanic was now tinkering with an old Ford taxi. Seemingly, the dealers you were looking for had vanished from the face of the earth. Were these actually the same houses? You'd rub your eyes, but that didn't help either. When hallucination becomes as everyday a phenomenon as a cigarette, the doors of perception, like perception itself, are crafted from a substance more deceptive than intoxication.

And when the boundaries of perception are blurred, other yardsticks lose their legitimacy too. Ede and I devised our own scam. It involved picking up one of the clueless young foreigners who were pouring into the city in ever greater numbers and who wanted to score a kilo of gear before boarding their Pan Am or Qantas flight, so they could play the experienced globetrotter and travelling sales rep for hashish back on their campuses in the Midwest or New South Wales. You ran into them everywhere in the Pudding Shop and teahouses around the Blue Mosque: blonde, sun-tanned, ever cheerful boys and girls on their Europe trip, sitting together in their hotel rooms playing guitar, singing protest songs and swearing they'd never go to Vietnam, to kill. They made Ede, myself and the few other long-term German residents on the Bosporus feel like ancient Asians, steeped in the ruthless philosophy of opium: if you have something, it will be taken from you. If you have nothing, you will die. And like all philosophers we thought it was only fair to pass on some of our knowledge to the commu-nity – before they listened to anybody else. Finding suitable victims was easy. When you live on the edge you develop an eye for travellers' luggage. So one of us would make a beeline for the boy or couple – of course, we only sought out those who were absolutely non-violent and looked a bit stoned – and bring them to the hotel. The room was decorated appropriately. The easel with a painting made an excellent impression, and from there people's gaze wandered instinctively to the corner with Ede's entire oeuvre. In the other corner my well-thumbed paperbacks caught the eye, as did my heap of carefully folded airmail editions of the London *Times*. When we started passing round a joint, the atmosphere was truly 'beat', and ever since Kerouac 'beat' had been the key to unlocking the souls of these young Americans.

Business was always speedily concluded. Beats are really cool people who have little time for everyday waffle. One of us would vanish with the dough – with *all* the dough, of course, because we were practically only helping out with these deals as a favour – and the other would hang around with the sucker up in our beatnik pad, with a view of the Blue Mosque and the sea, and roll joints. As it got dark the contours of the mosques faded away and the seagulls flew arabesques around the minarets. The music from the teahouses also helped. The conversation ebbed to a trickle. Peace.

'Shouldn't he be back soon, man?'

'What? Oh, yeah.'

'I mean, it's getting kinda late …'

'Sometimes they have to wait till it gets dark.'

'Oh.'

Then we'd give them a few pills, a little speed to pep them up, and soon they'd look agitated whenever the door to the roof extension creaked below. Their movements became rapid, they'd start talking, and the more they talked the more you had them under your control. You can't confide in a stranger how dreadful it was when your girlfriend ran off with a Hell's Angel that time, and then the next moment tell that stranger outright that he's a crook and a fraudster, part of a band of Turkish and German gangsters. Not if you're really cool. We did come across the other type too, but Ede easily dealt with those. He could appear pretty menacing if he rolled up his sleeves, showing off arms ravaged by addiction, and attacked his canvases with a razor blade. They'd all heard of Van Gogh. By the end they were clinging to every last hope, and because you were starting to get edgy as well, you'd take them to Tophane. One look at the desolate, barely lit square on the main street – the drunken gypsies, the mangy dogs, the beggars in rags, the babbling, toothless whores and the men in dark suits who suddenly appeared from the darkness and scrutinised them with cold eyes – and they were seized by fear and started to panic. But then you'd take them to one of the teahouses, where opium addicts wrapped in tatters waited salivating for their dealers, while huge cockroaches fell from the ceiling into their tea glasses – not that they actually fell, but the suckers *saw* them falling – and you chatted to the hunchback – 'You OK? Me OK too' – until the message was loud and clear: Run for your life!

By the time I got back to our room it would already be reeking of turpentine and oil paints and Ede would have managed to stain his bedclothes.

'So, how did it go?'

'How do you think it went?'

'Will we see the guy again?'

'You'd never recognise him.'

There was a lump of opium on the bedside table. All around us the whores were shrieking. I rarely felt like having sex. I lay down and opened up my notebook at the chapter I was writing. The Rapidograph was full of ink. A new swindle, a new picture, a new chapter. What was it that Faulkner said? 'I'd steal from my grandmother if it would help me write.' I didn't know precisely what he meant by that (you never knew precisely what these people meant by that), but one thing was sure: I was writing.

l Raw Material Raw Material Raw Material Raw l
terial Raw Material Raw Material Raw Material
l Raw Material Raw Material Raw Material Raw l
aterial Raw Material Raw Material Raw Material

two

It was drummed into me pretty early on that you have to make something of your life. On the other hand I suffered attacks of apathy as well as recurrent inflammations of the throat, which didn't stop when they removed my tonsils. Melancholic shivering fits which flared up time and again when I caught sight of the fires on the desolate fields in autumn after the potato harvest, the ravens hanging in the trees, the red hair of a girl who lived nearby. Nothing helped save to retreat to bed and read, or write myself. After two brief flirtations with politics and religion, it was clear to me at the age of eighteen that to be a writer was the only vocation in which I could live out my apathy and yet perhaps still make something of my life.

However, all the good books had already been written. They were in bookshops or on my shelves at home, and thus I couldn't help falling under the influence of hedonists such as Henry Miller or Kerouac – but I grew up in the Frankfurt 50 district. You could only write honestly about the things you had learned or experienced at first hand, and the technique only came when you'd had a serious enough crack at the writing. And so I was lying in our pad in Istanbul, filling up the Turkish oilcloth notebooks; for the first time I was having a serious crack at prose. I'd seen out my civilian service in a specialist clinic for lung and chest diseases, and now I was writing a novel about a young man doing his civilian service in a specialist clinic for lung and chest diseases. I found there was a lot I was able to pack in – the crazy Catholic nurses, the erotic adventures with the auxiliaries, the eccentric cancer patients, the stuffy bureaucrats, the morphine which was easy to get your hands on. I had difficulties writing about dying people, however, and then my sentences kept getting longer.

'This sentence never ends,' Ede said. I liked to read him passages that had turned out well. He had a Turkish girl in his bed, some tripped-out chick who hung about in the area around Sultan Ahmed and who was being sought by the police and her rich parents from Izmir. That was anything but cool in my eyes – I mean, we were working without a safety net – but Ede wasn't cool any more. His pictures were getting more and more colourful and he was talking about putting on an exhibition.

'It's down to the technique,' I said. 'It's a stream of consciousness à la Joyce. Ever read *Ulysses*?'

The Turkish girl groaned from somewhere beneath the covers. Our candles cast fantastical shadows. Ede lit another cigarette. 'I think it's got more to do with the Desoxyn,' he said. 'You know how speed works – you start a sentence, then you get carried away and ramble on and on.'

'Are you saying that Joyce took Desoxyn?'

'Maybe his brain would have worked like that even without Desoxyn.'

'Precisely because he'd worked out a particular technique.'

'Writers!' Ede said dismissively. 'With you lot everything

has to go via the brain.' He swore. The Turkish girl had bitten him. 'Painting, on the other hand – not even music is as direct.' He stubbed out his cigarette, grabbed the Turkish girl and pulled her on top of him. Finally she managed to undo his flies and it could begin. Poor Ede. She worked him with her teeth and claws. The bed shook mightily and our cat fled to me. Then the first cockerels crowed nearby and those over in Üsküdar responded. A pale strip of light appeared on the filthy windowpane. The Turkish girl was panting as if fighting for her life. Maybe she was. What was it, anyway, life? Maybe the cat knew, but she preferred to clean her ear. My God, Ede, come on. I skimmed the final sentence. It was still far too short. Everything had to be packed in, into a sentence just as into this room, where everything sat side by side, including death. Ah! Death. Death was missing from this sentence. On the way to the ward, where he was going to help himself again from the poison cabinet, the hero would have to be intercepted by the manic-depressive consultant who'd take him to the cold chamber where the corpses … that was it! All the story was lacking was a bit of vampirism. I started to write, but it was getting lighter now, and those two in the other bed were groaning and behaving as if they were ripping out each other's guts. How could I write like this? What would Joyce have done? I got up, took my coat from the hook and left.

I liked the city best early in the morning. It was good to be alive. The wind blowing in from the Horn cleared my head. I went to a milk bar, where porters and apprentices were having breakfast, ate a bowl of sweet noodles and drank hot, sweetened milk. At this time of day even the spies and informers were just simple men who'd survived another night. I wandered down to Sirkeçi station and waited for the newspaper kiosks to open. The train to Germany was already on the tracks. I had no desire to get on it. I bought a *Times*. Spring '68. It seemed as if something was brewing in Paris, Berlin and Prague. I sat down in the teahouse on the corner and read the paper. It looked interesting. The Yanks were taking a beating in Vietnam. Who knew what the Turks thought of that. We heard that American sailors had been stabbed to death in Tophane and elsewhere. Rumours. Hopefully the two of them would finish their sex session soon. I wanted to continue writing. I could hear ships' horns in the harbour. Then it struck me: If you do actually finish the thing, what are you going to do with it? Are you going to bundle up these oilcloth notebooks and send them to Germany? And to whom? Do you imagine some important publisher's going to read it and send you money? And then you'll pay off your debts at the hotel and perhaps move into the Pierre Loti and buy a kilo of opium and write another book? I looked at my hands. Old scars and new ones, and scabs. Opium and Nembutal destroyed your veins. I wasn't wearing any socks, my shoes had holes in the soles and were a size too small. My trousers, once green, were now colourless; the corduroy was fraying. You could buy new shirts for a few lira, but when you'd got used to one you were loath to be separated from it. Just as you were loath to be separated from Istanbul, from the hole you'd made cosy for yourself with the scars and the apathy and the Rapidographs and the view of the sea. I wanted to stay in this hole for as long as I could. Life was meaningless anyway.

three

Ede started selling. His pictures hung in the Pudding Shop and hippie hotels, in souvenir kiosks and kebab stalls. He made vague remarks about an exhibition at the Hilton. Odd characters appeared up on the roof – young Turks in three-piece suits with needles in the jacket pockets; a German with a red beard, who babbled something about commissions in Damascus and Amman; gruff street-fighters who showed us the wounds they'd picked up on the barricades of the Boul'Miche. We had a flourishing trade in art, a flourishing trade in passports and a flourishing circle of weirdos and informers. A real model even made a guest appearance with two hat boxes. My production came to a virtual halt.

'What you need, Harry,' Ede said, 'is a typewriter.'

'What I need,' I said, 'are some plastic veins.'

When Ede got something into his head he went through with it. Down in Galata we found a shop selling second-hand typewriters. The cheapest model with a German keyboard cost as much as we needed to live for two months. We thought a Turkish one would do. It was the first typewriter I bought with my own money. The money may not have been entirely clean, but then blood stuck to any needle, didn't it? The typewriter had a green metal casing. A solid object in a grey plastic box. A tool. When you looked at it you couldn't help spitting on your hands. Now we'd see whether I'd made any progress during those cold nights with flickering candles, the purring cat, the spirit on the floor and the Rapidographs which filled notebook after notebook.

But as soon as I started with the typewriter, problems arose that I hadn't encountered before. In the daytime our room saw an endless procession of characters coming and going, and at night I couldn't type properly – people wanted to go to sleep. My paper supply vanished rapidly, but for use in the loo rather than the typewriter. While Ede continued to assault his canvases at night – he'd put on a bit of weight and liked to paint women with enormous breasts – I sulked in a corner, leafing through my notebooks.

'You need to get yourself into a different rhythm,' Ede said. 'The best thing would be to rent another room and set up some sort of office. And then you could keep fixed hours. Who writes by hand any more, for God's sake? People must think you're keeping a diary.'

I tossed the notebooks onto my other possessions. 'Why don't we go back, Ede? Revolution's breaking out across Europe and we're up here on this roof masquerading as artists.'

'Believe me, I know those types who are playing at revolution. They're the windbags from Club Voltaire. My paintings will be hanging in the Museum of Modern Art before they manage a revolution in Stuttgart.'

'Listen, Ede, back in Germany I was a correspondent for *Freedom*. Kropotkin founded that when he was in exile in

London. Surely you're not trying to tell me I don't know a revolutionary situation when I see one?'

'But there's nothing in the news about anarchy in Britain, Harry.'

'They need a while longer. And besides, we'd get heroin on our health insurance.'

'Don't let yourself be bullied now,' Ede said. 'When I first worked with a real canvas I wanted to ditch it all too. It passes. You've just got to get used to the typewriter.'

'Should I sleep with it, or what?'

'Why don't you start by writing letters? Being a writer is still a profession amongst the Turks. I don't mean being an author, but a writer. You'd be best off starting as a writer. There are hundreds of foreigners living here; just think of the opportunities that offers. Who else has got a type-writer? And if you're a good writer, you'll also become a good author.'

'Che Guevara is dead and you're spouting all that crap at me!'

'Don't imagine for a moment that Che would have told you any different. Pass me the tube of Prussian blue, would you?'

The following day I sat at that bloody machine and tried with one finger to type out the first few pages from my first notebook. It turned out that I'd written the long sentences fairly early on. And as you have to write such long sentences very rapidly to avoid losing the thread, it took me a while to decipher them, and even longer to get to the bottom of their meaning. Most of it was shit. I was on the verge of tears. Someone cleared their throat. It was Mahmud, the hotel porter, a man of around thirty who was treated little better than a dog, and so had started to behave like one. Now he was looking wide-eyed. He stretched out a hand and touched the typewriter with reverence, making a series of clicking noises as he stared in awe. I drank the tea he'd brought me. He laughed, vanished, and returned with the boss. The boss was a rotund figure with light skin, calculating eyes and a friendly looking chin that couldn't negate the eyes. He examined the typewriter, passed a knowing comment, and that afternoon I was in business. I wrote their letters. I wrote for my rent.

1 Raw Material Raw Material Raw Material Raw 1
terial Raw Material Raw Material Raw Material
1 Raw Material Raw Material Raw Material Raw 1
aterial Raw Material Raw Material Raw Material

four

In summer the French and Austrians poured into Istanbul. Hordes of hippies from Vienna and Paris, the Tyrol and Brittany, transforming the intimate atmosphere which had prevailed till then into a supposedly libertarian free-for-all. They did it in public in the parks, they started begging, they stole and cheated without any finesse, they spouted non-sense and very quickly dragged down general conversation to a miserable level. And for each one who disappeared off to the East, another two would turn up the next day.

There were serious waves of arrests. Sentences became harsher. Twenty years for a kilo, three years for ten grams, an American shot dead for pulling out a gun while being arrested. The first Vietnam veterans appeared. Black Congolese dopeheads from Katanga. The season of love and peace was long gone. We were rapidly approaching the season of hell.

The Pudding Shop wasn't selling paintings any more and I'd stopped writing for good. No long sentences and no letters for the boss. A sweltering summer descended on the city. Demonstrations in the university district. Road blocks. Night-time curfews. In the teahouses they read aloud articles about hippies and stared at us. I was no hippie, I had no trouble with the police, but nor was I a writer any more and certainly not an author. On the day I pawned my typewriter, the boss presented us with an astronomical bill. His tone was unmistakably clear: if you don't pay soon you'll be out on your ear. But by now the roof was far more than just accommodation. Up there was our home. The roof was our sanctuary. Anywhere else and we'd have been gone in a day. It was clear what was needed: a sting.

We kept our hands off the Americans. I mean, we didn't fancy one of them suddenly pulling a Colt on us. There was no one else save a countryman of ours who we'd known for a while now. A risky undertaking, but you couldn't afford to have feelings in this business, and it was getting too late for misgivings. We could only leave and enter the hotel when the boss wasn't around. He assumed that we didn't have any papers, but we still had our identity cards; we always kept them on us. We set up the sham deal, but on the day we were going to pull it off Ede took an excessive dose of Desoxyn and was hit by an attack of total paranoia, so he was out of it. It all went belly up. The guy was on my tail for hours. He got wind of what we were up to and didn't want to part with his money. An electrical tension seemed to hang over the entire city, like a long-overdue storm. Instead of the two or three thousand Turkish lira I'd expected, I only had a thousand when I finally got on the ferry to Karaköy. Still no storm. I imagined I was surrounded by police. I walked through Karaköy and toyed with the idea of taking a hotel room for the night. If the lightning was going to strike anywhere, it would be over there in Istanbul, over Sultan Ahmed and Cağaloğlu. But I urgently needed a fix. I wouldn't get anything in Karaköy. I was shaking with exhaustion and humiliation. All this craziness for four hundred marks, instead of working on the revolution or a novel. I hadn't held a girl in my arms for a year. What I needed were my notebooks – twelve months of work – then I'd flee. I'd had enough of Istanbul. But where would I flee to? West or East? I made my way back to the ferry. How peaceful the men over in the teahouse were. How pleasant the serenity of the Orient. A beautiful spot. It was good that I couldn't stay. Good that I'd never come back.

l Raw Material Raw Material Raw Material Raw l
terial Raw Material Raw Material Raw Material
l Raw Material Raw Material Raw Material Raw l
aterial Raw Material Raw Material Raw Material

five

The police prison was close to the station, not far from Cağaloğlu. An entrance hall with offices and small cells, a gallery with further offices and cells, and a holding cell the size of a gymnasium which stank like a mass grave. I had to surrender my glasses, identity card and belt. The folded banknotes were in a small side pocket of the swimming trunks I was wearing instead of pants. The French, of course, made a huge racket, especially the girls: '*Salauds! Fascistes!*' The most frenzied amongst them earned a truncheon blow and were dragged off to isolated cells. The rest of us were led into the big cage.

I discovered that the round-ups had started at lunchtime. They'd caught me on our roof just as I was about to shoot up. Ede was there too, but he must have managed to slip away. Or had he made some private deal? Of the one hundred and fifty or so people in the cage I only knew a few old timers. You could recognise them by their short hair, wan complexions and the fact that, rather than complaining and protesting, they immediately started eking out tiny advantages for themselves – from the newspaper to sit on to the capsule of Nembutal to ward off the cold turkey. But after a few hours on the chilly floor we were all in withdrawal – on that horror trip the opium poppy furies punish their impotent lovers with.

I sat on my newspaper with my knees tucked up, as far from the others as possible, my arms around my legs, staring myopically at a night-time landscape inhabited by figures from the nightmares of Hieronymus Bosch. It was as if all the drugs and poisons I'd been pumping into myself for years were attempting to discharge themselves from my metabolism at once, and thus fighting ferociously over every pore. And when they'd left my useless body, like vampires they entered the metabolisms of those junkies they could still dine on. It wasn't a pretty picture, but what made me really worried was the thought of my notebooks.

You've got to get your notebooks, I told myself, the moment my fever allowed me to piece together a clear thought. With your notebooks you can prove to the court that for you drugs were an assignment. An assignment and a crucial experience. Think of all those writers who've praised the virtues of opium! Do you really imagine that Pierre Loti never smoked opium? There's even a street named after him in Istanbul! What's more, it's perfectly clear from these note-books that my novel is anything but an apologia for opium. On the contrary. It's a strong warning! A report from the abyss! Your Honour! Turkey of all places, as an opium-pro-ducing country, should not impede my mission as a writer, let alone punish it, but encourage my every effort! I'm thinking of publishing privately, sponsored by the Ministry for Tourism! Give me back my rooftop sanctuary, provide me with a typewriter with a German keyboard, and I will show you the forces that are unleashed in a young writer if he's only given the chance! German–Turkish cultural cooperation! Tophane working group!

All of a sudden I realised that nothing was going to happen to me here. I was even able to get up and move around. I saw what a bad state the others were in. Some seemed to be on the verge of dying. A French guy, whose arms consisted of nothing but open, festering wounds, appeared to be attempting suicide by banging his head repeatedly against the wall. His friends were trying to stop him, but he whined so horrifically that they gave up. Finally, the Turks fetched the guards and he was hauled off. Others tried to divert themselves through sex. That didn't look any better. In between this lot were the silently suffering old timers, who dealt with the Turks and guards in whispers. From time to time the French girls in the gallery cells would start screeching their obscene slogans. Then the pigs would grab their truncheons and give them a good thrashing. And interrogations took place the whole time. A few smart detectives in well-fitting suits would unlock the cells, pick out and handcuff the ones they wanted and lead them away. None of them came back. The pigs seemed to have a list. It was the longest night of my life, but I never had the feeling that I was on that list. I did, however, make the discovery that on nights like this it's well worth occupying your mind with myths.

After all, I was the only one of these ragged, corroded, slobbering figures who was on the way to becoming a writer. And what could be better for a writer than to sit in all this filth and practise survival? Writers belonged in places like this. It was places like this where myths were born, evolved and triumphed. I thought of Gorky, Algren, Fallada. The time I'd spent with their books was now paying off. Other people had muscles, dough or nice arses to help them get by in hell. Writers had their myths. Or so I thought.

The following lunchtime they took us out and bundled us into two buses. This led to feverish speculation.

'They're dropping all of us off at our hotels!'

'They're deporting us to the islands!'

'You watch. They're going to take us out of the city and shoot us!'

One of the old timers had managed to get hold of a small bottle of opium tincture, and I bought some of it off him. We had a little water and enough cigarettes, and I enjoyed the lengthy bus ride to the border. After the long, hot summer the landscape was burned out. Veils of dust drifted over dried-up river beds. Yellow pyramids of pumpkins beside petrol stations and teahouses. The occasional glimpse of the sea, shimmering like a Fata Morgana. The overcrowded buses stopping in tiny, squat villages, the children selling sweet ring-shaped pastries and lemonade, the peasants with their flat caps and knotted handkerchiefs, the women kneeling in the fields, stray dogs, the odd bird of prey circling above a minaret. I knew I'd soon be writing about all this.

They locked us in the station at Edirne and left it to the border guards to decide what to do with us. The collage disintegrated. There were guys lying on the ground, wanking. Others were trying to shoot up their own saliva. A few hip Canadians had got people at the consulate to bring their luggage to the jail, and were now handing out blocks of hash to the station manager, the border police and the customs officials. I think they still had enough left over. The only language they understood here was money. They packed us onto a train that was meant to take us to Bulgaria, but the train was stopped at the Bulgarian border and sent back. After the opium was finished I bought a bottle of cheap brandy, and at some point the following morning reached Salonika. I still had my identity card, around five hundred Turkish lira, my glasses and the rags on my body, but my novel was gone. Promising myself that I would write the next one to the end, I set off back for Germany. When, a week later, I rang the bell at my parents' house, my mother opened the door. I saw the look of horror on her face. I weighed forty-five kilos.

1 Raw Material Raw Material Raw Material Raw 1
terial Raw Material Raw Material Raw Material
1 Raw Material Raw Material Raw Material Raw 1
aterial Raw Material Raw Material Raw Materia

six

We arrived at Berlin Tempelhof at eight o'clock in the morning. It was the beginning of December and the sky was a lead plate from which icicles hung. Caspar said it wasn't far. He was a blond Adonis with a slyly cold laugh which was made for winter. He was twenty-three and claimed to be an anarchist. We took the metro to Schöneberg. Caspar was travelling without luggage. I was wearing a heavy winter coat and had a suitcase jam-packed with books, sweaters, socks, pants, notebooks, pamphlets, scarves, woollen gloves, records, medicines stolen from hospital supplies and manuscripts. We were entering the Berlin underground – he to make revolution and I to gather material for my new novel. Of course, I took care not to mention this. I was an anarchist too.

The commune was not far from the metro, which at this point was an elevated railway. A bleary-eyed young woman opened the door. We were expected and she let us in. I found it barely warmer than outside, where dead pigeons were lying on heaps of snow. The members of the commune were camped under blankets, coats and pillows on a sea of mattresses. Despite the stove it was about as cosy as a family crypt. Some of the communards gradually emerged from their covers and cast me strange looks. They took me for a spy right away. I soon got used to these looks. Berlin was full of black looks and the city had never been short of spies.

'We've just come to the decision that we're all sleeping together,' explained Sonja, who'd let us in. She seemed to be the oldest one there and something like the leader of the commune. She was also the prettiest. 'Otherwise we'll never be rid of this bourgeois crap,' she added. Her smile could mean many different things.

Caspar just nodded and buried himself in a map of the city. He played the tough actionist, interested solely in facts. 'We only need accommodation here temporarily,' he explained. 'A base.' He looked around meaningfully.

'We'll have to discuss that first,' a communard piped up.

'We won't get anywhere by discussing,' Caspar said.

'But you can't just turn up here and use us as you see fit,' the communard retorted. 'When we take action, we do it together. We've done away with all of that individualistic shit here.'

Now look what you've got yourself into, I thought. Maybe going in the other direction would have been a better bet, back at the border. It wouldn't have been much warmer up on the roof at this time of year, but by God at least you had your peace and quiet – Ede at the easel, the purring cat, the national anthem in the playground, and the persistent scratching of the Rapidograph. I banished such thoughts. I knew that nothing ever comes round again. I said I was willing to fetch breakfast. I still had two hundred marks on me. I may have been a spy, but that day I was a Croesus too.

Breakfast was the main meal of the day. It consisted of tea, coffee, cocoa, fruit yoghurt, rolls, margarine, charcuterie, curd cheese, sliced cheese, perhaps some fish or cold meats, cucumbers, fruit, chocolate and, if there were any, some joints. Otherwise we smoked Schwarzer Krauser tobacco, rolled in Abadie papers. The newspapers were important too. The tabloids were the preferred reading, and there was the occasional *Frankfurter Rundschau* when more sophisticated journalism was called for. Although most people in the commune were students or ex-students, the level of political discussion barely rose above that of vaguely left-wing pub talk. Revolution appeared to be something that first you had to undertake in yourself, for yourself, around yourself, in sexual matters especially, but also mentally, and all the time, even when washing up or taking a crap. After a while I wondered whether I hadn't left more behind in Turkey than just my notebooks. Then they started talking about drugs and I knew that I had the key to their minds. The talk was all of a new consciousness. All I had to do was turn the key.

l Raw Material Raw Material Raw Material Raw l
terial Raw Material Raw Material Raw Material
l Raw Material Ra——————Raw Material Raw l
aterial Raw Material Raw Material Raw Materia

seven

The tables had been lined up lengthways and piled high with printed sheets of paper. These were photocopies of pages 118 to 148 of Wilhelm Reich's *The Function of the Orgasm*. We were making a pirate edition. Now the sheets of paper had to be collated. To do this we had to walk around the tables in single file, grab the pages one by one, and put our pile onto a separate table. Sweeping the shop floor of a factory would have seemed like an artistic undertaking by comparison. Putting together copies of *The Function of the Orgasm* reminded me of the punishments we were handed out at school: Write out one hundred times: *I will never do that again.*

'I think we'd be better off discussing why I *don't* orgasm,' Hilde said. She was a young chick from the Hanover area and had studied education for a semester before moving into the commune with her boyfriend. 'I haven't had one since we've all started sleeping together.'

'We have to see this through,' Baby said. Baby pretended to be gay, but he was sleeping with Sonja. He looked like a girl, but he was the only man in the commune before Caspar and I turned up. 'If we don't sell at least a hundred copies tomorrow, our electricity will be cut off. Come on, Hilde, get going!'

The gas had already been cut off.

'And I thought communes had abolished stress,' Hilde said. 'Sometimes I even feel stressed making breakfast. Who fancies coming to Go?'

We all went. Mister Go had rock music and a light show. The most popular images were snapshots from the Vietnam War. The walls flickered with GIs launching attacks and dying, monks on fire, Vietcong being executed. To a soundtrack with music that was new to me: The Doors, Jefferson Airplane, Cream, Jimi Hendrix. Dealers with flowing hair and Mao badges on their Indian shirts; wrestling types with earrings and musk aftershave; ethereal graces from Siemensstadt or Neheim-Hüsten who wanted to swap their hairdressing apprenticeship for free love or a speed bomb, but instead woke up in a basement flat in Kreuzberg with a rusty needle sticking out of their arm; future political commissars with white nylon shirts and the collected works of Enver Hoxha committed to memory as well as complete lists of people to be lined up and shot; and street kids in search of their first rush – all of these huddled under the light show with its reminders of the Asian revolution, and The Doors trying to give the child a name: 'Father, I want to kill you.' When you left the building, there were the police cars on the corner, their flashing blue lights like a scornful commentary on the exploding collages in your head.

'What do you want to do, Sonja?'

'What do you mean?'

Four in the morning. Snowflakes were melting on the neon lights in Potsdamer Strasse. The favourite song of the silent majority droned out of some beer hall: Heintje's 'Mama'.

'I mean, what do you want to do later?'

'There is no "later" any more.'

'As simple as that?'

'"Later" has been abolished. There is only now.'

'What about in ten years' time?'

'In ten years' time it'll still be now.'

'Are you saying time stands still?'

'Harry, you really turn me off.'

I sat down in the room with the bay window, from where I could see the elevated railway, watching the red lights of a train vanish beneath Nollendorfplatz or emerge from under it. I swallowed a few tablets of Rosimon-Neu and got down to my poetry. I was writing poems again, but no longer the lyrical stuff from my schooldays. They contained occasional references to Istanbul and to the long lines of prose from my lost oilcloth notebooks. Every night I wrote four or five poems and then read them to Manni, a young guy who had run away from something in Brunswick. He had long hair, tight jeans, suede boots, sunglasses and was never without some gear. He flitted around the commune like a moth around a light. We smoked, he put on records, I wrote. Then I read my poems out to him.

'Yeah, man, yeah.'

Ede had been a harsher critic. But maybe I'd got better too. There. Another train. The red lights ran off into the darkness.

'Manni, how do you see things?'

'What things, man?'

'I mean, what do you want to do?'

'Oh, that. Hey, something will come up.'

'So you've no plans, then?'

'Well, I'd love to move in here. I think there's room for expansion in this place.'

'So you fancy selling *The Function of the Orgasm*?'

'Well, you've got to have dough, man. Sure, they'll get rid of it in the future, but for the time being you've got to have some. But selling books isn't really my bag, you know? I'm more the practical type.'

'So, what do you have in mind?'

'Well, I see opportunities in junk. Junk is red hot at the moment, man. And then there's acid. The first time they were all on a trip. Wow! You won't need all that politics any more.'

'Are you sure?'

'Listen, man, this is how I see it: acid's gonna change the world more than Mao Tse-tung.'

'But how do you see your own future, Manni? What's going to become of you?'

'My motto is: "Be cool". I'm sure there'll be something to do here, I've already checked it out with Sonja. And if not, I've got this compadre in Brunswick. We want to go to India sometime. I think that's where you get a real perspective.'

'In India?'

'Yeah, you know, Buddha and stuff. Hey, man, what do you think of my boots? I could get you a pair if you want. Cool, aren't they?'

Manni put on a record. Vanilla Fudge. My fingers were stiff with cold. And the red lights ran off into the daylight.

eight

Commune One thought New Year's Eve was the right time to go on a trip, and we were in on it too. It was only five days later, when still no one had got any sleep, that we realised it hadn't been acid, but STP, a drug straight from the Devil's own laboratory. It combined the hallucinogenic effects of LSD with the violent stimulation of the amphetamine. Maybe the perfect means of opening up new possibilities at a flagging nudist party in Hollywood, but a pretty risky way to be ordained into the acid age, bang in the middle of this front-line city as it celebrated the New Year. And long after the used firecrackers and rockets had been cleared up, explosives were still going off in the communes, tearing holes in the brains of those living there.

Naked people on the steps. Five days spent listening to the Beatles' *White Album* and then finding out as clear as day that Revolution No. 9 meant exactly that: Revolution No. 9 – 1789, 1830, 1848, 1871, 1917, 1918/19, 1949, 1959, 1969: the blind will see and the mute will sing. 'While My Guitar Gently Weeps'. Never sleep again. Twenty-two years spent looking for the 'you', only to discover definitively that there is only an 'I', and it wears dirty underpants, green socks with holes in them, has yellow stained teeth and a red hole in the middle of its forehead. Yes, I have to separate from my 'I'. Separations, stormy reunions in institutions and at sausage stalls. A heap of records were broken, a heap of books torn up, televisions demolished, windows broken, lips bitten, Mao bibles set on fire, cocks brought forth, appointments cancelled, tears shed and backs turned, looks analysed, tights not found, words forgotten, language renounced, cocks not chopped off after all, keys lost, pillows clutched, flats found again. 'I' and 'you' found again, crusts of bread celebrated, poems written. The poems were from me, but as nobody could listen and it appeared as if nobody would be able to listen in the future either, I threw them all away. I guess poems weren't my cup of tea after all.

An American girl had turned up in a dirty sari, nine months pregnant. Someone on Formentera had given her this address. Go to Berlin, it's groovy. Revolution, you know. She'd been dropping acid for a year and now she had it in her head that she wanted to give birth to her child in a commune. On a trip, naturally. She still had a whole strip of blotting paper. Caspar and I bundled her into a clinic in Mariendorf and now she was there, between the wives of postal workers and ticket collectors from the Berlin public transport company, babbling mantras and demanding her blotting paper. We sent a telegram to her father in Chicago, and a few days later we were sitting with him in an expensive Chinese restaurant on the Kurfürstendamm. He was a short, polite man, grey at the temples, wearing a flannel suit and a melancholy smile, desperate to understand why his daughter was drifting around the world in a sari, and

why we wanted to blow this world to bits. The communards thought his melancholy was bourgeois, one of those
lousy capitalist tricks, and as they proceeded to embarrass
our host and the Chinese waiters with their Berlin anarchist
posturing, it became clear to me that I still didn't know
where I belonged. I had the suspicion, in fact, that I didn't
belong anywhere at all. Perhaps my ridiculous literary ambition was just as bourgeois as the Chicago businessman's suit.
On the other hand, I could hardly imagine that I would cut
a good figure if I'd been in his shoes. And the literary world?
It was as far away for me as the moon.

The American girl gave birth to a baby girl and drifted
on. The electricity company threatened to cut us off again.
Winter seemed as if it would never end. Caspar made
contact with Iranian bomb-makers. I hung around with
passport forgers. All of a sudden there were drugs everywhere. Things fell apart.

l Raw Material Raw Material Raw Material Raw l
terial Raw Material Raw Material Raw Material
l Raw Material Raw   Raw Material Raw l
aterial Raw Material Raw Material Raw Materia

nine

The flat was in a grisly state. The heap of rubbish in the kitchen made it unusable. Lumps of frozen spaghetti, piles of filthy plates. Musical instruments that nobody played any more littered all over the place. Suitcases in which abolished private property was hibernating. Record sleeves used for scribbling lists on. *8 p.m. Audimax! Everyone!* or *Gerhard: laundry*. But no one was washing anything any more, and amongst the general assembly of students we looked like tramps at an SPD party conference. And everywhere *The Function of the Orgasm*, in every nook and cranny leftover copies of Wilhelm Reich, the long-abandoned attempt to participate in production and barter.

I wanted to give up writing for good. It seemed not only unimportant, but also a pretentious attempt to put a buffer between me and things as they stared me in the eyes on a daily basis, a black market of feelings, values, demands. Set against the authenticity of the frozen spaghetti and the mountains of books, each sentence pretending it had something to say could only come across as obscene and ridiculous. And yet I still wanted to make something of my life.

Having spent time poring over an atlas I'd got hold of, now I'd found what I was looking for. 'Got it!' I said, marking a spot in the Indian Ocean. 'And it's not so hard to get there.'

'Get where?' said Sonja.

'To the Seychelles, see?'

I had an ally, Jan, a nineteen-year-old big baby from Friesland, who was in Berlin hiding from military service. A working-class child who'd already been to sea, he survived without difficulty amongst the students and pseudo-intellectuals. For Jan the Seychelles were exactly the right place. We worked out various routes to get there – via Africa, via India – the two of us acted as if we were old hands in the tropics, as if we knew where you ate coconuts and yams, and in which ports you could sign up as a seaman on board a ship. Listening to us, you'd think the Seychelles were the last paradise on earth and the only place where a commune from West Berlin could survive the apocalypse and achieve the highest degree of human consciousness. On an icy-cold Sunday in February, with four marks ninety-five in the communal kitty and the termination notice for the flat on the table, where no hearty breakfast had been enjoyed in a long time, nor any copies of *The Function of the Orgasm* collated, while a Siberian storm raged over Schöneberg, our tales of a life of freedom on white beaches, of adventures with sharks and gargantuan supplies of hash from Mombasa and Madras, made quite an impression, even on a sceptical big-mouth such as Sonja.

'Great revolutionaries you are, all the same!'

'We can make revolution in the Seychelles.'

'You're talking through your arse.'

'One thing's for sure: rather the Seychelles than here.'

Even Caspar, who was frustrated because he still hadn't managed to blow up Schöneberg town hall, or at least the Gedächtniskirche, gave the Seychelles the revolutionary stamp of approval. As we had learned from our time at school, university and with the German Socialist Student Union, we procured literature the following day from the Institute of Oriental Studies. The snow was so deep that even the buses could barely move. From the books we learned that the Seychelles were British and essentially just waiting for us to liberate them. There wasn't much besides fish and coconuts, but let's face it we weren't exactly spoiled, and the dispossessed British would leave us what we needed. The only question was how to get there. I suggested rustling up some money – someone must have an aunt or grandmother with a postal savings book or part of an inheritance that could be paid out – and sending one of us to Istanbul. In winter the price per kilo for the Turks was pretty low, and in Berlin you got five marks a gram. It was a vague commercial calculation, but they accepted it and, as I had expected, I was charged with bringing the stuff back.

I'd lost my identity card and so got my acquaintances, the passport forgers, to make me one. I falsified my own student ID, which I could use to buy a cheap student ticket in Frankfurt from Turkish Airlines. When I landed in Istanbul winter was almost over. It had only been five months since the bus with heavily armed policemen had transported us to Edirne, and I'd already spent two winters in the city, but everything now seemed to have changed. Berlin had changed Istanbul. People's faces seemed much harsher, colder than before. I avoided the Cağaloğlu district. I had more money in my pocket than Ede and I'd ever had before, but I was determined not to tell him if I saw him. I didn't see him.

I met one of the Austrians from the previous summer and lodged in his doss house in the university area. He was still on opium, the old routine: all day long dozing and slobbering in bed; traipsing round the teahouses in the evenings. I'd had enough of that. Nobody recognised me in Tophane. Posters for political parties were stuck to the walls and overnight inscriptions appeared that were not hard to decipher as revolutionary slogans. I met another friend of the dirty needle who told me that Ede was in Germany, so-and-so in prison, so-and-so dead, so-and-so in Kathmandu, and that my notebooks were in the safe of our hotel. I didn't go there. I wanted to forget them altogether. Even if I was going to write again at some point, that stuff was farcical, those endless sentences about the pasty youth in the clinic and the stuttering attempts to stylise the passages where he fucked the nurse. I stood around the fires where in the evenings rubbish and charcoal was burned in the streets and alleys around the markets, with the porters, the people who sold trusses and teaspoons, the children, the dogs. I wished the others from the commune were there, and that we were already on our way to the Seychelles, somewhere we could understand something of the life around us and also participate in it. I envied those men who spent their nights sleeping in caves, corrugated-iron huts or unfinished new builds, I envied their communality, even though I knew nothing of their community. Maybe there was still a chance in Berlin after all. I got the gear. It was more expensive than I'd assumed and the quality wasn't that great either, but in any case I had the feeling that this was not the right way. Hadn't I suggested it in Berlin so I could get away? Now I wanted to go back, no matter what I brought with me. On the final evening the Austrian persuaded me to have some opium. Then I bought some off him. I went through customs at Frankfurt with the whole lot of it in a battered suitcase. The officer asked, 'Any ham, salami or meat in there?'

In Berlin it was still winter. I'd only been away a week, but as soon as I got back I realised the Seychelles project was a dead duck. Jan had been caught during an identity-card check and deported from Berlin back to West Germany proper. Richard Nixon, America's new president, would be coming to the city in the next few days. Everyone was behaving so secretly, as if they'd personally built the bomb which was going to blow him sky-high. Only Manni still showed an interest in the gear. The place was teeming with plain-clothed policemen. We started flogging our stuff nonetheless. When Nixon arrived I was in the crowd at the Gedächtniskirche. A few snowballs were thrown. Employees hung out the open windows of office blocks, waving paper flags.

1 Raw Material Raw Material Raw Material Raw 1
terial Raw Material Raw Material Raw Material
1 Raw Material Raw M   l Raw Material Raw 1
aterial Raw Material Raw Material Raw Materia

ten

The main auditorium of the Technical University was packed. That evening's topic for debate was the forthcoming vote for federal president, which was taking place in Berlin. As ever, the list of speakers was endless. Practically no one was thinking of Heinemann as a candidate. I was standing right at the back of the room amongst the rank and file, taking care not to become separated from Sarah. Sarah was nineteen and reminded me of the Song of Songs: 'Behold, thou art fair, my love; behold, thou art fair; thou hast doves' eyes within thy locks: thy hair is as a flock of goats, that appear from mount Gilead.' Last summer she'd sent a photo of herself to me in Istanbul; she was leaning against a tree in the Englischer Garten in Munich, and when Ede saw it he said, 'If there's anyone who's going to pull you out of the shit, it'll be her.' Now she was in Berlin too, and I was determined not to be parted from her again.

The crowd jeered and shouted down a young socialist. It was all part of a ritual in which the leaders of the radicals played at being the Bolshevik bosses, and the students and dropouts in the auditorium the riotous masses of St Petersburg. In truth it was much simpler: the leaders were enthroned on the podium and engaged in high politics, while the rank and file stood below, believing in the historical moment. Skilful direction brought the room to boiling point and at the decisive moment the slogan was uttered: 'Onto the streets!'

We were still a tight mass in Hardenbergstrasse, but when we got to America House, where the police lay in wait, the crowd soon dissipated. It struck me that I had twenty LSD trips in my pocket, which I'd swapped for a few of the blocks I'd got off the Turk. As I hurried away I looked around for Sarah. She was behind me, being shoved along rather than moving of her own accord. In the police floodlights and nocturnal glow of Hardenbergstrasse Sarah looked far too beautiful and fragile. I tried to grab her and battle my way out to the side, but those advancing from behind dragged me along with them. Stones were being hurled at America House, but word got round that we were to take the Kurfürstendamm, and so we charged onwards, past Zoo station. Stones were everywhere on the ground; I picked up a couple myself – smooth, grey cobbles. I'd soon forgotten the LSD, and Sarah too. I charged with the crowd. There was the Ku'damm, the colourful façades, the onlookers, the massive vehicles with their water cannons. We were coming from all sides, we were storming. There was Café Kranzler, temple of the bourgeoisie, there were the police, chains of uniformed men that entangled us. No sooner had the echoes of our war cries died down than the first screams of those being beaten by truncheons resounded in the street. I threw a stone, then turned and saw a policeman charging towards me at full pelt. I dropped the other stone and ducked. The truncheon only hit me as I bent down, a second blow found my arm, and another policeman hauled me off to a patrol car, but let me go when a new troop of assailants broke through and made for Kranzler. Cautiously I stood up again. No one appeared to be watching me. I slipped through a kind of no man's land to the corner of Joachimsthaler. There were stones everywhere, protesters bent over injured bodies, those arrested held temporarily in wrist locks by the police. I felt cold and thought that our attempt to take the Ku'damm had become a complete farce and would be far better without me. I looked for Sarah and found her at a metro station. I took her in my arms. She was wearing a fur coat and an old, thick cloth jacket, but through all our winter clothes I could still feel her breasts which bore the promise of springtime.

Via a circuitous route we arrived at the flat near Savigny-platz, where Boleslaw and his girlfriend, Sylvia, were waiting. They'd been living in a commune in Potsdamer Strasse and had now moved into this grand, nine-room apartment belonging to two scientists who worked at Siemens and who were trying to find a synthesis between computer science and anarchism. As far as I was concerned, their flat was paradise: an enormous kitchen where everything functioned, a refrigerator filled to the brim, ceramic stoves, comfortable sofas and leather armchairs everywhere, pictures hanging from the panelled walls, two bathrooms, two cats, books. I offered them all a trip. Sarah was still together with a friend of Boleslaw's, an ascetic philosophy student in his seventeenth semester, who lived in a tiny hovel without any hot water in Steglitz. I wanted, of course, to prise her away from him. That night we all took a trip, and in such surroundings I sensed I was coming closer to the world of literature.

I sat with Sarah in Boleslaw and Sylvia's room. To my mind these were the nicest people I'd come into contact with in Berlin. They were good-looking, they were educated without trumpeting it, they'd travelled widely, and they had artistic leanings without pretending to be artists. Their anarchism was an intellectual provocation, but they, too, had picked up stones in the street, and told the state precisely what they thought of it in court. And one day there was no doubt that this society would give them the space they were asking for. I looked down at myself. I felt like a filthy little drug-dealer from Tophane. I could sense the dirt oozing from my every pore. '2,000 Light Years from Home'. That's how I perceived myself too. Sarah lit an incense stick. She was so breathtakingly beautiful; how could I imagine that she'd be the one to save me from all this shit? The beauty of the Orient flowed in waves from her face and transformed the wall into the Taj Mahal. Sylvia snuggled up to Boleslaw, who smiled at me. I was sweating. I rolled a joint. That was one thing I could do. Although it was good to be able to do at least something, I felt I'd have to demonstrate a little more if I was going to win over Sarah, Boleslaw and Sylvia. The three of them seemed to be fusing into one, together with the candlelight, the music, the smell of the incense. I was sitting beside them like a lump of frozen spaghetti. I was sitting beside them like a heap of unsaleable copies of *The Function of the Orgasm*. I was back in Istanbul, sitting on the roof, the snow seeping through the walls, the fog-horns wailing, the pigeons scrabbling at the holes in the plaster, the schoolchildren below filing into the playground and singing the national anthem. Were I sitting there, I could write again. Although I didn't have my notebooks or a Rapidograph, this biro would do, this sheet of paper with computer formulae on the back. I started writing.

The following morning Sarah went to fetch her things from Steglitz, and we moved into the maid's room beside the kitchen. Heinemann was elected president.

eleven

Sarah was studying medicine in Göttingen. The semester began in mid-April. A week later she fetched me from the station. She showed me around the city. I rang Boleslaw from a telephone box.

'Boleslaw,' I said, 'you know I'm not the type to just play along with something.'

'What was that, Harry? I can barely understand what you're saying.'

'I'm trying to tell you how ghastly Göttingen is. I don't think I'll survive here.'

'Why, has she given you the shove?'

'No. Not yet.'

'I think what you're suffering from is culture shock. It'll pass.'

He was right.

We found somewhere to stay in Düstere Strasse. A grey, crooked house right out of the Middle Ages, which belonged to a working-class couple – that's to say she worked and brought up the children, while he sat in the garden in his vest, drinking beer. The toilet was in a wooden shed in the yard, and our room at the top of the stairs. It contained a wash basin, Sarah's desk, Sarah's chair, a bed and a cupboard. With her record player and my holdall it was almost at bursting point, but Sarah still managed to find space for her books and a hotplate. The window was a skylight through which you could see the clouds. In the room next-door was another student who was getting on a bit. On the evening we moved in, I heard the clickety-clack of a typewriter. I sat on the bed and watched Sarah getting ready to go out. She was wearing some beautiful old family jewellery: brooches, bangles, earrings. I put on Bob Dylan, but could still hear the clacking. It was louder than 'Mr Tambourine Man'.

'Sarah,' I said, 'I don't think I ought to write by hand again. You know, those long sentences. Truly dreadful.'

I'd told her all the important things about me.

'Maybe you can borrow his typewriter.'

'You know I find it tricky with students.'

'So what am I, then?'

'That's different.'

Further down Düstere Strasse was a pub. With his red face, green woollen cardigan, braces and baggy trousers made from tatty material, the landlord was a figure straight out of Wilhelm Busch. We called him Uncle Just. For two marks eighty you got a chop with fried potatoes and gravy, and beer was sixty pfennigs. In the low-ceilinged, smoky bar, where the same six or seven regulars were forever nursing a beer and offering in dialect scornful commentaries on local politics, the decline in moral standards and the impending relegation of Göttingen 05, we sat like an anxious but optimistic young couple, ate our fried potatoes and did some calculations. Sarah got four hundred marks a month from home, and my mother occasionally sent me something too. In certain student circles, moreover, hash was now popular. A year ago in Istanbul things had looked very different. I tucked in heartily and also had a second beer. I'd always been keen on beer, but over time opium ruined your appetite for everything except opium.

That night I dreamed I was a puma, roaming with other pumas through somewhere which in my dream was the South American uplands, but looked like a mixed forest in medieval Germany. I could feel the forest floor beneath my paws, the moss, the pine needles. Through my nostrils I breathed in air which was so pure that even in the shade a puma could taste every ray of sunshine in it. I climbed trees and leaped across clearings, I played with my companions and watched sympathetically as the birds of prey circled above the bluffs, stalking their quarry. I was a puma. I'd never felt so good in a dream. I awoke and there was Sarah's warm body, her long hair over my face. I could have jumped for joy.

We found a small out-of-the-way shop which sold typewriters. I told the sales assistant what I was looking for: a model made to last for ever, but also easy to use and cheap – in other words, a top-notch product of German manufacturing. She didn't have to think for long.

'There's only one model for you,' she said. 'That's the Olympia Splendid 33.'

I looked at it. The case was made out of light-coloured, but hard-wearing plastic, very durable. Inside it said: *Typewriter and case made in Western Germany.* That sounded confident, assured. Which is what the machine looked like: compact, sensible and conscious of its value. I tried the keys. Well, I could live with the font. I felt my heart pound. I could write with this. The shop's label was affixed to the back, white writing on a black background with a gold edge: Hatopp & Son OHG, Office Machinery and Office Furniture, 34 Göttingen, Papendiek 32, Tel. 59 39 3. Olympia Wilhelmshaven. From there it had come to Hatopp & Son, and now it was mine. All I had to do was nod. I lifted it up. The solid casing had been made to last for years. If you smashed the thing on someone's head, that would be the end of him. A typewriter was a weapon. I must never forget that. I'd always felt I had to defend myself against the world. Here in Papendiek I'd finally found my weapon. I put it back on the counter and nodded to Sarah. She wrote out a postal cheque. My beloved was giving me a typewriter as a present. She believed in me. I carried the thing back through Göttingen. I believed too. I was almost twenty-five. I was on my way. Back home, I inserted a sheet of paper into the machine. I knew already what I was going to write. Only four words: *Stamboul Blues: A Novel.* I thought: I'd like to see someone else do this. I inserted the next sheet and lit a cigarette. So, this was it: I was on my way. These weren't notebooks any more, and there was no Rapidograph, no snow seeping through the cracks, and the only panorama the scraps of the firmament through the skylight. Now there was nothing but sheets of white paper and the hard thumping of the keys. Although I could only type with one finger, I found that to be the perfect speed. In any case, it all depended on *what* you were writing. And there, I told myself, you've got an advantage if you stick with what you've seen.

twelve

Our trip to Amsterdam was not a success. We went with a student friend of Sarah's. That spring everyone was heading for Amsterdam, and I had to offer Sarah something too. I was suspicious of Holland from the outset – flat, clean, sedate, more German than Germany – and I loathed Amsterdam from the moment we set foot in it. The canals left me cold, I didn't like those cafés that looked like antique shops, and I didn't like the hippies, who seemed to have appropriated everything. They'd got on my nerves in Istanbul, and they already owned this city, or so it appeared. Paradiso, they said, Paradiso, we must go to Paradiso. The first thing I saw in Paradiso was one of the hippies I'd been deported with. I went up to him and asked how things were going. He just stared at me, shrugged, shook his long hair and said, 'Karma, man. It's all karma.'

'Let's go,' I told Sarah.

She just gave me one of her long, dark looks and then followed me.

We spent the night in some café which rented beds, but the following morning, a Sunday, I was up at six. I went outside and there was another canal. On the corner a café was open, beside it a sort of flea market. Everyone there looked as if they were artists, teachers, socialist councillors, youth pastors, antiques dealers, LSD dealers, rock musicians, vegetarians or devotees of Zen Buddhism. I'd often been out and about at this hour of day in Istanbul, and in Berlin and before that in Frankfurt. I enjoyed wandering around large market halls, train stations, parks, snack bars, tram depots, late-night bars, teahouses where the only sounds that really counted were the gurgling of hookahs, the rattling of dice and the call to prayer of the muezzins. Perhaps all that existed in Amsterdam, too, but I had no desire to go looking for it. I wanted to go back to our small room, to my pipe, to the Splendid 33 and the heap of typed paper. Perhaps you'd get on with them if you spoke their language, I thought; after all, you're not someone who hauls crates around large market halls and is destroyed in Tophane by opium and poverty. But I hadn't spoken their language either, and yet they'd let me sit with them and watch. The Dutch looked at me warily. I didn't buy anything, I didn't say anything, I didn't have a bicycle, I didn't perform somersaults, I didn't whip out a flute and start playing 'Strawberry Fields Forever', I didn't chalk 'The Night Watch' on the pavement, and nor was I passing around a three-paper joint with the Stars & Stripes. I paid for my coffee warily and left.

Eventually Sarah came with me. We hitch-hiked. My thumb in the wind yet again; I'd been doing it for years, but this time I had Sarah with me, and I thought, in four hours' time you'll be sitting in front of your typewriter. Not a chance. When they saw Sarah, they stopped; when they saw me, they put their foot down again. That afternoon we were still in Holland, Sunday afternoon in Holland, stranded in the area where the last German Kaiser consumed his pension and chopped wood: Doorn. In the end we had to escape by bus. And the longer we stood by the roadsides and motorways, the more palpably I felt as if I was already starting to lose Sarah. She was nineteen and I twenty-five, but at times I must have come across as an old grump in his late fifties who'd had it with the rest of humanity. Back home in our tiny room I was sure of her; amongst other people she flitted around like a butterfly. I scented a rival in even the least interesting of her fellow students, and each hour in a lecture theatre or the institute was a potential sixty minutes to cheat on me. Not that she would have been consciously unfaithful, not yet, but she was so open to any interest shown to her – and which man wouldn't have shown her some? – that it was only a matter of time before she followed this interest into their bed. I had to try to bind her to me, she with her Jewish background and strong penchant for the Orient, but on that grey, overcast spring day in Holland I already surmised that the bond between us would not be long lasting. She was a genuine Oriental, forever in search of Jerusalem, whereas for me the Orient was merely a foil for my apathy, my weakness for opium, my literary dreams. Her Orient was in the blood; my Orient was the *Stamboul Blues*.

An English soldier and his family took us to Hildesheim, where we found ourselves roaming the streets at five in the morning. We sat down outside the station. Everything was closed. The cathedral a pale silhouette. Packages of newspapers smacked against the pavement. Pigeons on slate roofs.

The first lorries, grey faces behind steering wheels. We walked in the direction of Göttingen and ate warm pieces of streusel cake out of a bag. Rape fields. Smoke from factories. The first sales reps on the roads. Tanks with green leaves covering the barrels. From time to time I put my arm around Sarah; she looked at me, seriously but affectionately. That morning the most beautiful girl in the world was mine, and although the countryside around us wasn't beautiful, it became gradually familiar; the countryside and I both came from this sort of background. A pharmaceutical rep picked us up. The pharmaceutical industry was booming. We all did what we could.

Sarah opened the skylight and let the sunshine in. Its rays warmed Sarah's medicine textbooks, her Koran, my Olympia and the pile of typed pages. Before I crawled into bed next to Sarah, I read the last section again. I sensed that it wasn't going to be easy, but then no one was born a writer. You became a writer. I snuggled up to Sarah. She was waiting. No one was born a lover, either. Sarah was a good teacher. That morning we made love as if we had more to extinguish than a lost weekend in Holland.

l Raw Material Raw Material Raw Material Raw l
terial Raw Material Raw Material Raw Material
l Raw Material Raw Material Raw Material Raw l
aterial Raw Material Raw Material Raw Materia

thirteen

I was a beginner. Nothing that had been written before counted. That was the point of the radical change, the revolution I still believed in despite the Berlin blues. We needed to find new material and new ways of expressing it. A new literature. Nineteen forty-five would have been an apposite time for this, too, but what did we get in (West) Germany? Group 47. I couldn't give a toss about what those people were writing. But even the new stuff, which Sarah showed me now and then, was pretty uninteresting. Clever students. Either artificially complex or written with that bombastic pathos I knew from the German Socialist Student Union. A new literature it was not.

That was something I only found with American writers. William Burroughs, for example. When we first got hold of *Naked Lunch* in Istanbul, Ede and I, we didn't like it. All that shagging, and almost all of it between men, had turned us off. We thought it gave the writing a bad name. Junkies can be more prudish than pastors. Now I read it more closely (and sexually satisfied), and with my street English also read the American edition of *The Soft Machine*, and discovered that this could be the language and aesthetic of a new literature. And as far as addiction was concerned, Burroughs went straight for the vein.

Like *The Soft Machine*, *Stamboul Blues* had to be a pioneering work. The novel in its traditional form was simply hopeless for what I wanted to describe. Addiction destroys individuality, so individual characters could be jettisoned, followed by the linear story. And while we're on the matter, classical sentence construction, subject, predicate, object could go too. None of those can describe what happens when opiates blast the grey cells. I tried explaining all this to Sarah when she got home in the evenings from university and read what I'd written that day. But I'd always had a real struggle with theory.

'Surely you dreamed that,' Sarah said, pointing to the place. It was a passage where two junkies are on their way to a city in Turkey. Landing up in some desolate village, they are pumped full of drugs and detained. A paranoid delirium.

'If I dreamed things like that,' I said, 'I'd rather hang myself.'

'So where does it come from, then?'

There was a heroic answer and an honest one. I tried to come up with a mixture of the two.

'Look, Sarah, when I sit at the typewriter in the mornings, all of a sudden a memory flashes in my mind – the fear we really felt last year when Hermes and I went to Bursa to score gear, and we were scared of going anywhere, because everyone gave us evil looks – and the memory triggers a certain image, that's what I start with, and then the next one comes automatically … I write for three or four hours, as if I'd tapped a source, and then suddenly it dries up.'

'Don't you think it's like that with all writers?'

'No I don't. When I read what people write over here …'

'Don't be so easily offended. I think what you write is rather unusual, too. I just wonder who would publish it.'

That was the sore point. A sense of foreboding hovered over me about this. But I didn't have much of an idea about the industry myself. Someone would notice the talent which had matured entirely unobserved. And if they didn't recognise it, surely they'd pounce on the subject matter. I already had a winning tagline for the book: addiction – a report from the inside. For God's sake, even the magazines lying about at Uncle Just's were writing about the topic. And here was where the literary response to it had come to fruition.

'Maybe the unusual needs a bit longer in Germany,' I said confidently to Sarah. 'But it *will* make a breakthrough. What are you doing?'

'Getting dressed for the party.'

'What party?'

'You remember, the spring party.'

I'd put it to the back of my mind. Sarah's friends, students. They'd planned a spring party in the country, at which everyone was going to let their imagination run riot – costumes, sketches, music. 'Let your dreams come true'; 'You are me too'.

'I thought we'd go for a nice walk and then have dinner at Uncle Just's.'

'But we do that every day.'

'What's so bad about it?'

She only needed to look at me and I knew. I wanted to give her a kiss, but she turned away. The party was a complete success. Lambrusco, flowing robes and horseflies.

I sneaked away and went to Just's to eat a chop and drink beer. I also read *Quick*. I had a fatal partiality for normal life, something which Sarah didn't understand. LSD and Burroughs and *Stamboul Blues*, but also a couple of small beers and the regional election results in Baden-Württemberg.

l Raw Material Raw Material Raw Material Raw l
terial Raw Material Raw Material Raw Material
l Raw Material Raw Material Raw Material Raw l
aterial Raw Material Raw Material Raw Materia

fourteen

By autumn I had one hundred and seventeen pages of text with one-and-a-half line spacing. I felt that was enough. Anybody who read these one hundred and seventeen pages must surely know what I was about. It was time to find a publisher. How did you do such a thing? I didn't know anybody in publishing. I didn't know any writers. No, that's wrong – I'd once met V. O. Stomps in the Taunus district, when I was in the sixth form. I'd slipped a selection of poems between the empty bottles of schnapps, but never heard back from him. Perhaps he didn't like the fact that I'd turned up with a girlfriend. Perhaps he didn't like the poems and he'd used them as scrap paper. In any case he was not the right person for *Stamboul Blues*. I needed a proper publishing house, a publisher who had a feeling for new literature and would offer me his best whisky while recounting anecdotes about Hemingway.

I had an aversion to bookshops, so I sent Sarah. She came back with the addresses of a few publishing houses, which one of the trainees had given her. I only had the original and one carbon copy of my text. Photocopying was expensive. And why bother? I thought. Even if the first publishing house didn't jump enthusiastically on *Stamboul*

Blues, it didn't take long to read one hundred and seventeen pages, then I could send the thing straight off to the next one. I perused the list. Suhrkamp, Rowohlt, Luchterhand. I plumped for Suhrkamp. After all, I came from Frankfurt, and what's more Suhrkamp had a reputation as a progressive publisher. They were bound to know something good when they saw it. I had to wait about four weeks for a reply. The manuscript was enclosed. Hollow phrases: 'Read with great interest ... not right for our list. Best regards ...'

'It doesn't matter,' I said to Sarah, who didn't know whether I was shocked. 'They'll soon realise what they've let slip through their fingers. Who've we got now? Rowohlt. Rowohlt's good. Hemingway, Miller, Nelson Algren. I fit in perfectly.'

She gave me a look which betrayed utter scepticism, but she took the packet to the post office all the same. I poured myself a small glass of whisky. Whisky was another drug you had to learn how to handle. I thought of Ede. Ede, I said to him, wherever you are: we had a good schooling.

Rowohlt took six weeks to decide that the time was not yet ripe for *Stamboul Blues*. I found the rejection easier to deal with than the time it had taken for the people to decide on it. Although I understood that they had other manuscripts to read too, one hundred and seventeen pages were a piece of cake; I could get through that in three hours. If each time the package sat for weeks or months gathering coffee stains on some desk, it could be an eternity before I found the right publisher. I hit upon a smart idea. Why not make it easier for the readers and split up the manuscript? Thirty pages were as good as one hundred and seventeen. Maybe it would even stimulate curiosity. So I assembled four similar sized sections of *Stamboul Blues* and drafted an accompanying letter, varying it only slightly for the four different publishing houses I sent it to.

'I think you should get the new addresses from a different bookshop, Sarah – preferably from several.'

'Why several?'

'What do you think it looks like if you go to the same bookshop every month to get addresses of publishing houses? Leave no traces.'

Sarah knew that I was taking speed again and sometimes had paranoid episodes, but she'd never experienced this sort of paranoia. She got the addresses. I tramped through the city for hours on end. The wind blew the leaves over the ramparts. I could feel the approach of winter. It would be a hard one. I couldn't go on waiting for ever for one reader to throw themselves at their publisher: 'I've got it! That's it!' 'What?' 'What we've been waiting for for twenty years!' I decided to become otherwise employed. Sarah had plenty on her plate anyway with her mid-term examinations; I couldn't just sit around at home the whole time, expending fresh air. I suspected in any case that the love between us was almost spent.

The editorial department of the *Tageblatt* was in the same building as the printing works, and you could feel the pounding of the presses all the way up to the top floors. The features section was housed in a sombre cubbyhole with a view onto the rear courtyard. A woman with grey hair, glasses and a tired but not unfriendly face looked up from a manuscript when I cleared my throat. A younger woman in a long, scruffy cloak, who was busy browsing a bookshelf, didn't stir. Just wait, I thought, soon my book will be there too.

'So, you'd like to work for us on a freelance basis? Please take a seat, Herr Gelb.'

I sat down and lit a filterless Camel. This is how careers must have begun. The friendly old lady – editor of the features section and also responsible for the supplement – introduced me to the sloven.

'Our book reviewer. What area were you thinking of? Have you written reviews before? I see, that might be slightly difficult.'

'Listen,' I said, flicking my ash onto a galley proof, 'I'll do anything for you – reportage, essays, opinion pieces.'

She gave me a weary smile. 'Well, maybe we can find something for you after all. Actually, our film critic is currently indisposed; perhaps you'd like to write some film reviews?'

'I'm an expert in thrillers.'

'Right, what's on today? Oh yes, here: *Hilfe, ich liebe Zwillinge* with Georg Thomalla. It's bound to be a big hit – Uschi Glas is in it too – we need to send someone along to that. I don't see any thrillers in the current programme.' She looked at me, tired, resigned and yet a little bit curious. 'Would you like to do it?'

I stubbed out my cigarette. Great careers often have the most bizarre beginnings.

'You'll have the review this evening.'

'By half past seven, mind you, and precisely thirty lines, Herr Gelb!'

The sloven let out a triumphant laugh when I left. It

wasn't until I was in the street that it occurred to me I'd forgotten to ask about the fee.

My review of the popular hit *Hilfe, ich liebe Zwillinge* appeared in the Saturday edition of *Tageblatt*. The following Wednesday the postman brought me my fee: seven marks eighty. The film had lasted two hours, and it had taken me two further hours to write the review, during which time I'd smoked half a packet of cigarettes and drunk three whiskies, not counting the trip through the autumn storm to the editorial office, where I'd spent another three-quarters of an hour discussing with the book reviewer whether satire was an inappropriate stylistic approach for criticism from a left-wing perspective. I decided to pay a visit to the labour exchange the following day. I needed money. And there was still no answer from Kiepenheuer & Witsch.

The mail-order kitchenware company was the far side of the railway. Crows sat in the tops of the bare trees. The first snow of the year fell in mushy streaks. It was just after seven in the morning and I could hear the roaring of the lorries on the motorway. Sarah had given me her winter coat. Although the buttons were on the wrong side, it kept me warm. I also had a thick scarf and a cap with earflaps, and a package with sandwiches and a copy of the *Frankfurter Rundschau* – every inch the serious young assistant who'd voted for Willy Brandt and looked into the future with eyes full of belief (I'd stopped reading the *Tageblatt*).

I obtained a position in Fräulein Lücke and Frau Klemmer's office. Frau Klemmer was the younger of the two;

Fräulein Lücke hadn't missed a day's work since 1946, and was something like the éminence grise of the firm. My job consisted of preparing invoices. I was good at mental arithmetic and had neat handwriting. My future was secure. The firm's money-spinners were Teflon-coated pots and Teflon-coated pans. The contractors couldn't deliver fast enough to satisfy the need of German housewives for Teflon-coated pots and pans. Day and night the huge juggernauts arrived from the motorways and unloaded Teflon-coated kitchenware. I was witness to a major boom. Only Fräulein Lücke remained sceptical.

'I've been in this business for so long now,' she said. 'Believe me, children, this Teflon craze will soon be over. Even space doesn't go on for ever. And then people will start to realise how much better goulash tastes from Granny's old cast-iron casserole, let alone schnitzel. I've yet to fry a schnitzel that I've really liked in a Teflon-coated pan. And who knows? In the end Teflon might be poisonous.'

'Oh please don't go on, Fräulein Lücke!' said the warehouse manager, who used to come to our office for a coffee. 'You know jolly well that without Teflon we might as well close this business tomorrow.'

'Oh yes, progress,' Fräulein Lücke said, adjusting her glasses and giving me a smile. I was her student. The two of us knew the score. Sometimes she'd slip me a salami roll, too. To both our satisfaction the number of complaints piled up, but Teflon stayed number one all the same.

When I got home, Sarah would have already made dinner, or we'd go out to Uncle Just's, the Greek place, or the Italian. There was always a whisky to hand and I saw very little of Sarah's friends. After all, I was the wage earner now; I earned eight hundred marks a month and had the prospect of a Christmas bonus. Teflon coating, wherever you looked. The blessing of space travel. I thought about a flat, I thought about a television set, I thought about Ede. What hole was he passed out in, or was he now exhibiting in the Museum of Modern Art? But most of all, on my way through the cold darkness of the mornings, and with my head on Sarah's chest just before going to sleep, I thought about *Stamboul Blues*. I tried to picture what sort of people they were who dictated to their secretaries '… we don't see any possibility …' or typed themselves '… the problem seems to be your inadequate reflection of the outside world'. Were they similar to the teachers and professors, booksellers and gallery owners, editors and doctors I had known? Had that legendary V. O. Stomps really been such an outsider, or in reality the incarnation of everything that everyone in this industry wanted to be? I seemed to have virtually no chance. My *Blues* had not yet found its way to a Boleslaw. There probably wasn't a Boleslaw in the business. I saw myself in ten years' time in Fräulein Lücke's job, and when the Teflon craze was over, well, I'd always predicted it, Fräulein Lücke and I: 'You see, children? The good old casserole!' I saw myself finally being accepted at Uncle Just's regulars' table, sitting for the FDP on the local council – for in my position you have to represent the middle classes. I also had a little garden and on Sundays my blonde Mausi would allow me an extra shag so that I could get through the difficult week to come. Sometimes I'd think of Sarah in all this. Since I'd become a novelist, I'd started to fantasise like any bourgeois dreamer. I relished the despair as I wallowed in this morass. If you don't want me, no problem. There were far more subtle forms of retreat from the commercial world of literature than looking for gold in Africa. Teflon sounded absolutely perfect.

In December Sarah went to her parents in Munich. No sooner had her train left the station than I felt gripped by flu. I lay shivering and freezing in bed, in surrender to my hallucinations, when the postman knocked. He had a letter. The letter was from a writer in Munich who worked for a publishing house there. 'If the rest of your manuscript is like these thirty pages, I see a good chance of your being published by this house.' I read the letter about forty-five times, while downing half a bottle of whisky. Then I put on my new favourite record: The Rolling Stones' 'You can't always get what you want, but if you try some time you might find you get what you need …'. Well, I thought, my teeth chattering, there has to be a bit of talent in there, too. Let it bleed.

l Raw Material Raw Material Raw Material Raw l
terial Raw Material Raw Material Raw Material
l Raw Material Ra***** ***aw Material Raw l
aterial Raw Material Raw Material Raw Material

fifteen

The roads in Schwabing were iced up, and in my Italian loafers I skidded across the pavement, although I felt more as if I were gliding. The Göttingen flu had come from Asia, and I had lain as if in a coma for a week before I was able to go to Munich. My only suit, blue pinstripes with a waistcoat, hung loose on my emaciated body. I'd been reading a lot of Joseph Roth recently, and I thought I knew the secret of the Trottas of this world: schnapps and brandy. I glided.

The writer had a 'studio' in one of those houses from the Jugendstil era, the sort where dentists, designers, advertising people and affluent young widows lived. With each large, gliding step I took, I put more distance between myself and the opium dens. The first thing I saw when the writer opened the door was a poster with Allen Ginsberg sitting on a toilet, dressed in nothing but a top hat. *Legalise Pot*. Then there were the walls of books, of course, the cultivated disorder of piles of manuscripts, luggage and endless cushions scattered about the floor, the whisky glasses in the fading light, the view out to the snow-covered front garden. It was one of the first January days of the new decade. The writer had a short-trimmed beard, he dressed with deliberate casualness, and wore an expression that was supposed to look melancholic.

'Bourbon or Scotch?' he asked. 'I've been more into bourbon recently. I'm sorry I've got so little time to spare, but as you can see, I've got to go to Rome tomorrow.'

He sipped his bourbon, I my Scotch. The Scotch was good. I remained silent.

'So,' he said. 'Your book ...'

I handed over the remaining eighty-seven pages.

'And all this is authentic?'

I nodded. Maybe you should show him your scars, I thought, but let it be. After all, I was sitting opposite a writer and literary adviser, a giant of the publishing industry – not the doctor at the mail-order kitchenware company.

'Well,' he said after a pause. 'I was quite impressed. I mean, it was a little expressionistic. You need to go easy on the adjectives.'

Something I'd heard often enough; they all said that.

'Of course, this is just a first draft,' I said. 'I'm well aware that a lot of work still needs to be done. And I've already got something new in my mind. If I had a publisher ...'

He cast me a melancholy look and changed the subject. He wanted to know something about mind-altering drugs. Then he talked for a bit about Rome. Munich. London. The pauses became longer. I had no idea what was expected of me. Here I was, the author of an authentic if somewhat expressionistic manuscript about the effect of hard drugs, looking in my suit like a bank clerk on his way to the Barmer Ersatzkasse pulmonary sanatorium in Bad Aibling. After twenty minutes I put on Sarah's coat. Both of us were relieved to have come through the encounter unscathed.

sixteen

In January came a hailstorm of rejections. The publishing industry seemed to have returned from its winter break with good resolutions for the new decade; now desks were cleared and dud manuscripts sent back that had been piling up since the autumn. Oh yes, and there was that *Stamboul Blues* as well, thirty pages, who does this man think he is? Please return his scribblings, Fräulein Meyer-Endruleit, you know what to write: *Regrettably, we have no room on our lists until 1979.* But I wasn't going to be kept down that easily. There was a whole host of publishers in West Germany, and I'd kept the Swiss and Austrians up my sleeve. I would have also sent off to ones in the GDR, but they weren't listed in the directories Sarah consulted in the bookshops. I'd jacked in my job at the mail-order kitchenware company. I was living off my savings, trudging to the post office through the snowy streets and sending off my packages. I'd eye the other customers in the queue suspiciously. I could see at once if any of them were potential competition. They'd also have that haunted look and the anxious frown when the post-office worker stuck 'Recorded Delivery' on the packet. The postal service was making a fortune out of failed writers. I'd trudge back via the dentist and have yet another tooth extracted. It was an effective way of combating boredom, and always a good excuse to sink a few schnapps in the evening.

Sarah was unhappy with this. She sat on her bed, reading the Koran, the Sufis, Krishnamurti, Gurdjieff, Sri Aurobindo. Her eyes had a curious sheen, which assumed a metallic glint when she scrutinised me slurping my whisky and reading Fallada. I liked Fallada. *Who Once Eats out of the Tin Bowl*, *Wolf amongst Wolves*. He had a feeling for the night. A German junkie. Sarah read him, too, as a deterrent. Snow fell onto the skylight until it was white all over. The aging student was clacking away at his typewriter. A ten-finger typist. I'd stopped writing temporarily, apart from my covering letters to readers: 'Dear Sir or Madam, Please find enclosed a few chapters from my first novel. It's about …' I was finding this increasingly difficult. What was it about? Nothing that sparked any interest, that much was certain. I heard from Boleslaw that Sylvia had left him and was now living in a psychoanalytical commune in London. After that I heard nothing more from Boleslaw. Berlin was further away than Istanbul. I thought: You've just got to give them another book. Productivity is the advantage of the autodidact. Anyone can shift their arse onto a warm seat and study German. Besides, I already had a title for the new book: *Schmargendorf City Blues*. One more blues and I'd have a trilogy.

On the spur of the moment Sarah flew to see her relatives in New York. The 1970s were shaping up dreadfully. After three evenings at Uncle Just's I scraped together the last of my money and bought a ticket to Istanbul. The freezing-cold Orient Express struggled through the snowdrifts in the Balkans for forty-eight hours. In Belgrade the restaurant car was uncoupled. Huddled closely amongst the Turkish workers and their unbelievable supplies of bread, tinned meat, cheese, stuffed cabbage leaves, coffee, peppers, sweets, music cassettes and good humour, were a few pale figures in old, very long raincoats, Indian saris and plimsolls riddled with holes, counting down the hours until they'd be sitting back in their lice-infested corner of the Gülhane Hotel, cooking up a shot of opium in the rusty communal spoon. I had nothing against this; in fact I had something similar in mind myself. After twenty-seven rejections for *Stamboul Blues* I felt that opium was the only thing I could still rely on.

I was wrong. After one day in Istanbul I wanted to leave again. Now that I'd written the book I felt somehow ridiculous roaming the streets of Tophane. What was I doing here? I'd sunk from witness to tourist; all I needed now was to whip out a pocket camera: Please! It won't take long! Just one for the family album. A car drove past, spraying mud all over my coat. I paid tribute to the spirits, the dead, and to those who still wished to live, then moved on.

I spent a few more days sitting around in the old cafés. Occasionally someone I'd known from before emerged from the shadows. We sat there like geriatrics, consuming sweet tea, nut pastries and memories. I heard only vague rumours about Ede. My notebooks were still in the hotel safe. I didn't go to fetch them. The girls seemed prettier now. Maybe I hadn't been properly aware of them before. There were a few things I hadn't been properly aware of before: the way people whispered, the hostile looks, the rising prices, the proclamations on the walls, Fascist processions, the filth which the rain washed down into the slums from the hills. Fish heads, melon rinds, rusty soup tins, condoms, dead rats that looked different from Dalí paintings, blue stones to ward off the evil eye, plastic dolls' arms, mouldy orange peel. At dawn it seemed as if myriad fleas were leaping out of the smouldering heaps of burned rubbish on the Golden Horn, from which stray dogs and beggars scrabbled what the princesses of the night had left them. Taxis rattled across Galata bridge. Soviet freighters bobbing up and down in the harbour. The hammer and sickle over Tophane. It was colder in Istanbul than in Göttingen. When I left I thought: this is for good. The sea was grey.

Sarah wasn't back yet. There was a card from her in the post box. I took it upstairs, turned on the gas stove and sat there for ages, breathing in the gassy air as I tried to fathom what Sarah had written to me. The card was sent from Chicago. Sarah always liked to be obscure in her expression, but this time I understood even less. The clearest sentence was: 'I can give you nothing except my consciousness.' I lay down on the cold bed and thought, you're going to have to find yourself another one soon. Another bed in another city. I looked through the rest of the post. The only difference between the large and small publishing houses seemed to be that the rejections from the former came quicker and those from the latter sounded less assured.

l Raw Material Raw Material Raw Material Raw l
terial Raw Material Raw Material Raw Material
l Raw Material Raw Material Raw Material Raw l
aterial Raw Material Raw Material Raw Materia

seventeen

Blackish-blue flies droned against the windowpane. Fat things glistening toxically. No surprise, really: we were in the country, after all. The sun set them into a frenzy, this Lower Saxon cabbage-and-turnip sun, sitting atop the Galgenberg like Wotan's crown. The flies buzzed against the dusty glass, unable to grasp why the window remained closed. It made them unruly, and then there was the incessant clattering of the travel typewriter. No typewriter had ever clattered here before. Here, in this village on the highway in Göttingen district, only wooden clogs and milk churns normally clattered.

Sarah had decided that we should move out to the country, and she'd found this spacious old flat which had once been home to farmhands. On the mayor's farm, it cost two hundred marks for a hundred square metres, and ensured we were the envy of everybody. From the very first day I knew this was the beginning of the end. Sarah, suntanned, with Mother Earth on the turnip fields, while I started swallowing amphetamines again and sat in the cigarette fug of my room with Burroughs, Fallada and textbooks about drug-related crime. I kept the curtains tightly closed and followed Sarah's every movement. I read her letters

69

too, of course, and soon identified my deadly foe, one of those boyish types, I assumed, which Ede and I had preyed upon in Istanbul, Love and Peace idlers with their sleeping bags, their guitars, their mindless drivel about Woodstock, togetherness, karma. I'd never trusted those characters an inch. All they were after was a cheap fuck, especially the ones who always banged on about consciousness. *Om.* Bankrolled by Daddy through the 'Third World', financed by tooth decay, Standard Oil and the arms industry, but preaching asceticism, the soya bean, Yin and Yang and cosmic rays. Freeloaders. I tried to explain this all to Sarah, but it only made things worse. She sat there in her harem pants and threw the I Ching with English pennies. Whole nights passed like this, with her gleaming eyes never failing to watch me swallow another few Ritalin pills. She became saintly. I became thin. And the letters from Chicago arrived on a daily basis.

But my failure in love could not stop me from writing. I was working on my second book. Production is everything. *Schmargendorf City Blues* progressed at a pace. One reason for this was that I'd reflected on my notebooks in Cağaloğlu, on those carefree, lovefree sessions in the cold Turkish nights, when I'd abandoned myself to the rhythm of long sentences. Punctuation marks are a distraction altogether, I decided; it wasn't just literature that had to be abolished, but the terror of punctuation. All that was needed was a vertical line, which gave pages-long sentences a rhythm I simply called jazz staccato, Göttingen bebop. I was writing about a ghost town called Schmargendorf City, about tramps and old SS men, swarms of crows on the gables of condemned houses, where morphine addicts with lung diseases injected through the sleeves of Salvation Army uniforms, and cross-eyed orphans played with the bones of Martin Bormann, while the commune in the attic participated in deviant sex games when they weren't folding pirate copies of *Golem* as they sang witches' songs. All of this underlain with the long, wistful inner monologues of a first-person narrator seeking in this ghost town the traces of a lover who'd left him many years before under mysterious circumstances – a political crime could not be ruled out. Occasionally I leaped up to swat a fly which had snuck into the room in spite of my precautionary measures. Then I took a gulp of cold Nescafé, lit a Camel, and carried on working. Within three weeks I'd managed to write over a hundred pages. When I was writing I forgot all else. It was just a pity that I couldn't write for twenty-four hours, followed by a further twenty-four hours, just write for every hour of my stupid life. But the amphetamines helped. I wrote for twelve hours, fourteen hours, sixteen hours, then I stuffed myself with sleeping tablets and dozed. In my dozing state I could barely make Sarah out. We had separate beds.

'Please close the window,' I said, the smoking cigarette between my lips. 'These flies are driving me mad while I'm trying to write. The flies and this sun.'

Sarah didn't reply. The window remained open. I raised my head. I was in full flow. Sarah was standing at the window, the sun fell on her brown, chubby, healthy face, and the flies were buzzing around the typewriter.

'If you shut out the sun, your book will never amount to

anything,' Sarah said. 'It's only corpses that don't need any sun, but then corpses can't write books.'

'You don't say.'

'I can sense your hostility, your hostility is so strong that I can scarcely breathe.'

I stubbed out the cigarette. My fingers were yellow from the nicotine, and the dirt beneath my nails looked revolting. I could feel abscesses in my mouth, which was parched, as if it had never had anything to drink other than words.

'Has the post arrived yet?'

Sarah gave me a hard stare. The sun was playing with her hair, which shimmered copper. She smiled, a smile I knew by now. It was a smile expressing sorrow for the inanities of an incorrigible race of people condemned to extinction – and the awareness of belonging to those heading for new shores where the Messiah was already waiting to have his feet kissed. Or his cock, that tiny, but sacred cock which was directly connected to the origin of the universe.

'We need to break up,' Sarah said.

I swallowed. I hadn't expected it to come so quickly. Especially now that I was already halfway through the second *Blues*. Didn't I have a right to a new consciousness? I mean, I was a writer, even if no publisher had made that official yet. I'd had work published, I was on the way. And now Miss Sanctimonious was dropping a bombshell to stop me from progressing any further. Paradiso, I thought. It all began in Paradiso. She wanted to sit with them in a circle, chanting Om, whereas I wanted to be alone with her, smoking opium, drinking whisky, and talking about my adventures in Tophane and the books I was going to write. All the complications in the world stemmed from the fact that women can't be alone.

Downstairs, the front door clattered.

'That must be the postman,' I said, flicking away the flies from my forearms. Sarah was already at the door to our flat. I could see straightaway that Chicago had struck again, a really long letter. Well, let him scribble as much as he liked, he'd never be a writer. There was post for me, too, but a letter rather than a returned manuscript. One of the small avant-garde publishing houses that I'd sent the first *Blues* to. 'Read with interest … very positive feedback from our external reader … if you're ever in Frankfurt …'

I read it three times, then took a gulp of cold Nescafé and lit a cigarette with gusto. So that was it. Literature interfered in life; it blew life apart. A pyrotechnic display of images. One moment total despair, the next back on top of the world, a rapid journey, the light at the end of the tunnel in sight. Chicago devastated. Success is better than karma, success *is* karma. The Chinese were all in favour of success. Everyone's in favour of success apart from Sarah, and she's got a nice fat inheritance up her sleeve. Now that I had practically made it as a writer, she'd think twice about leaving me. I could already hear the Indian music coming from her room; leave her. It's what she needed, just as the turnip fields needed their Galgenberg sun. The rest of us needed success, then we were going to take on the whole of America. I looked again at the letter. You couldn't exactly call it a direct commitment, but it was the best I'd had so far. I took page 109 out of the Olympia, inserted a blank one, gave the typewriter a gentle pat and tapped away: '… I'm also in the middle of writing my second novel, which I think will be finished in the summer. But we can chat about this when I …'

I did not omit a single comma. Next-door the sitar was lamenting. I got up and closed the window. A fly attacked me. I flicked it away to the wall, grabbed the rolled-up newspaper and waited for it to land on a patch of sun. Then I swatted it dead. I felt like a killer. The sitar sobbed even louder. I sat back at the typewriter. To withdraw your love from a man was akin to murder, but with a typewriter he'd survive.

l Raw Material Raw Material Raw Material Raw |
terial Raw Material Raw Material Raw Material
l Raw Material Raw Material Raw Material Raw |
aterial Raw Material Raw Material Raw Materia

eighteen

Gutowsky was a short, portly guy about my age. I could picture him as the son of the sweet factory boss somewhere in the Levant, but now Destiny seemed to have selected him to be my first publisher. I was wearing shining loafers and a tie; he was in white jeans and a T-shirt. His bachelor flat on Hochstrasse was stuffed full of books and he served Chianti. Then he showed me his avant-garde list. I'd never heard of any of the authors, but the slim volumes were carefully put together and had striking covers. With its gleaming silver jacket, one book stood out from all others, printed on enlarged lines from the original manuscript. A German author with the name of a Polish poet: Anatol Stern. As I leafed through the book I was amazed. I, with my vertical lines, was an altar boy compared with this. On some pages the text was divided into columns, there were passages in bold, and as far as punctuation was concerned Stern seemed to have dispensed with rules altogether.

'Stern uses the cut-up technique,' Gutowsky explained.

'What's that?'

He cast me a wary look. 'Don't you know? The Burroughs method?'

I avoided his gaze. 'Burroughs? Of course I know him.'

'Louis Schneider said at once that your work was heading in the direction of cut-up. That's why we want you on our list. The German cut-up authors. We're about to publish one of Burroughs's texts too. It slots perfectly into our list.'

I took another sip of Chianti. 'Who's Lou Schneider?'

'He's our external reader, translator and chief adviser for the cut-up list. You should go and see him in Mannheim as soon as you can.'

'Hmm,' I said. 'The fact is, I'm rather broke at the moment.'

He twisted his mouth, as if he'd just discovered a new cavity in one of his molars. Money was evidently a painful subject for Gutowsky.

'OK, then,' he said after a stifling pause. 'Come to the office tomorrow and we'll give you the fare to Mannheim. Look,' he added, as if he now had to make up some lost ground, 'we're a little short at the moment. The good old revenue office. But when I publish your book, of course you'll get an advance.'

'And what direction is that heading in?'

'Five hundred marks,' Gutowsky said with a squeak in his voice, as if he'd just revealed the absolute limit of what he could afford.

You'll have plenty more fun with this chap, I told myself, as I wandered up to the hash meadow with Anatol Stern's book in my pocket. That summer drugs were cheaper than books, unless you were writing them yourself.

Lou Schneider fetched me from the station in Mannheim. He must have had a nose for junkies and ex-junkies, because he picked me out of the crowd as an experienced detective might a wanted pickpocket. He looked more like a crime reporter from an American gangster film than an external reader for an avant-garde publishing house, but then again I knew I didn't exactly have the air of an aspiring young author about to publish his first novel with Suhrkamp or Hanser. He lived in the attic of an old house in the centre of town. A cat prowled around his flat. The coffee was strong. We smoked the same brand of cigarettes.

'Good work,' he said, rapping his knuckle on the manuscript of *Stamboul Blues*. 'Just a few lines to edit out here and there, some quicker entries into scenes and transitions, then it'll be superb.'

'Really?'

'Sure thing, *amigo*. Take the beginning. If you delete the first two lines and go straight into the toilet where the two guys are shooting up, then bang – you've got the scene licked. Just get rid of the ceremony – who wants Martin Walser when they can have Burroughs?'

'Ask the booksellers.'

'Oh yes, it drags a bit here. And then again here, in chapter two: introducing that old Lasker-Schüler woman all of a sudden, it jars somewhat. She doesn't belong at all.'

'But I began with poetry.'

'There's only been one good German poet, and that was Dr Gottfried Benn. But even Dr Benn can only exist as a shadow in this text. In person, however, Dr Benway could appear in disguise. Doc Benway, do you remember?'

I really had read my Burroughs. 'Of course. But in my book he's called Dr Tox.'

'Right, and in that chapter there isn't anything that needs changing.'

In an hour we'd gone through the manuscript. Although I had nothing to compare him to, I couldn't imagine a more capable professional than Lou Schneider. All the waiting and anxiety had paid off. As a publisher, Gutowsky was neither fish nor fowl, but Lou Schneider was the whole menu including wine, coffee and the cognac at the end.

nineteen

As I was still enrolled at Johann Wolfgang von Goethe University, even though I hadn't been to a lecture since 1965, I managed to get a job with the Bundesbank. I worked in the foreign exchange department, observing the financial world in Tokyo, Buenos Aires, Rio. It was an easy job. You collated, did some calculations, wore a tie and learned something of other employees' worries. They were married at twenty-five, and at thirty were looking to build a house. At forty they started to lose their hair and to work out what promotions they would need to retire with this or that pension. I taught a trainee how to play poker, and when the weather was fine we would play outside during our lunch break. We were joined by a third player, then word soon got around and the boss banned it. For employees of the German Bundesbank, gambling games were taboo.

'How do you hope to make it, then?' I asked.

'With the Bundesbank, of course,' they'd say. They were full of optimism. The future lay ahead of them as if on a serving tray. It was a beautiful summer and the summers ahead would be even lovelier. In Berlin Andreas Baader was sprung from prison. Ulrike Meinhof, who had gone underground, called for armed struggle. At lunchtime I'd go to the hash meadow and get myself some morphine stolen from pharmacies. It cost ten marks a phial. I'd given up writing my second book, but reworked *Stamboul Blues* using Schneider's suggestions. Gutowsky's promises sounded increasingly vague. An excerpt should have already appeared in their catalogue. I consoled myself. You can always console yourself in summer. And the phials helped.

Sometimes I'd visit Anatol Stern after work. He lived in Westend with his wife and daughter. Stern's main job was as a pilot; he only wrote on the side, mostly in the hotels where the crews stayed: Karachi, Bombay, Bangkok, New York, Los Angeles, Rio. His wife was extraordinarily attractive and hospitable. Their flat always seemed to be teeming with hippies and junkies, but I gradually realised that these were literature students, models, shop-owners, artists and authors. All of them wore long, flowing robes, had long, wafting hair, and were adorned with chains, rings, neck scarves, pigtails and glass beads. Joints and teapots were constantly being passed round. The way they behaved to each other was somehow quite fluid, their relationships followed rituals that I didn't understand. There was a lot of talk about sexual liberation – Gutowsky had already entered the soft-porn market – but people rarely touched each other and I had no idea if they were all sleeping together or changing partners all the time. Nobody slept with me. Lou Schneider was seldom there, and Anatol Stern was the only person I was able to talk to. I was finding cut-up a struggle.

'OK, so I cut up the pages. But what then?'

'Then you rearrange the bits and put the sentences together differently.'

'And then?'

'Well, you might get a new image, a sense that's remained hidden till then, maybe just a surprising adjective, sometimes a key to the door which was locked before. Or you throw the whole lot away. It's hard graft.'

'Hmm.'

'Texts have to open up new areas of consciousness. Why else bother writing? Texts are trips through time and space.'

I didn't even have a driving licence. Anatol turned on the television. News. Images flickered on the screen without any sound. Bombings in Vietnam. The invasion of Cambodia. Nixon. Kissinger. Something new: wanted posters of Germans. Then Anatol set up the tape recorder. The squeaking voice of an American reading an unbelievably obscene text in the style of a communiqué from a military commander. William Burroughs. Very impressive.

As Anatol told me, cut-up had existed since 1959. Back then the gurus of the Beat Generation would sit around in a hotel in rue Gît-le-Cœur in Paris: Burroughs, Brion Gysin, Harold Norse, Gregory Corso, Ginsberg and all their entourage. One day Gysin laughed so much he fell under the table, having arranged two bits of newspaper in such a way that General Eisenhower had suddenly turned up at the Mexican border where he was arrested for murdering prostitutes. Burroughs seized on the coincidence straightaway and developed it into a method which included not only scissors and newspaper columns, but tapes and films too. Experimental literature. I couldn't imagine Algren or Fallada working like that. They were storytellers.

'We need to bring literature into the age of space travel,'

Anatol Stern said, putting on his pilot's uniform. He was a handsome, friendly man. Even the uniform looked good on him. He said goodbye and set off for Dakar, Johannesburg, Rio. I walked with some of the models, artists and authors, but only as far as the station. They talked about films, light shows, the Stones, their last trip, meetings in Munich, London, Rome. I took the metro to Eschenheimer Turm and got myself a few more phials. Then the long trek home. Dornbusch, Eschersheim, Heddernheim. They were building everywhere. My mother had made dinner. Whether it was linear narrative or cut-up, all in all my prospects looked hopeless.

I finished my stint as a temporary employee. In Munich I saw Sarah again. When we were together, she'd hated needles, but now one of her friends or bedfellows had got her hooked and she wanted a shot from me. I gave her one. We went to bed together again. It was a warm night, very stuffy. There was a party at the Academy, the music echoed down the street. Sirens somewhere, the fire brigade. Drunkards bawled outside the Arri cinema. I pulled Sarah close to me, stuck a finger up her arse, sucked on her tits until she screamed; I wanted to keep my cock in her pussy for ever. Where was Asia that night? Where was America? When dawn broke we still hadn't slept. We could hear the racket of the metro construction works, the trams, the jets of water from the vehicles cleaning the streets. Pigeons cooed outside the window. Then I did get to sleep after all, and when I woke up Sarah was already dressed and consulting the I Ching. This time the pennies didn't fall for me, either.

l Raw Material Raw Material Raw Material Raw l
terial Raw Material Raw Material Raw Material
l Raw Material Raw Material Raw Material Raw l
aterial Raw Material Raw Material Raw Material

twenty

There had been an outbreak of cholera in Istanbul. I went back there. Perhaps this time I'll die, I thought; maybe cholera will get me where opium and the police failed. But I got the vaccination. They wouldn't allow you in otherwise.

I'd always spent the forty-eight hours on the train sitting or standing; this time I treated myself to a couchette. I'd written a story for *twen* about a trip to Istanbul, which was never published, but at least they'd paid a kill fee, and Sarah promised to send some money too. My plan was to take a look at the cholera and then this time to travel further, just for once to cross bloody Anatolia and see Teheran and Isfahan. I'd never heard another word from Ede, but now I sensed that I'd see him again, I'd bump into him in Tophane and the two of us would immediately take the night express to Ankara.

The couchette was a waste of time. The train stopped in Sofia. It was shunted onto a siding and then it just stood there. All the Bulgarians did was give a shrug. They'd never been what you might call forthcoming with information or communicative. Rumours whizzed around the mild October night. The Turks have closed the border. The Bulgarians have closed the border. The train's going back. The tickets are no longer valid. The Bulgarians are keeping us here. The Bulgarians are carrying out mandatory vaccinations. We left the train in small groups and filtered into the station. At eleven o'clock at night Sofia's train station is not the most hospitable place in Europe, but there was a café open, where rail workers, policemen, farmers and travellers with no fixed destination were fortifying themselves with beer, schnapps and shashliks. They had local currency. We didn't. On the international currency markets no doubt the lev had risen sharply that evening. At dawn the following morning the train trundled on to Turkey. I didn't bother trying to reclaim my couchette.

In Svilengrad I bought a bottle of brandy, and from there we were ferried to the border in buses. We had to walk the last part through the dust to the Turkish frontier. Bulgarian soldiers chivvied us along. Two years previously Turkish soldiers had thrown me out of their country in a similar manner; now this was how I was returning. They took their time at the border. Anybody wishing to go to Istanbul while cholera was raging could only be a spy or a madman. Spies and madmen could wait. When I got my passport back, stamped, the bottle of brandy was empty. For the first time I entered Turkey on foot and off my head.

The five hundred mosques of Istanbul were gleaming; all the gold of the Golden Horn. This time I went back to our old hotel. They were all still there, in the shabby reception area, with the portrait of Atatürk on the wall, the scarred bureau, the smoking stove, the tatty carpet, the samovar and the safe in the wall where my notebooks lay, as if it were only yesterday that I'd been hauled down from the roof and into prison. I had a strange feeling – was it only two years? Not two hundred, or two seconds? Was this the trip through time and space? Cut-up? They wanted to give me back the notebooks; I said leave them in the safe. Security. They laughed and slapped me on the shoulder. Even old Ane was still there, the Macedonian cleaning lady, the slave of the clan, who all day long slid on her knees around the hovel with mop and bucket, seven days a week, three hundred and sixty-five days a year. She was so lowly that she was the only one who could afford to laugh with total freedom.

No one was allowed to stay on the roof any more – they'd probably wanted to stop the bakshish – and I'd already thought that Ede, paintbrush between his teeth, would meet me at the door and ask if I'd brought him some yoghurt. I took a room on the top floor, lay down on the narrow bed, stared at the stone ceiling with its faded green paint, and waited for Istanbul to take me in her arms again. There were the pigeons, there were the seagulls, there was the screaming of little children and sometimes the recalcitrant braying of a donkey, too. There was the roaring traffic, the millions of car hooters between Sultan Ahmed and Beyoğlu, between Üsküdar and Kadiköy, the ship sirens, factory sirens, foghorns, the trains leaving Sirkeçi. There were the five hundred loudspeakers of the mosques, with which the voices of muezzins called even the wind to prayer. There was the wind, which in spite of the October sun, carried the first harbinger of the winter frosts. The expectant meowing of cats on heat mingled with the husky enticements of the gypsy whores; the tambourine they used to make the bear dance with the radio advertisements for Coca-Cola and Persil. From thousands of dimly lit rooms, from hostels and haunts, the caz reached out to me, the dangerous melancholy of Anatolian blues, which always seemed to say: What is life? Throw it away and you haven't lost a thing. There was the stench of urine, the smells from the food stalls, raki, sweet milk and tea, salted nuts, damp walls, candle wax, sugared pastry rings, disinfectant spray, Turkish tobacco, crackling logs, fried fish, the iodine from the sea air, hash. And then the cacophony of the main street: shrill hooting, police sirens, the clanging of shop grilles, rattling windowpanes, whistles, hundreds upon hundreds of badly soled shoes on cobblestones, orders, truncheon blows, cries of pain, shots in the night, or was it backfiring? I no longer had any right to be embraced by Istanbul.

I was standing in a long queue outside the vaccination centre in Galata to have a second cholera jab when somebody poked me in the shoulder. It was Jonas, one of our Frankfurt clique, a passionate junkie who also had a Section 51.1 hunting licence. Jonas had always been short but broad, with powerful shoulders, a bull's neck, a prominent nose in a face strangely refined by his addiction, a fool, gambler, man of honour, a lone wolf with bloodshot eyes he used to scour a world in search of survival opportunities, a world which long ago had let him know that such opportunities were no more. Now Jonas looked even smaller, contracted, almost dwarf-like with his head that was too large and shaven, a sign that he'd just been released from prison, and like an old man with his watery eyes and those white hands whose bones shimmered through the surface of the skin. His voice sounded as if it were filtered through cotton wool.

'Back home again, are we?'

'Just passing through, Jonas, as ever.'

That made him laugh. It was not an attractive laugh, but then again it was not something Jonas was known for. His laugh could make the blood of junkies freeze in their syringes.

'We'll see how the cholera turns you on, eh? Come on, I've got something better for you.'

He had a room in a hole in the wall of the old fort. A tomb which would have shocked a Spartan. The old ritual, the old stories, the newer stories. For eighteen months Jonas had been dragged and kicked through jail and the loony bin. Now he spoke Turkish with a Russian accent and spoke very highly of a small prison in the countryside, where he'd risen to become a hairdresser's assistant. His job had consisted of shampooing the customers – men who'd gone to prison as children so that the elder brother, who had committed a murder, could feed the family; men whose cold cell floor was the only place on earth they felt secure; men whose last enemies were guards and rats. They had all eaten the same food, done the same things, harboured the same fears. It almost sounded as if Jonas had discovered the ideal life which we in our Berlin commune had dreamed of – no demands, no possessions, no ambition. Jonas was in prison in Istanbul when the cholera outbreak began, and then he was released. One morning they had carried out thirty coffins that had been made in the prison when the epidemic hit. The deceased had knocked together their own coffins.

'What about you?' Jonas asked. 'Have you finally finished that book you always wanted to write?'

'Uh-huh.'

'I see, so what now?'

'I plan to write another one.'

'Why would you want to do that?'

I couldn't come up with an answer and left soon afterwards.

The rainy period started, and wet patches appeared on the ceiling. Then the water started dripping onto the bed. I moved down one floor to share with a Frenchman, a tall, spindly guy from Normandy, whose slang I barely understood. He had the face and hands of a farm boy and the body of a Chinaman who'd been smoking opium for sixty years. He sat on the edge of his bed and gave himself a shot, said, '*Oh, le flatch,*' by which he probably meant 'flash', and collapsed into a heap, the needle sticking from his arm. For simplicity's sake I called him Flatsch after that.

In November I ran out of money. I'd tried to organise a few minor deals, but soon discovered that I no longer had the nerve. I saw nothing but police all over the place, and when I didn't see police I saw ghosts. A reasonably friendly Swede suggested I accompany him on the overland route to Kabul, before the mountains became impassable. He was waiting for money. When the money was there I sorted out everything at the bank for him, then I asked him to advance me two hundred lira. I didn't want to be in debt to the hotel again. He made a pinched, Swedish, social-welfare face, and I left him standing there outside the bank with his down sleeping bag, cowboy boots and blue eyes. No harm done, I thought; somewhere there's always a Swede standing outside a bank, waiting for someone to show him where the entrance is.

Flatsch only ever left the room to go to the loo or score opium. He spent nothing on food. He was satisfied with what I gave him – the odd piece of chocolate, half an orange, or a hunk of bread with goat's cheese. When he was halfway lucid he'd talk in fragments about an aunt in Normandy he wanted to visit. It remained a mystery what he was doing in Istanbul. He'd grown up in a tiny village and his aunt lived in another village. He'd wanted to visit her to help out with the harvest, but he'd ended up in Paris instead and now he was sitting here, dreaming of apple trees. I probed further. Someone had told him about India. In India, they'd said, everyone was happy. Poor, but happy. Flatsch had also been poor, but happiness had evaded him. So now he was in Istanbul in winter, the cold room, the opium, the stranger lying on the other bed, reading or asking him questions he didn't understand.

'*Pourquoi tu veux être heureux, Flatsch? Le bonheur n'existe pas.*'

'*Comment?*'

I could foresee that he would die here. I had to disappear or I was going to get into big difficulties. I wrote to Germany. Sarah sent money, Stern sent money. I got some opium for Flatsch, left everything there for him that I couldn't carry on my person, and skipped town again. Winter had arrived early. Snowflakes swirled above the mosques and put the slums under water. This time I knew it was for good. I was someone who was only ever passing through.

twenty-one

I went to meet William S. Burroughs at three o'clock in the afternoon in his sparsely furnished apartment in Duke Street, not far from Piccadilly Circus. He was wearing a black, three-piece suit which reminded me of the suits worn by my grandfather, a primary school headmaster, a white shirt and black tie. I'd put on my pinstripe suit again, with a white shirt and tie. Burroughs was tall, gaunt and slightly stooped when he walked. He'd turned white at the temples and his mouth was a narrow, bloodless line.

'Tea or coffee?'

'Coffee.'

'Black or white?'

'White, please.'

We both had a cup of Nescafé and sat at a brightly polished table. Burroughs had his back to the window. Through his glasses he fixed me with his gaze. His eyes were blue and radiated the unshakeable authority of a high court judge who's seen all manner of corruption, and even when every bribe is added together it still doesn't amount to enough for him.

'What kind of magazine is it you're working for?'

I said a few words about *twen*. My English was not

particularly fluent in itself, but now I found my thick German accent disagreeable. It didn't seem to bother Burroughs. Maybe he had some sort of perverse sympathy for the Germans.

'And this article you mentioned?'

I'd been commissioned by *twen* to write a report about hard drugs. Lou Schneider had established contact with Burroughs while *twen* had paid for my flight to London and given me substantial expenses up front. I was on my way – and how! I tried to explain to Burroughs that I'd been a junkie myself for four years, and in my report I also wanted to write about how one could get off the gear. Burroughs had managed it with apomorphine. Apomorphine was unknown in Germany. That's why I was here. He lit another cigarette. He smoked filterless Senior Service. Chain-smoked them.

'What sort of stuff did you take?'

'Oh, opium mainly.'

'What? Raw opium? You didn't take it intravenously did you?'

'Yes, I did.'

'Young man,' Burroughs said, with the hint of a smile, 'you must have been out of your mind.'

He gave me a short lecture on the effects of raw opium. What he said was more or less true, even if he didn't know it from experience. He'd always had clean stuff, but of course he'd been around when opium devotees coughed up lumps of their liver. It was getting dark in the room, but he didn't switch any lights on. He gave me a summary of what he knew about apomorphine. Under the supervision of an

English doctor called Dent, it had finally allowed him after fifteen years to conquer his addiction, his metabolic disorder. 'The good doctor is no longer with us, I'm sorry to say,' Burroughs said, standing up to make more Nescafé, 'but both his nurses are still practising. I could give you their addresses if you like. And then we've got a doctor in France who does a course of apomorphine treatment, and another in Switzerland.'

He sought out the addresses for me and noticed that I was gazing in fascination at the only picture in the room. At first glance it was nothing more than a wild arrangement of colours around some lettering, but as you looked at it longer you saw strange rhythms and structures, all of which varied the lettering.

'It's by Brion Gysin, the painter and cut-up collaborator,' Burroughs said. 'You should take a look at it when you've taken a psychedelic drug – although I have to advise some people against this. For many contemporaries it's better if the doors remain locked.'

'So you wouldn't recommend cut-up to everyone either?'

He gave me another economical, wolfish smile.

'Listen here, son. One man can take a whole spoonful of raw opium, while another drops dead when he's inoculated against smallpox. Are you a writer? I don't wish to be indiscreet, but you don't look much like a reporter to me.'

I told him that I hoped to be published soon, and by the house where Lou Schneider worked.

'Really? How interesting.'

He vanished into the next room, returned a moment later and handed me a magazine-format booklet wrapped in brown packing paper: *William Burroughs: APO-33 Bulletin.* The subtitle was: *A Report on the Synthesis of the Apomorphine Formula.*

'You can keep it,' he said. 'A small contribution to health care.' He laughed, but this staccato ha-ha-ha came from a rather dark place. 'The apomorphine formula,' he said, sitting back down, 'is a contribution to the cleansing and decontamination of the planet. Decontamination from what? From illness, dependency, ignorance, prejudice and stupidity. The question is, are the people in power now interested in this decontamination? Young man, you know what the answer to that is.'

He talked until his face was completely in shadow. Clouds of smoke billowed through the room; I thought somewhere I could hear the ticking of a clock which suddenly went quiet again. Burroughs's voice was raw, cold and utterly fastidious, a precisely functioning cog in a machine, and it perfectly fitted his raw, cold and utterly fastidious sentences, sentences that reminded me of Dashiell Hammett. I stared at him through the smoke, and all of a sudden I thought I was listening to a Chinaman polluted with opiates in a Hong Kong slum, a triad boss talking about the last internal butchery, interrupted by forced, guttural laughter. Then I was sitting opposite a Texan marshal informing me that, on his deathbed, Wyatt Earp had revealed to him the location of the treasure of Sierra Madre; and finally I realised that William Burroughs was the reincarnation of Sherlock Holmes – a Sherlock Holmes who now had to waste his entire time crawling through the cesspits of our consciousness and the rubbish tips of the powerful, and solve his last major case, the Case of the Naked Lunch, the naked, polluted mouthful on the rusty fork. Whodunnit?

When it was eventually dark in the room, Burroughs cleared his throat. 'Don't forget to send me the article.'

The interview was over.

The girl's name was Bärbel. She wanted to work for *twen*, too, and the somewhat helpless editor had sent her to meet me in Hamburg. Bärbel had a pretty face with a button nose, she came from Mannheim, and told completely incoherent stories. I wanted to go to bed with Bärbel straightaway – my cock had to forget Sarah even if my head couldn't – but Bärbel was sitting in this dark, crammed, perfumed photographer's flat somewhere in Eppendorf, getting on my nerves with her stories. Then she showed me a gun, a double-action revolver with mother-of-pearl grip. It looked like a toy gun, a lady's gun, maybe all right for gas cartridges. I spun the cylinder, took a sniff. Nothing. Still, it felt pretty good. Later, when the others had forgotten about it, I slipped the revolver into my bag.

I was only able to stick it out for a day, then I left for the station with Bärbel. The train to Munich stopped late that evening in Göttingen; I got off with Bärbel, we took a taxi, and at midnight we were standing in the snowy country road, waking Sarah with our knocking. Sarah came and opened the door. She was wearing a long dressing gown and offered us some of her home-made bread. It seemed to be all she lived off, the stuff was rock-hard, the stove cold, the three of us went to bed, me between the two girls, who were soon gently snoring. A full moon hung in the window.

I tried waking the girls by stroking them; their snoring got quieter, they groaned slightly in their sleep, I could feel their dreams, but also sensed I had no place in them. The shadow in the moon looked like Burroughs.

The article came out and could be found in every kiosk. Although my name wasn't on the cover, the editorial team had given my report a brash headline and printed the picture of a sweet blonde to lure the public. I roamed the cafés in Frankfurt city centre. People were reading *Der Spiegel*, *Stern*, *Quick*, tedious things like *Autoillustrierte* or *Pardon*; but where was *twen*? There, in Café Schwille, I saw a reader, long hair, nickel glasses, you bet! I stole carefully up to him and peered over his shoulder. Leafing indifferently through *twen*, he paused for a moment when he came to the blonde, paused again at the Tuscan farmhouses, then put the magazine away and picked up the features section of the *Rundschau*. Anyway, I didn't give a shit about these sorts of readers, what counted were the insiders. *Der Spiegel* and *Stern* would have to follow suit now; they always followed suit and it was perfectly obvious that they wouldn't pass me by. I could see the interviews already, 'A Contribution to the Decontamination of the Planet', and I'd have nothing against throwing in an essay either, a reportage, although of course I'd still remain tied to *my* paper.

Der Spiegel and *Stern* didn't get in touch. Apparently *twen*'s circulation had fallen rapidly, and it would fold two months later. And Gutowsky's publishing house was on the verge of bankruptcy.

twenty-two

I'd had a close look at Burroughs's *APO-33*. It was a cut-up
text written in columns and assembled from anecdotes,
stories and newspaper reports, which appeared in his novels
as insets and movable pieces, like a trail of blood. There
were also characters and sentences or phrases from books by
Graham Greene and Joseph Conrad.

The text was broken up by photographs, snapshots,
picture montages – Chinese banners, newspaper kiosks,
book covers, houses, a bar and a hotel in Gibraltar, a drawing
of a pirate flag. A text as bulletin, a book as magazine, I liked
that. I was fixed on having a book, and if Gutowsky went
bust I'd be out on the street again, where it was becoming
bloody uncomfortable, and I'd be without Sarah, too. I saw
myself typing letters again: 'Dear Sir or Madam, Please find
enclosed … working on a second book … very grateful for
a swift response …' Besides, I'd already ticked off most publishing houses; those that remained were firms whose names
didn't inspire great confidence, such as Werkbund-Verlag
Stolberg/Westfalen, or Verlagskollektiv Roter Mohn/Berlin-
Neukölln. I might as well save the postage. Perhaps it would
be helpful to begin with a witty, quickly put-together cut-up
piece in magazine format, and when the piece created a furore

I would already have one whole *Blues*, plus half another one in place: Would you care for any more? I could be pretty confident that a booklet in the style of *APO-33* would cause a furore – you only had to take a look at what was piled high in the bookshops: sociology, 'vox pop', 'Third World', soft porn. According to the critics, the great vanguard of German writers were suffering from severe creative crises, or getting involved in politics, entire libraries were flying from the shelves of the lower floors, and every banner proclaimed the end of literature – or at least its transformation into the Socialist Collective of Authors. Maybe Lou Schneider and Anatol Stern were right after all, and cut-up was the only suitable response that individualists could give these days.

I got straight down to work.

I was back in Göttingen, but the flat I was visiting was slightly larger than the one in Düstere Strasse. Clint Kluge was a gangly thirty-year-old with long blond hair and a bandana that he wore in the modern fashion. His wife and daughter were blonde, too, both of them would be crotchety, and then become soft and plaintive, also in the modern fashion. Stern and Schneider had set their sights on Kluge as a publisher because he had connections with printers from his work as promoter and manager of a students' and artists' club that I'd carefully avoided during my time here in Göttingen. What was the point? Now I was sitting at the kitchen table with Clint Kluge, cultural giant and future publisher, drinking tea, spattering my trousers and outlining my ideas about the book Kluge wanted to publish. I even had a title already: *Ice Box*.

'It's meant symbolically,' I explained to Clint. 'Just as addiction freezes your metabolism, civilisation freezes all of humanity, and it's only when we've detoxified ourselves …'

'Super,' Clint said. 'I get it. The title is fine. Adele, could you take her to kindergarten earlier today? We need to work in peace.'

Adele went into a huff, which I could understand. It was minus ten outside. Yes, I already had a decent title up my sleeve, even though the book wouldn't come out till March at the earliest, and then the crocuses would be blooming once more. But it ought to be a long-term seller, too. This time I decided I wouldn't manage the financial aspect of my book as poorly as I had with Gutowsky, who in spite of our contract still hadn't come up with the promised five hundred marks.

'So all there's left now is the question of a contract,' I said, spreading some more cream cheese onto a crispbread. 'I mean, it would be best if we sorted that out in advance. What sort of advance were you …'

Clint Kluge did not make a pained face; he had a different ploy – he simply laughed. He had a fairly large, flat face, so his laugh was fairly large and flat too. It could have easily filled a television screen.

'Advance? You've got to get that out of your head right now – I'm just starting up my publishing business, where on earth am I going to get an advance from? And I'm the one taking all the risk, aren't I? I've got to pay the printer, all the costs that stack up, not forgetting postage, marketing, I mean, I can't walk the length and breadth of Germany to peddle the book. Look, Harry, let me make you a fair proposition: as soon as enough money's come in to cover the rough costs, we'll split the profits fifty–fifty. Deal?'

'When do you think the rough costs will be covered, then?'

'Well, we're bound to flog five hundred copies fast, and that should deal with the printing costs.'

'If you say so, Clint … so, shall we draw up a contract?'

'Oh, contract … sure, we could do … but come on, friends can just shake on it, can't they?'

It was new to me that we were friends, but his face expressed such disarming honesty – as big as a television screen – that I could hardly say no if I didn't want to look like a whinger. So I nodded and took some more crispbread. I don't particularly like crispbread, but it was still nicer than that macrobiotic stuff which was served everywhere now.

Clint Kluge turned up in Frankfurt with a package of books. There it was: Harry Gelb, *Ice Box*. My first book. Or at least the first that had made its way to a printer's. We'd had the manuscript reproduced exactly as it had come out of the typewriter, added a few modest photomontages, bits torn out of newspapers, recipes etc. The text was quite a jumble – even *Schmargendorf City Blues* looked linear and comprehensible by comparison – but this was the time of experimentation, shifts in consciousness, new paths. In a word: underground. If *Ice Box* wasn't underground, then what was it? Kluge went straight off to a rock concert, taking a pile with him. When he returned he'd sold three copies. The book cost three marks fifty. Well, you couldn't expect too much too quickly.

'What did the people think of it?' I asked Kluge. 'Surely they flicked through it and said something.'

'Oh, you know what they're like. Some idiot who writes for the *Rundschau* muttered something about a lack of originality. They see cut-up and then you're pigeonholed immediately.'

'So typically German,' Anatol Stern said. 'Those are people who all lead the same, completely interchangeable existence, identical furniture, identical books, identical food, identical women, whom they fuck in an absolutely identical way. They talk the same, they vote the same, they go on holiday to the same Greek island, look the same, smoke the same brand of cigarettes, drive the same make of car, listen to the same music, and are conditioned so that they will all appear at the same time in the same place when one or other of their gurus gives the right word. But if writers with similar experiences and views, using similar stylistic methods, come in the end to similar – and yet on an individual level completely different – results, then these zombies resound unanimously, "Lack of originality!"'

'And this is in a country,' Lou Schneider said with his fierce FBI voice, 'where every year literature seminars unleash a dozen Bachmann copies and Uwe Johnson imitators on humanity. Mamma mia!'

'Don't worry,' Clint Kluge said to me. 'I'll sell your book.'

All the same, I began looking for a job.

twenty-three

In Stiftstrasse was an old jazz bar, Zero, where now they were putting on live rock music. It was the new 'in' place and also called itself a rendezvous. Clumps of GIs stood outside the entrance, waiting for someone decent to rendezvous with, and on the other side of the street plain-clothed policemen were parked and taking photographs. Zero was the hottest joint in town; I only went there if it couldn't be avoided. I'd stopped shooting up and, besides, I had no desire to get into trouble with the drugs squad.

One evening I was standing at the bar when I saw someone playing table football who I knew from years back, from the jazz-bar days. I chatted to him for a while. Paulus had been studying pharmacy and enjoyed experimenting with amphetamines; now he was working in Zero.

'What sort of work can you do here?'

He told me he was friendly with the two managers and he'd been employed on a fixed wage, as a sort of head dogsbody.

'You seem to be having more fun here than you did studying pharmacy.'

Paulus grinned and scrutinised me though his rimless spectacles. 'What about you, man? We're reading big stories by you in *twen* now. Are you still shooting up?'

'I've stopped.'

'Glad to hear it.' He stared at me a while longer, then took a deep drag on his Roth-Händle and said, 'Listen, we were just wondering whether we ought to do a newspaper ourselves. You see it's going to take off here, it's going to be big – you know, underground, counterculture. If you're interested in taking part, come back tomorrow afternoon. Someone like you would be just right for the paper.'

It took me no more than a minute to see it that way too.

The following afternoon I turned up at two on the dot. I'd just taken out a subscription to *Newsweek* and, armed with the latest edition, *The Times*, the *FAZ* and some underground publications from London, I felt professionally kitted out. The managers of Zero were sitting with Paulus in a cubbyhole behind the stage, going through bills and getting themselves in the mood for the evening with a pinch of coke. One was called Carl Dorfmann, a tall, broad-shouldered, PE-teacher sort; the other was a slightly more delicate, darker and shiftier version of Dorfmann, and he was called Wolf Westenberger. They were types I'd never really met before: young, smart wheeler-dealers, fluent in the jargon of subculture, aping its rituals and customs while exploiting it at the same time. The time when we'd dreamed of anarchy in a freezing Berlin winter now seemed far off. Here, in this cubbyhole with the cocaine and cash box on the table, subculture was all of a sudden something quite real and commercially viable, like vacuum cleaners, carpets or modern art. Eagerly, I breathed in this air. I'd had enough of frozen lumps of spaghetti. Besides, I'd always enjoyed befuddling my brain with a project. And although the projects that were buzzing around here seemed gargantuan, I felt they were perfectly feasible, more feasible, at any rate, than Ede's ramblings back in Istanbul about typewriters, exhibitions and the Museum of Modern Art.

'I don't, however, have a whole lot of experience in putting together newspapers,' I admitted truthfully.

'That'll come,' Carl Dorfmann said. 'We didn't have much experience with stuff like Zero either – and now we're number one in Frankfurt. And once the paper's up and running, we should give serious consideration as to whether we enter into communal politics.'

'Of course,' said Paulus, who in the past I'd come to value as a sceptical scientist. 'If the politicians aren't capable of responding to our needs, then we must become politicians ourselves. In Amsterdam the Provos have been elected onto the city council.'

'This trouble with the chief of police has got to stop,' Wolf Westenberger said. 'A raid every night and we'll be closing.'

'We need a new image,' Dorfmann said, arranging a few specks of coke.

'That's why we're doing this meditation thing now too,' Paulus said.

'What meditation thing?' I asked apprehensively.

'Butzmann's doing it, the former happening-artist,' Paulus said. 'Now he's got a meditation circle that meets here once a week. In summer they go to the Grüneburgpark and do levitation exercises, and this way they reduce aggression in the drugs scene. The city contributes something; we often meet with the councillor in charge of cultural affairs.'

'When I heard what that theatre rakes in, and just how much they subsidise each seat in the opera,' Dorfmann said, 'I was flabbergasted, Wolf, I really was. And what do we get? We take the young people off the streets, we stage rock music, organise cultural activities, set up painting groups, kindergartens for single mothers, a little bit of therapy here, a little bit there, meditation, a newspaper – isn't that culture?'

'Someone from *Spiegel*'s coming next week,' Paulus said. 'Whatsisname? That guy who's always writing those long, meticulous reports. Now he's going to focus on the scene. We'll give him a real welcome, Butzmann will do him some meditation, he's made a name as an artist, too; it'll be the perfect PR for us.'

'Which means those council people won't drop in any more,' Dorfmann said.

'What ideas did you have for this newspaper?' Westenberger asked me. I could see how the roles were divided up. Dorfmann did the talking, Westenberger called the shots and Paulus was a kind of figurehead, but he also had to fill in as doorman. He was wondering what role they had envisaged for me. All I knew was that I had a foot in the door.

'Well,' I said, 'it depends what you've got in mind. Of course we could start very small and then build the thing up, or we could make a splash right away. In London they've had a large underground press scene for years – *IT*, *OZ*, *Friends*. Now, Frankfurt's not as big as London, but we should be thinking along these lines if we want to end up with something more than a collection of our own sermons. We need to include communal politics, the music scene, literature, sport, everything that concerns us. Reportages, information, entertainment, education. One page for drug-users, and one that says what's happening at Eintracht Frankfurt. Record tips, demonstrations, the rubbish-collection scandal, the new cut-up series published by Gutowsky, and the decline of Westend. The paper that no one in Frankfurt can avoid. A platform for freaks and hash cakes for progressives in newspaper form. Zero for the entire city. Here we go into the colourful Seventies! Flower power and Zero power. It's going to cost a bit, of course.'

I could see that I'd hit on the right style. Where else could you find a rock club where the managers produced a progressive underground paper with an international flavour? It would allow them to be visible in London, Amsterdam, New York. *Zero*, the magazine which gave *Pardon* and *twen* the kiss of death. A lead story in *Spiegel*, and then the advertising business and an island in the Caribbean. We all had our dreams.

'We'll do it,' Carl Dorfmann said, offering me a pinch of coke. Westenberger nodded and Paulus suggested a game of table football to celebrate. The managers had particularly liked the bit about Eintracht Frankfurt. Both of them were season-ticket holders at the Waldstadion and the Bieberer Berg. You can tell these sorts of things.

The next day I began with a monthly salary of eight hundred marks plus expenses.

'For the time being we'll do it here,' Dorfmann said. 'Later on we'll rent some proper editorial offices.' He also set up an editorial account at the bank, which I had access to.

This was the set-up: a desk was moved into the artists' dressing room, where in one corner Westenberger, his cowboy boots on the table, spent the whole day on the phone to agents and musicians in London. 'Hey, Rod, how are you? When are you coming to Frankfurt, Rod?' I was given a telephone, I bought a few packets of index cards, drew a sign, Zero Magazine – Editorial Office, and stuck it to the dressing-room door. The girls who served at the bar were flabbergasted, but they felt uneasy about me. They preferred the musicians. It'll come, I thought, but now's the time for some hard graft.

I called the first editorial meeting. The editorial team was to consist of the editor-in-chief, Paulus, Wentz the designer, and Butzmann the happening-and-meditation artist. Wentz, a man around forty with a permanent smile, was the only true professional amongst us; he could cope with the layout and understood something about printing. His rock posters were all over the city. He was a typical designer, who turned up on the first day with a plastic case in pop colours, looking slightly queer, but he was a very hard worker. Butzmann, with his waist-length straggly hair and big bushy beard, had already been through all the current avant-garde phases. He'd said farewell to this type of art, and now just drifted about with his posse of dope-smoking disciples, most of them from the batik scene. I gave him the task of designing the centrefold, which could be a little rosy and mystical. That gave him plenty to be getting on with and I seldom saw him. Paulus wanted immediately to run a pharmacologically scientific series on drugs. I thought this was redundant, given that some evenings at Zero you could hardly see your hand in front of your face for all the chillum smoke, but so long as it made him happy I was fine with it. Naturally, Wentz had approached the paper with wide eyes, immediately seeing a magnificent playground where he could give free rein to his designer's tics. Now he came with the craziest typefaces and incredibly eye-catching graphics, as well as a photo series which he wanted to sign Herr Asahi (after his camera). All too brash in my opinion, but Wentz was the cultural guru of the team, so I turned a blind eye. The publishers reserved the right to approve every line. We all needed our playground. Compared to what went on in the cubbyhole in the afternoons, Butzmann's crowd and their meditation exercises were about as crazy as a Samaritans' coffee morning.

It took me a few days to understand what was going on in those heads, the 'vibrations', as the process was now known. Finally, it dawned on me. This was a business – pure commerce – whose protagonists probably had a murky past, or at least a not entirely spotless one. Given that their lifestyle, as well as the lifestyles of those they earned their money with and everyone they earned their money from, was equally tarnished, not to say criminal (anyone who smoked a joint was guilty of an offence), they'd come up with the brilliant idea of spinning a fine web of culture around this business, cultural hustling and bustling, active involvement in what the Frankfurt councillor for cultural matters, the highest communication guru Hilmar Hoffmann, never tired of calling 'culture for all'. But culture in this sense was pure optimism, rosy-cheeked, pie-in-the-sky, ecstatic for technology, horny for popularity, lustful for the future. We were all young. No one had any worries. Bob Dylan gave expression to it and everybody bought it: New Morning. New Morning Frankfurt. New Morning Deutsche Bank. New Morning *Zero* magazine. New Morning publishers all over the world.

'We need a press release,' I said. 'People have to know that we exist.' We were with a friend of Dorfmann's, a model, drinking Bacardi, and vodka with bitter lemon, and listening to New Morning music, the whole lot of us.

'You're right,' Dorfmann said. 'Have fifty thousand printed and distributed throughout the city.'

I sat in a corner and dashed it off: 'Zero Press Release No. 1 – Red Morning'. I was still struggling with New Morning. I gave the scrap of paper to Dorfmann, who read it through.

'No, no, no,' he fussed. 'It's far too political, we can't have that.'

He gave it to Paulus. Paulus shook his Beatles hairdo. 'Why are you so aggressive, Harry?'

'Shit!' Westenberger cried after taking a look at it. 'Do you want the city to close us down?'

Aha. The penny had dropped at last. I sat back in the corner. This time I needed ten minutes at most. I had a new headline: What Use Was Timothy Leary? Above it I put: The Revolution Is Over – We Have Won. They read it.

'That's it,' Dorfmann said, filling my glass with Bacardi. That night I thought of the Teflon firm, the Bundesbank. I'd earned eight hundred marks there, too. But I hadn't lied half as much for it.

twenty-four

Putting together a paper was a job, and I knuckled down. By now the publishers were convinced that the magazine was going to be a success, so we had to have the best printing possible, no expense was to be spared. We had lead typesetting, we had newsprint, we had red as a second colour, Wentz and Butzmann drizzled and thrust and sprayed their reds over the double-page spreads, I sat until late at night in the artists' dressing room, drinking vodka and making myself understood on the telephone over the noise of the music. I spoke to Lou Schneider, I spoke to Anatol Stern, I already had a network of correspondents in London, the Rhineland, Göttingen and all over Frankfurt am Main. I asked for an assistant – who had ever heard of an editorial team without an assistant? – but the girls at Zero preferred cleaning up rock stars' vomit to a career in the newspaper industry.

Lunatics turned up – pale German students from Upper Franconia in traditional collarless jackets, who placed on the desk weighty piles of single-spaced poems and tracts they had personally typed out, and put themselves forward as stringers; and every evening Wentz and Paulus would arrive and present me with their new findings.

'Here,' Paulus said with his dopehead smile. '"If a proposition is not necessary it is meaningless and approaching meaning zero." Wittgenstein. Isn't that hot?'

'What do you want me to do with it?'

'I thought we might put little inserts everywhere with Wittgenstein quotes. The man's just mind-blowing. He was already zero before *Zero* existed.'

'I thought we were making a newspaper.'

'A *new* paper. New Morning!'

'Here,' Wentz announced. 'I've got an advert. A small advert, but every little bit helps, Mr Editor.'

I read the small advert. *Emma sailing two brass beds.*

'Surely it should read *selling.*'

'But then there wouldn't be any joke.'

'All right. But what about the comic strip?'

'Let me outline what I've got in mind. I'm going to put two columns here. In this one I'll just put comic symbols – flowers, letters, characters, numbers. And in the right-hand one I won't put anything; the readers will have to make up their own story. Because doing it yourself is always better than having it done for you.'

'I thought we were going to run a serialised comic strip. Isn't what you're suggesting a bit childish? I mean, who's going to sit down at home, cut these snippets out with scissors and then stick them together?'

But Wentz had already received the publishers' blessing, and besides, he *believed* in this crap. I was producing an underground newspaper in Germany; I was doing it with two disco owners, a student in his eighteenth semester and a progressive design pedagogue.

Wentz lived in some godforsaken town in the Offenbach district. Offenbach was the domain of designers.

'Cut-up is all well and good,' he said, 'and I certainly don't want to stick my oar into the political side, but a paper like this has got to be human, it must radiate human warmth, we need to bring goodness, the others bring badness,' and he took me to an ice-cream parlour in his godforsaken town.

'Tonio,' Wentz said, introducing me to the owner, 'comes from an old family of glassblowers in the Veneto, and he's collected the old proverbs his father used to tell the children. The father's sixty-six now, and was here quite recently, so we wrote down his proverbs. I think they'd be really useful for our paper.'

Wentz wanted the sayings to appear on page three and he got his way. Instead of the great local reportage I'd dreamed of, we now had old proverbs from the Veneto, as they'd been written down in an ice-cream parlour, glassblower's proverbs: 'You can't make holes in water', 'Washing the head of an ass is a waste of soap', 'Heaven helps those that helps themselves', and then, of course, Butzmann came along with his gang and wooden-bead necklaces and Indian shirts, and he had put something to paper, too – an overview of personal space and time. The conclusion was: it is not this or that, but paradise. He got the rest of page three. I gave him a proper talking to.

'I'll tell you this, man: if the thing doesn't sell then all this proverb crap is going to be out on its arse.'

'You shouldn't just think of sales,' Butzmann said. For a moment I gave him a stare. I needed this moment, then I knew. Butzmann was the hardest salesman of us all.

The bosses noticed how much I was slogging my guts out, every day from eleven till one or two in the morning, and occasionally they'd take me to the football, Waldstadion, Bieberer Berg, to eat spare ribs, on a small train trip through the region, or to one of their meetings with the chief of police or the councillor in charge of cultural affairs. The chief of police wanted to close Zero down; the councillor saw the club as part of his plan for the city as a media hub. In all the new metro stations he wanted to install video studios, televisions, wired stories, do-it-yourself films, workshops on all B-levels, informal communication, pottery courses for the space age. Looking at the chief of police you could see that he, too, was thinking of video, of a do-it-yourself cinema, cabled communication, cameras filming silently on all levels. They belonged to the same party, the party that August Bebel and Wilhelm Liebknecht had founded one hundred years previously. So this was space-age social democracy. Zero was made to comply with strict conditions. Well, when I looked at the paper we'd just printed, those gentlemen could be well satisfied.

Given the hellish printing costs – almost eight thousand marks for ten thousand copies of the twelve-page paper – I was obviously forced to reduce the author fees to practically nothing. That I managed, but then the publishers came and set the price at one mark fifty per copy – madness. I tried to explain – apart from my editorial there was nothing in the paper you couldn't get anywhere else, that's if you wanted to read it in the first place – but I soon realised that these swinging young entrepreneurs in the underground scene were no more than contemporary versions of those archetypical small-capitalist penny pinchers who had given this narrow-minded and stuffy Central German Uplands region its characteristic stench. They'd forked out so much and now they wanted to see the cash come rolling in, and it made not a blind bit of difference when I worked out for them that by selling the thing at one-fifty they'd see less than if they sold it for one mark. But to have their names on the masthead as publishers, well, maybe that would impress their wheeler-dealer friends, their rock stars, their models.

Our first edition was due to appear in Frankfurt on 1 May. To mark the occasion, the bosses had dreamed up a nice little coke-fuelled vision: dozens of saucily dressed Zero girls would be posted at all strategic points in the city centre, and sell the paper like hot cakes. Little materialised of their vision of super saleswomen; it rained on 1 May, and after two or three hours the two girls who had coyly slipped off with their packages of newspapers between the student demonstrators and the beer drinkers wandering about Hauptwache, tossed the packages into a corner, settled up for the few copies they'd managed to flog and cleared off home to put on some dry jeans.

'We need to do it ourselves,' I explained to Paulus, and with a packet we trawled the venues where the hippies, students, actors and artist crowd hung out. They didn't exactly tear the paper out of our hands, either; in the artists' cellar we were given a plate of bread and schmaltz and a glass of red wine. Of course, that evening Zero was absolutely littered with the paper, Butzmann's magic Zero ring, his double-page spread, was everywhere. I went up to the disc-jockey on the platform, took the microphone and gave a short speech, a summary of my editorial: 'Changes within ourselves ... subvert manipulation ... techniques of liberation ... don't let your minds get burned out ... principle of life ... contemplation and action ... we've won ... if we want to ...' Rod Stewart sounded better, but when I stood up there in the dark, where the lamps of the mixing console glowed like insects' eyes, the crowd below me a mass of flesh and smoke and sex and hunger and muffled yelling, I had the peculiar feeling that all this now made sense – from the roof in Istanbul, the commune in Berlin and Sarah's lap, to here in Zero with a newspaper in my hand: New Morning! Butzmann's levitation exercises, the Veneto glassblower's proverbs, Wittgenstein. 'The world is everything that is the case', a bit of pharmacology, the designer's tics from the Offenbach district, Emma sailing brass beds, cut-up, the expansion of consciousness, and we'd even squeezed the bird expert into the paper, also from the Offenbach district, found by Wentz, the old bird expert from the millpond, 'I'd like to start going into schools, that's where you've got to begin,' and half the junk in small print, but that's not what mattered any more: New Morning! I was a guru, everyone was a guru, everyone was a newspaper. New Morning.

When I came back down and, amongst the junkies and the dealers, the GIs and the plain-clothed police, the con men and the conned, the crooks and the gurus, looked for a quiet corner with my vodka, a reduction in consciousness, a woman who wanted to be my guru, I met Babs. She was the sister of the last mug we'd duped in Istanbul on the day we were busted. She was dressed up to the nines, her long, black hair shone as if lacquered, her red mouth promised the sensuality of the Kama Sutra. Her eyes were circled by the yellow shadow of addiction. She was there with some blacks. Her brother was in prison again. I suddenly realised how many of us were addicts, how many of us who thought they could burn for ever had almost burned out for good. I moved to the bar. At least I was getting served a bit more rapidly these days. A Mediterranean type spoke to me, a short man with shaggy black hair, a wild moustache, animated eyes and an energetic face furrowed with harsh lines. I put him in his late thirties. He had the paper in front of him and asked whether I was the editor. Then he shook my hand and bought us both a drink.

'I'm looking for someone,' said Dmitri, the Greek, 'to help me work on a screenplay. I'm a film director and I've been living in Germany for two years. I've written a screenplay, but the German's poor.'

'What's it about?'

'Ha,' he said with a laugh. 'Rockers, students, revolutionaries, the CIA, traitors, death. It's about politics, do you get it? About life in its entirety.'

Dmitri accompanied me to the last metro. I learned that he'd managed to escape from the secret police at the very last moment with the rolls of his first film. This was in 1967 when the CIA brought the Junta to power. He was working as a bank trainee and hoped to have this latest project screened on television. Then I was sitting in the metro, looking through the paper. It would be hard to find anything more amateurish with such extravagant pretensions, I thought, but all the same you did it and nobody can take that away from you.

And there it was in print, too: Editor-in-chief Harry Gelb. But one thing's for sure – those fools are not going to mess around with your work any more. That's the end of glass-blowing wisdom, do-it-yourself comics, levitation exercises and snippets, whether they be from Wittgenstein or Wentz. And as for the publishers, they needed standing up to. They needed to be undermined. If only they *had* put Eintracht Frankfurt in the paper with their season tickets, their fan T-shirts, their big talk. There'd been enough big talk, now it was time to make a real magazine. Underground, but not in the underground scene. We'd had our little romp around the playground; the next edition would be compiled behind closed doors. What did Burroughs say? 'For many contemporaries it's better if the doors remain locked.' The man was right. If you really wanted to achieve something, you had to keep the crowd at a distance, the crowd of hangers-on, contributors, wafflers. If you haven't got a good team, I told myself as the metro rolled into Nordwestzentrum station, then do the paper yourself.

l Raw Material Raw Material Raw Material Raw l
terial Raw Material Raw Material Raw Material
l Raw Material Raw Material Raw Material Raw l
aterial Raw Material Raw Material Raw Materia

twenty-five

I found a room in Wolfgangstrasse, near the city centre, one of those student digs let out by widowed house owners with dyed-blonde perms and eyes the colour of old family safes. We fetched the bare essentials from the jumble at Zero with a pick-up truck, then I got back down to work. I wasn't just turning the magazine on its head, I was making a brand-new paper. All I intended to keep from the first edition were the masthead and imprint. There and then I also decided on a size of twenty-four pages and a cover price of one mark. I wasn't planning to make newspaper history, but for eight hundred marks a month I felt I had an obligation to do the best I could, and the best would be if I refused to allow anyone to butt in.

It came in handy that I was now a co-publisher of another magazine. Louis Schneider and Anatol Stern had decided that the time was ripe for a stylish in-house publication of cut-up conspiracy, and had invited me to come on board. In Stern's Volvo we dashed to Göttingen, and in two days and one night we put together *Ufo*. Schneider was not a professional designer and had never been to the Offenbach district in his life, but when it came to producing slick layouts, there weren't many professionals who'd be able to teach him anything. He'd been doing this sort of thing since he was a student, and after knocking back a few screwdrivers he put together *Ufo*'s twenty-four-page layout with incredible speed and skill, as if he'd done nothing in his life except work with Letraset and paste columns. Clint Kluge, the publisher of *Ice Box*, and now *Ufo* too, sat there open mouthed.

'Wow, Lou!' he exclaimed. 'That's totally professional!'

Lou fanned away the cigarette smoke and peered through his thick glasses at a photomontage, which he moved a millimetre to the left.

'Oh,' he said drily, without taking the Camel from his mouth, 'you should have seen me putting together this little magazine with Jim Silver in the East Village, *Seven-Up-Sisters*, or whatever it was called. You practically had to stick the Letraset on with a spray gun, otherwise the cockroaches would have eaten it off the paper. Those cockroaches must have really dug Letraset! Weird. And every quarter of an hour one of those nigger junkies would fall dopily from the fire escape; you needed a steady hand to align your captions. Yup, Clint, compared to that, this is like a weekend with the parish magazine.'

Having watched Schneider and Wentz, I felt I'd be able to put together *Zero* magazine by myself, if necessary. OK, I probably wouldn't win the art directors' prize, but now I wanted to make a real underground paper.

'We need a bit of action in it,' I told Bramstein, the only German student I'd given some freelance work to. Although he, too, was pale and ghostly with his long, straw-like hair, *and*, of course, he wrote heaps of poems, he did have a car, a girlfriend with perky tits, a healthy thirst and he came from the Palatinate. As a rule, people from the Palatinate were not quite as insane as those from Upper Franconia, the Allgäu, Dithmarschen, or anybody from Offenbach.

'Feature the Black Panthers,' Bramstein suggested. 'There's the trial of Black Panthers on at the moment in Zweibrücken; that sort of stuff will go down brilliantly – Power to the People!'

'Good idea. What shall I do? Copy it out of the *Rundschau*?'

'I'll go there myself.'

He went and wrote a wild, but not entirely informative report on the trial.

'We'll put it on the back page,' I said, 'with that photo of them raising their handcuffed fists in the Black Power salute, and I'll insert a speech bubble saying "Kill the pigs!".'

'Can't wait to see what your publishers are going to say to that,' Bramstein said.

'This time the first thing they'll see is the finished product. When I look at the sales figures they won't have much choice but to swallow it. Six hundred through Montanus, three hundred and fifty via other bookshops, two hundred direct sales – if they want to wallpaper the Eintracht clubhouse with their magazine then let them go ahead. A juicy trial is the best thing that could happen to them, isn't it? Why do you think they weren't mentioned in *Der Spiegel*'s underground report? I'll tell you: because they're feeble little busybodies of the sort you can find anywhere, even in Dietzenbach or Büdingen. But feature a trial for defamation of the state, glorification of violence and whatever else, just imagine the splash that will make! They'll follow suit, *Spiegel, Stern*. I know they will, they always follow suit.'

'Yes, but those clauses have now been liberalised,' Bramstein said. Students of German always had a tendency towards defeatism.

'I know the chief of police,' I said, to conclude the discussion. 'The moment he gets a glimpse of the magazine, he'll see red. Then he'll be out for blood.'

I also got involved with the sales side. I did a tour of the Rhineland, the Ruhr. I got off the train in Bottrop, marched along the railway embankment, then down the street with the brick houses until I found the place I was looking for. Aldo Moll met me with a huge yawn and a bottle of beer. He was working for Krupp as a programmer, and when he'd finished his afternoon siesta he would sit in a storeroom and investigate counterculture.

I'd never seen anything like it – piled high to the ceiling was an encyclopaedic collection of material that brought to the light of day cottage industries and libertarian groups, macrobiotics and health-sandal freaks, anthroposophs and anarcho-syndicalists, advocates of armed struggle and all the sanctimonious followers of non-violence, handmade paper and silk-screen printing in West Germany, Switzerland and Austria. Aldo Moll had made it his hobby, nay his revolutionary task, his life's work to ensure that this light was as bright as possible. Here, in his storeroom, which reeked of stale beer, cold sweat and printer's ink, was the relay station for all those untold scatterbrains, wheeler-dealers, political and religious fanatics, prospective and outgoing writers, earnest book makers and whirling dervishes of all varieties of irrationalism, who evidently made up what Moll called 'the scene'. I looked at the stuff for half an hour until it dawned on me that the publishers of *Zero* magazine had misjudged the situation. Well, I'd misjudged it, too; more than that, I'd been totally unaware of these blossoming gardens where utter bullshit formed the weeds against which the flowers of reason had to prevail ever more tenaciously. He also had a pile of *Ice Box*, although I was unsure whether that counted as weeds, too. Yes, blossoming gardens, German counter-culture was blossoming, it was blossoming especially in the hills along the Neckar, in the forests of Lower Bavaria and those of Upper Hesse, it was blossoming in the southern mountain ranges of the Allgäu, as well as in Rhenish Hesse and the Saarland; apparently it had overrun Kreuzberg in Berlin, too, so with our New Morning out of Frankfurt's Stiftstrasse we had arrived slightly late on the scene, but Aldo Moll viewed it differently.

'This is how I see it,' he said, handing me another beer. 'The great German underground paper is coming, and if your people in Frankfurt have the dough then obviously you'll be in the forefront of things.'

'You'll never accommodate all these hundreds of tiny factions,' I said. 'And who's going to take on the marketing? No, Aldo, you need a metropolis like London or New York for something like that. Minds have to be wired the same way, and in Kreuzberg and Idar-Oberstein minds are not wired the same way.'

'Don't say that,' Moll said, opening a flask of schnapps. 'Want a sip? I just can't work without the stuff. My wife moans, but sometimes I'm here in the middle of the night with my beard in the card index, honest I am.'

And his card index box truly was the apple of his eye, which was no surprise – he'd started with a few addresses of trade unionist readers from Bottrop and its environs, and now he sent his information sheet, which he cobbled together himself every two months, to more than fifteen hundred subscribers. Without Moll, the guys who produced *Red Compost Heap* in the eastern Odenwald, or south of Flensburg pushed onto the market the journal *Paths to Mahayana Buddhism*, would have had an even greater struggle to bring their product to the people.

'There's not much in there, to be honest,' he said. 'And it's expensive, too, you know? Another beer, Harry?'

'You wait for the next edition,' I said. I took another beer.

twenty-six

Now I spent every evening in my room in Wolfgangstrasse, typing and sweating and pasting the paper together. Without a bathroom, without a telephone, without a girlfriend it was a pretty lonely affair, and the lonelier I felt, the more radical my mood became. I took some speed and turned up the volume of AFN, *Night Beat*, *The Pete Smith Show*, the Stones, Lou Reed, The Doors, Janis Joplin. Then I drafted a new tag line: in the sewers of consciousness.

During these night-time sessions I got used to the radical mood, which didn't leave me during the day, either. Bramstein and I visited American bars, where dashing black men played pool and talked big. They taught us their revolutionary handshake, we smoked some pot, then I went to the editorial office, where Wolf Westenberger was on the phone: 'Hey Rod, when are you coming to Frankfurt?' He held his hand over the mouthpiece and looked at me: 'How's the magazine?'

I held up both thumbs.

Sometimes Wentz would help me with the layout, and when he cast an eye over the pages I saw that the hairs of his gentle soul stood on end like mountains, but he refrained from passing comment. That's your job, his eyes said; if you can't help yourself then do it. I admit, they seemed to be saying, you can't make an underground newspaper (whatever that is) with the glassblower, the bird expert and Herr Asahi, but – the eyes also said – if you're making it with nothing but Black Panthers, big tits and coarse sayings, with cut-up conspiracies and desperado posturing, then please remove me from your imprint. I removed him.

I had no reason at all to hate anyone, apart perhaps from the guys who took Sarah away from me – but could you hate Krishnamurti, the Sufis, Allah? – and yet all of a sudden this hatred was present, right in the middle of summer, a hot lump in my brain, which could only be soothed and cooled by the rattling of the typewriter and the Stones, even though it needed a completely different rattling, a much more horrific sound. I'd never felt as much hatred in Berlin, nor in Istanbul. Perhaps it was down to this hot, stuffy city, which let off its dynamism in the sky, celebrated every stock market recovery with a new high-rise, a city filled with an incessant droning, jackhammering, demolition balling, metro ramming. In the evenings poisonous air blew out from damaged lungs, a fatal dose, compared to which the pale opium dealers on hash meadow were peddling pure nectar. I climbed the stairs to my digs and turned on the light. The heat lingered in that tiny room. Desk, chair, mattress, a foldable plastic wardrobe, a few books, the transistor radio, the Olympia Splendid 33 – that was enough. I sat down and continued with the layout.

I'd demanded a free hand and been given it too; the bosses had enough on their plates. The police wanted to close Zero with a vengeance, and sent in the regulatory body first, which arrived with new rules and forms of harassment. The newspapers were full of articles about drugs, and they depicted Zero as a hellish quagmire, where innocent sons and daughters of the haute bourgeoisie were forced to commit perverse acts by foreign pushers, GI deserters in women's clothing, and criminal drug addicts from the laboratories of Dr Frankenstein. Nobody protested against the levitation exercises of Butzmann, the happening-artist, even though there was no reliable information about their long-term effects, and no one protested either against the entertainment tax that poured every day from Zero's coffers into the city's.

It was into this febrile atmosphere that I dropped my modest bomb, it carried the nondescript name *Zero No. 2* and was printed on yellow 80gsm paper. This time I'd made huge savings on the typesetting costs and had the layout printed using photo offset in a small-time outfit in Bergerstrasse. When I picked up the first copies the boss there gave me a very strange look – Oh well, I thought, maybe it's a bit much for a seasoned Social Democrat, but then again we're not that different. The Social Democrats began as a terror of the bourgeoisie too. We loaded a few stacks into Bramstein's old Renault 4 and drove to Stiftstrasse. I leafed through it on the way. I could see what the printer meant. You shouldn't stint on the ink ribbon when using offset. But if you ignored the places that were slightly difficult to read and the odd blunder with the layout, the thing looked very stylish – at least compared to the first edition. At any rate, Aldo Moll had some reading material for those long evenings with his card index and schnapps up in Bottrop.

We hauled the stack of papers into Zero. The cleaners had just started work, and in one corner an aunt from the parent-and-child group was practising her mime show with a few little brats. During the daytime the club really looked like nothing but a shed. The bosses were sitting up in their cubbyhole. I handed them two copies and withdrew with Bramstein to the dressing room. He buried himself in a newspaper and I started bagging up the first author copies. This time I'd had a mass of writers and it was not my intention to have engaged them for nothing. When the bosses finally got to grips with direct sales then we'd have a real chance of breaking even at least.

The bosses thought differently. Dorfmann yanked open the door. Scarlet face, visible beads of sweat, the beautiful yellow pages scrunched up in his hand. There was something particularly hysterical about the sight of his blue eyes – a small child in the sandpit whose favourite puppet has been broken by the local bad boy.

'You do understand that you're harming us with this, don't you?'

Behind him Westenberger called out, 'If this comes out we might as well shut up shop, do you hear? Close down.'

'I've never seen a case of commercial damage like it,' Dorfmann said.

'We can talk about that when we've seen the sales figures,' I said, scarlet-faced too.

'Our names are there in the imprint as publishers; do you really think we're going to allow this filth to be published in our names?'

'According to the press law I'm the man responsible

here,' I said, 'and I have no idea why there should be any difficulties ...'

'Here – "Kill the pigs", "Revolution is vital", "Smoke out the bastards", and these sadistic texts here ...'

'Satire,' I said. 'That's how *Pardon* earns its money every month ...'

'At least *Pardon* doesn't look as fucking awful as –'

'Don't let yourself get drawn into a discussion,' Westenberger called out from behind. 'That's enough! Finished! It's over!'

'We're shelving the magazine,' Dorfmann said.

'Give this edition a chance,' I said. 'It'll sell, you'll see ...'

'No we bloody well won't!' Westenberger bellowed.

'We're pulping the paper,' Dorfmann said. He looked like a broken man. Maybe I should have felt pity for him. He'd given me an opportunity – Westenberger had always been against me – and what had I done? I'd look like a broken man too. At some point. Just not now.

'If that's what you're going to do,' I said, 'then there's nothing more to say. Come on,' I said to Bramstein, who was staring awkwardly at the newspaper that had put his name in print for the first time. 'Freedom is being suppressed here.' I took a few copies with me. Westenberger looked as if he was going to tear them from my hands, but he let me be. Dorfmann, who had an eye for the big gesture, hurled the bundle of yellow papers into the corner in disgust. The mime-show aunt from the parent-and-child group had quietly been continuing with her rehearsal. Now she was Marcel Marceau and I was just a dimwit without a job.

twenty-seven

But this didn't mean I was without work. I embarked on the task of polishing Dmitri's screenplay. The Greek director was living in a garret flat in Kettenhofweg, and when the one next-door became free I moved in. It turned out that my new landlady was the same as my old one. Both rooms were barely more than poky dens with sloping walls and top-hung windows which the sun beat down upon, but up there beneath the roof we had the place pretty much to ourselves, and there was even a sort of bathroom. On one of the first nights I was awoken by a Greek war cry, and when I called out to ask what was wrong Dmitri opened my door and triumphantly held out his booty: a mouse.

Dmitri was a Macedonian, a farmer's son from that region to the north of Salonika which had suffered the worst during the civil war. He'd made his name in Athens as a left-wing theatre director. Disgusted by the communists who were devoted to Moscow, he'd joined the Trotskyites and belonged to a group which had smuggled weapons for Ben Bella during the power struggles in Algeria after the country had gained independence. It was from this period that Dmitri had retained a healthy loathing for every kind of ideology as well as officials and mandarins. The only people safe from his ridicule and hatred were his friends and women. He had but few friends, most of whom were in prison. His wife, a lawyer, had stayed in Athens. I asked whether she paid at least the occasional visit.

'Visit where?' he cried. 'This mousetrap here? Do you think this is a place for my wife?'

'I imagine she wouldn't care,' I said.

'Yes, because she's a woman. But I,' he said, 'do you know what I am? A man!'

Dmitri had gained his reputation as one of the best film-makers in Greece with a documentary about Lambrakis, the pacifist deputy who'd fallen victim to a conspiracy between the Fascists and the army. A few years later Costa-Gavras had seized on the topic and made the film Z, a global hit. Dmitri had nothing but ridicule and contempt for Costa-Gavras, as he did for the entire leftist camarilla that dominated the Greek population in exile. Using their contacts, others had a livelihood in France or West Germany if not a job; Dmitri, the ex-Trotskyite, was by day a courier in a bank, and in the evenings he sat in the airless garret, brooding over screenplay drafts and singing at the top of his voice Macedonian peasant songs, spiced with obscene verses he'd made up himself, in which gruesome things were done to colonels and Stalinists.

'What's going to happen to them?' I asked him. We were playing chess and he was holding his king in the air.

'What's going to happen to him? Ha ha! Can't you imagine? Do you think they'll just cut his head off? That would be far too good for the gentleman, wouldn't it?'

'So what will they do with Pattakos when they get him?'

'You Germans seem to have no imagination any more.'

'Fine, I'll give it some thought before I go to sleep tonight.'

He scowled as he stared at the board.

'I need a fuck, a fuck – that's the problem,' he said.

'Let's go to Club Voltaire. Maybe we'll find someone who'll want to go to bed with the two of us.'

He looked at me. 'Can I tell you something? Last year I found a girl who went with me, after a year, you understand. And when she sat naked over there on my bed, I realised it wasn't going to work, so I gave her a piece of cake and sent her home.'

'Why?'

He gazed at the chessboard and after a while said, 'The worst thing about this sort of exile is that for many people it's far more agreeable than at home. They live far better in Paris or Frankfurt than in Athens or Salonika. These bastards are worse than the Fascists. Fascists might beat us to death, but these bastards make us impotent. Checkmate! You ought to pay better attention. Another game?'

'I'd rather you sang something,' I said. 'I'd love to hear again what the peasants do to Melina Mercouri.'

There wasn't much more to do on the screenplay. Friends whose German was better than Dmitri's had already helped him, which meant that I just had to copy-edit the text and occasionally make the transitions flow more easily. Then Dmitri had fifteen copies bound and sent them to film councils and television editors. As he was widely known, if not widely liked, and probably no German film-maker of either the older or younger generation would come up with such a tough and exciting political thriller, I had little doubt that the film would soon be produced. Besides the material itself, this was 1971 and we had a Social Democratic chancellor in Bonn who was unequivocal about his bond with the Greek resistance, and solidarity was a word which had received the blessings of the highest cultural circles. Surely Dmitri would have it made with the councils and editors.

We went to Mainz. Dmitri had an appointment with the big cheese at ZDF television drama. He'd quit his post at the Bank für Gemeinwirtschaft, and as I didn't have a job either we were a bit short on money, but we still had enough for the train fare and some cigarettes, and it could only be a matter of days until Dmitri pocketed his first advance. I was accompanying him as co-author, Gutowsky had finally filed for bankruptcy, and the manuscript of *Stamboul Blues* was back in my drawer. I seemed to have no luck with books or the press. Film looked to be a more promising industry.

By the time we got to Mainz we were both bathed in sweat. High summer was not for people with empty pockets. We had no money for the tram and so walked to ZDF. The two of us had managed to overcome very different obstacles in the past, but as the perspiration ran down our faces and the damp patches on our shirts grew to the size of flannels, I had the distinct feeling that we were lagging behind. In Germany only tramps and snobs walked, and only tramps could think we were snobs.

The big cheese of TV drama welcomed us into his office, which was at a very pleasant temperature. He was middle-aged, wearing a crumpled sports jacket and an even more

crumpled expression; he looked like the deputy treasurer –
perhaps *he* was a snob. When we got to the subject, his face
added a few more crumples.

'Right, the screenplay,' he said to Dmitri. 'Really tense
stuff. I think it's good, I think the film has to be made. But,'
he then added, 'obviously it won't work in its current form.'

Dmitri lit a cigarette.

'Don't fly into a rage, now, Dmitri,' the big cheese said.
'Come on, you know me! All I'm going to do is tell you
what troubles us about the screenplay in its current form.
The rockers. You weren't to know this, Dmitri, but we've just
produced a film about rockers, the best rocker film ever.' He
mentioned a name which meant nothing to me. 'And it's the
best film he's ever made, too. Dmitri, you've got to understand that ZDF can't make back-to-back films about rockers,
I'd never get them to agree to that. I've got to see what we can
and can't do; I can't just make the decision by myself.'

'But my film's not meant to be a rocker film,' Dmitri said.
'It's a political film, the rockers just have a political function
as the lumpenproletariat for the students and as agents pro-
vocateurs for the secret services ...'

'You don't have to tell me that, Dmitri,' the big cheese
said, trying to appease him. 'As I said, I'd do the film like
a shot. It's just, well, seeing as you mention it, Dmitri, the
thing with the secret services ... I mean, have you researched
it properly? You know, I think it is possible that the secret
services have got their moles in the extra-parliamentary
opposition ... but the idea that this has led to deaths, well,
isn't that all a bit speculative?'

'A political film that doesn't speculate will never do itself justice,' I chipped in. 'The Italians, the French, they really go for it.'

The big cheese gave me a combative look. He didn't want to know anything about the French or Italians, seeing as he had enough trouble with this Greek.

'But the story's not authentic,' he said almost reproachfully. 'Both of you have to admit that. By contrast, this rocker film we've just produced – it's on in autumn, Dmitri, watch it. Obviously I'm not suggesting it as a model, but ...'

He left it at that. The big cheese of TV drama was playing the role of the little man in a big organisation with admirable dedication, and this little 'but' released him from all responsibility – Look, it was saying, what can I, a prisoner of this machine, possibly do? Look, the 'but' was saying, I've met my quota of controversy, but if you want to try again for the 1973–74 season, you know I'm always here and willing to help. Look, the 'but' called out, almost in desperation, there's nothing I'd rather do than have a long, proper discussion with the two of you about political films, maybe about the extra-parliamentary opposition, too, the secret services and ZDF's strategy and tactics, and why we made the rocker film by that young, well-known film-maker, but not the political thriller by the ex-Trotskyite Greek arms smuggler – even though, children, the 'but' said, concluding the discussion, you ought to know that without having to talk about it at length.

In the end, the big cheese had given us an hour and a half of his time. On our way back to the station, neither of us uttered any grievances. It was too hot for that, anyway.

At Hesse Television's third channel, a pale, long-haired

editor with owl-like eyes and tinted glasses was tearing the screenplay to shreds. His tone reminded me of those debilitating evenings in the German Socialist Student Union.

'In its current form,' he pontificated, 'I find this screenplay not only apolitical and irrelevant, but – and I'd like to emphasise this point – profoundly reactionary, not to say counter-revolutionary. At no point do you make clear where you stand politically, and this at a time when film-makers in particular adopt a clear stance. As it is, the screenplay is a totally superficial, unrelenting action film, which really doesn't fit in with what we do.'

Even Dmitri, who had substantial experience with these people, had to gulp. The hairs of his beard bristled. I found the rudeness almost impressive – straight from an academic upbringing at home, via the Adorno seminar, to this office of cultural bigwigs, a face that didn't bear a trace of real-life experience, a man who'd never gone hungry in his life, whose greatest threat had been from a professor when he told him after a sit-in to stop all that nonsense, that this man should then reprimand another who had proved his commitment and risked his life for it. That's what you called chutzpah.

My hatred grew. My scars started to burn at the idea that you could spend a few semesters in regular study, in order, perhaps, to scavenge such a job, and from there start writing fat books yourself or prevent others from writing them. I bumped into an old junkie, I immediately scored some gear again, made my way up to the garret and stuck the needle into my scarred veins. In this system there seemed to be no chance whatsoever of realising what you wanted to do. The ruling cliques had finally distributed the prizes amongst themselves – the right-wingers got business, the left-wingers culture. If you fell through the grate you stayed down below for ever. What sort of absurd naivety made us sit up on that roof for three years, Ede with his painting and me with my notebooks? What sort of immaculate conception had made us believe that one day we'd be able to hop straight from our petroleum-drenched and opium-poisoned *One Thousand and One Nights* dream to tread the stage of the German cultural world? If you've done that, may I join you? We'd have been better off going into advertising, I thought, giving myself another shot. The pharmaceutical industry probably had a whole host of junkies under contract. That was something you could still think about. As for culture, they use it to oil their hair or eat it with ketchup.

One evening I bumped into Babs. She could see at once that I was back on heroin, and without saying very much came upstairs with me. I'd known her for a number of years, and all of a sudden we were in bed together. I assumed that she wanted a fix, but she shook her head. She did, however, have that manic compulsion to talk, which many women had anyway, but which was even stronger if they took drugs. Her body had almost withered away, even though she was only a year older than me, and this withered nature gave everything Babs did or let be done to her its own sorrow, an oriental fadedness which was particularly arousing, musk and mustiness. My dulled, feverish brain made me believe I was shagging an Indian goddess. I could smell snakes, amber, essential oils. Her body was dark brown. I rode it like a mortally wounded white conqueror.

Afterwards Babs talked all night, she chain smoked her Roth-Händles and talked, absent-mindedly kneading my cock and occasionally biting my neck, as if to check whether I'd been properly hung and aged. Babs talked about her daughter, about her Indian, about her blacks, about her brother, back in prison again, about her mother, about her job, lost again, about her dreams, about her trips.

'Why don't you say anything?' she asked from time to time. 'Do you think you can just lie here the whole time, shagging me and saying nothing? Are you dumb?'

She bit me and I shoved her away.

'You're hurting me.'

'Oh, so you *can* open your mouth. Do you know what? You're perverse. There's no way you can just listen incessantly to what I'm saying without uttering a word yourself. Have you been like this for long?'

'Listen, Babs.'

Next-door, Dmitri started singing. The wall was fairly thin, and he must have heard everything. Now he was singing his obscene peasant songs. His voice sounded hoarse.

'Shall I go and give him a blow job?'

'Stop it, Babs.'

'I'll do it if you want me to. And I'll do it if you don't want me to as well.'

'I can well believe it.'

'Then I'll suck you off. You dig that, don't you? Say nothing, do nothing. How do you fancy that?'

She did it. I lay there listening to Babs sucking and Dmitri singing. A perfect world.

twenty-eight

I was sitting on the floor, watching the blood run down my forearms. My veins were totally shot. I got up, went to the telephone and called a doctor, who prescribed apomorphine in response to my article in *twen*. He promised to send me a prescription right away. The man was an Israeli. A German would never have done that.

Apomorphine was administered in large doses as an emetic where people had been poisoned or drunk an excess of alcohol. I'd read a few things on it, especially Dent's book and what Burroughs had written about his treatment. In scientific journals and consumer magazines he had for years availed himself of every opportunity to highlight the advantages of apomorphine, which in the main were that it drastically curtailed the horrors of withdrawal and reduced the fear. His Dr Dent had become a mythical figure in the Burroughs cosmos. The so-called experts had pounced on him in unison. The contempt was mutual. After five years on junk I realised that I had to go with either the apomorphine or the world of experts. If I now surrendered myself to the drug doctors, the specialist clinics, the therapists and social workers, the psychologists and quacks and their assistants from various departments; if I now let myself become a patient, I could kiss goodbye to my freedom for a long while – and to writing, too.

I stuck to the lowest dosage that the doctor had recommended, 0.1cc subcutaneously, and lay down immediately. I felt slightly ill, a vague light-headedness, a flickering before my eyes. I dozed off, woke again in a sweat an hour later and drank half a glass of water. I was fairly groggy. I lit a cigarette; it tasted perfectly normal. I looked at my arms, the scars, chunks of burned flesh. A clear case of self-mutilation. Odd. I fell asleep and woke again after an eternity that had lasted only five minutes. Life was a gaping black hole. Perhaps I should take another dose of apomorphine. I did, then fell asleep. I slept deeply, took another dose, slept again. The following day I was already able to eat something. After two days I was up on my feet. I was still quite weak, my knees were shaking, but I fancied a beer. Two days later I had a relapse which I immediately brought under control with a further dose of apomorphine. The following week the doctor rang.

'Did you really do it?'

'Yes, of course.'

'So how are you?'

'No complaints. I'm fine.'

'Listen, if it gets you in its clutches again, give me a call. You can come over here, too.'

'I've still got four phials left, Doctor,' I said. 'They'll last me the rest of my life.'

'Well,' he said, 'at least you've got an advantage over many other junkies: you know what you want to do with your life.'

I wasn't so sure any longer, but I agreed with him. It would have been futile to disappoint the man, particularly now. And I'd really had enough of this sort of stuff.

Somebody was thudding at the door downstairs which led up to the attic. It was Babs. I looked at the clock. Seven in the morning. She climbed the stairs, wobbling on her high heels. In the dim light her hair was as lustreless as her face. Her lips were swollen and her eyes unnaturally small. She was wearing a blouse which was half open, and had splashed on too much perfume. She tried focusing on me, which was not an unqualified success. It was as if her eyes didn't have the strength to manage a complete look.

'You must have something for me,' she said when she got up. I was wearing only my pants and felt ashamed that something was stirring below.

'A cup of coffee,' I said, 'if you can stomach coffee at the moment.'

'Stop making silly jokes,' Babs said. 'You know damn well what I need.'

'Sorry, Babs. I haven't got anything. I'm clean.'

'Clean?' She tried to laugh. It was such an effort that she started to sweat. 'Since when do you call that "clean"?'

'I've stopped taking that shit,' I said. 'I'm off it. For good.'

'Good for you,' she said. She wasn't trying to laugh any more. She needed all her strength to head for the next address on her list.

'Why don't you stop, too?' I said. I'd always had a leaning towards social work. 'With the stuff I've got here it's terribly simple. Apomorphine.'

Babs wasn't listening. She was fiddling with her blouse.

Maybe her brain had told her that the next address was far away and that the money for her gear would be reduced by the taxi fare. She'd rather have another try.

'I understand,' she said. 'You want to fuck me before you bring anything out. Well, what are you waiting for?'

'Babs,' I said. 'Listen to me, I've got nothing except this apomorphine. Give it a try. In two days you'll be off the stuff. It's child's play.'

She put out her hand and stroked my cheek. Her bitten lips were quivering.

'Don't worry about it,' she said, before tottering down the stairs. A little later I heard that Babs had jumped out of a fourth-floor window.

We were broke. Just covering the rent was a struggle. Dmitri tried to get a job in television, but although he could do just about anything connected with film, he couldn't even find work as an assistant cable puller. So I had an interview with the Bundesbank and in fact was taken on again. This time I was in the personnel department, and because the man I was supposed to be working under was off work with illness, I had an office to myself and spent the day updating the payroll for the medium- and lower-rank employees.

It was interesting for a few days. What solidity these card boxes harboured, what comfortable living! I could see precisely when each employee had started working for the Bundesbank, what salary they had started on and what they were getting now. With my staff lists I had all their details before my very eyes: this one lots of cars, this one lots of women, children, owned homes, lawnmowers, holidays, second car, refrigerators, colour televisions, fitted kitchens, washing machines, mopeds, baby outfits, family graves, plus a few thousand theatre and cinema tickets and truckloads of Böll, Lenz, Simmel, Grass! Things were dispatched from here to there – after all, people did move occasionally – you sucked up to the bosses and then got the house on the slopes of the Taunus, south facing. The world of the Bundesbank was well organised, so long as you didn't make any faux pas. You could be part of this too, I thought, just stick it out for a few more years and they'll give you a permanent post, then you'll have your regular seat in the staff restaurant and in your free time you can set up the Bundesbank writing club. It looked even more desperate than a career in the literature industry. Gutowsky's business had folded. I heard from Clint Kluge that the sales of *Ice Box* were slow. Once he sent me two hundred marks, and I took Dmitri out to dinner.

A few things started to get going politically. In Westend the first houses were squatted, mostly palatial joints which had gone to rack and ruin and were now targets of speculation. The SPD were in the firing line for letting the concrete tower blocks go up and taking backhanders from speculators, which clashed with the verbal socialism of their youth organisation. And the members of the Baader–Meinhof gang still hadn't been nabbed; on the contrary, the Red Army Faction seemed to be well organised and spreading their ideas amongst the people, or at least those who were prepared to listen. I picked up a few of their brochures and showed them to Dmitri. He read and returned them to me with a scornful look.

'If there's anything worse than an orthodox communist,' he said, 'it's a paranoid communist. Huh! This lot are loonies. Loonies with guns, just watch out!'

'There were some bits I didn't find too bad,' I said.

'If only they were real anarchists,' Dmitri said, setting up the chess pieces. 'But behind these slogans all I see are death squads. Marxism–Leninism! Vanguard of the proletariat! Bang, bang! What's wrong? Don't you want to start?'

I moved a pawn. 'But sometimes, Dmitri, I think that it would be a good thing if it all blew up here.'

He laughed. 'What? Just because your book isn't being printed you want revolution tomorrow?'

'That sounds funny coming from your mouth. After all, you were the one who smuggled weapons. And because you're one of those, you can't get your foot in the door here, either.'

'Maybe,' Dmitri said. 'But with the Germans the problem is different. Look at yourself, look at me and then look at those editors and those people like Kluge or Schlöndorff. They have a particular physiognomy; you can see straightaway that they belong together – same background, same university courses, same views, same life. And you, my friend, you and I, we don't look like that, and that's why it's hard for us. But just because they think it's smart to babble on about revolution now, it doesn't mean that the Red Army Faction's right. I'm Greek, I know what revolution is and how blood flows. And now I'm going to take your bishop!'

He took it, but I'd been learning and I gave him a bitter struggle. I admired Dmitri's toughness. For him, life in exile was a series of setbacks, insults, duress and daily disasters, and yet he stuck it out, even though it was ages since he'd believed in socialism, the revolution, or just that life would get better at all. He believed that he'd make another good film one day, and he hoped that at some stage he'd be living with his wife and child again, and see the generals hanged from the lamp posts. If you thought about it, that was rather a lot of hoping.

twenty-nine

We approached our destination at dawn, a troop of dark figures wrapped up thickly in parkas and leather jackets, beneath which we carried crowbars and car jacks. Our boots crunched on the early frost. We made it to the rear of the building, the basement, without being seen. Somewhere in the distance we could hear a police siren, but it wasn't getting any closer. The door wasn't a problem. We were soon in the empty house. It had four storeys, parquet flooring, tiled bathrooms, stucco angels on the ceilings, wrought-iron railings on the balconies, a broad, winding staircase, conservatories, and stood on Bockenheimer Landstrasse near insurance companies, banks, advertising agencies, university institutes and other occupied houses. A Persian estate agent and speculator in Westend planned to turn the house into an office building. Well, from today it was going to be our home for a while.

The occupation had been planned long in advance and was carried out by all the groups who were involved politically, from AG Westend to the anarchists. To prevent any freeloaders from taking advantage, anyone wanting to move in had to explain their motives before the plenum. Of course, there were holes in the system, for some liked to keep us in the dark about their purpose. These included the anarchists, who only wore dark clothes anyway, had black flags and tended to draw their ideals from the shadows of history rather than its sunny sides. The anarchists included me and Dmitri as my co-opted shadow. Both of us were fairly wet behind the ears as far as anarchism was concerned. In addition, Dmitri was expressly excluded from all campaigns. After all, he had another job now, one where he worked nights and slept during the day.

The preparatory plenary sessions were dominated by two factions: the Communist Student Union (KSV), which in terms of numbers was the strongest grouping; and Red Student Action: Law Division, in which the Dantons and Bossis of the future were earning their spurs. The anarchist representation was not of such high quality. It basically consisted of an out-of-work commis chef from Wiesbaden and me. On the other hand, we refused to allow ourselves to be trumped in verbal radicalism by any of these intense Maoists, and this aroused the sympathy of a group of rockers, a small band of stray lumpenproletariat that had become the darling of the students. Life in this house promised to be a lot of fun. Even a French girl wanted to join us, the girlfriend of one of these future provincial high-court judges, shyster lawyers or bank robbers. She was a graceful person, with fiery eyes, long, black hair and cat-like movements. Her name was Bernadette.

The first dispute arose when we insisted on attaching our black flag to one of the balconies. The KSV lot wanted to stop us, but after some plain words – 'Renegades! Traitors to the workers! Think of Spain!' – the commis chef prevailed.

By mid-morning we had as good as won our battle. Our supporters had the streets virtually to themselves, and many residents dropped in with warm clothing and warm wishes. The chief of police acquainted himself with the situation and disappeared again. One speaker after the other hailed an important victory. Listening to them, you might have thought we'd just stormed the Winter Palace in St Petersburg, back in 1917. Well, maybe there was a bit of that, too. History never repeats itself, and a life can become bloody long if you only look back at the defeats.

It had been agreed that no alcohol was to be drunk during the day, but of course the rockers didn't stick to this. A day without beer simply didn't count. In the name of anarchism we joined them, and by the evening we were on fine form. Instead of the 'Internationale', 'Red Wedding' and 'The East is Turning Red', the loudspeakers were pumping out the Stones, Jimi Hendrix, Ton Steine Scherben. We already had electricity, water and gas. Meals were cooked. The Italians from the Lotta Continua faction served up spaghetti. Really homely. Dmitri didn't hold back with his snide comments.

'You'll see,' he said to me, as he was getting ready for work. 'Soon they'll be fetching their books and furniture, and make it all domesticated here. After that we'll have timetables on the walls and Mao posters, followed swiftly by the stereo equipment, and then girlfriends, sisters and parents will come to visit. Rugs, houseplants, the collected works of Enver Hoxha, a cosy home. These are people who want it all: bourgeois and bohemian, career and revolution. Can you tell me how that works, eh?' he said, packing his sandwich in a plastic bag. 'Surely every revolutionary must know that if the system allows you anything you have to destroy it; you mustn't just make yourself comfortable. These people want to be revolutionaries, do they? They're the new Social Democrats.'

I wasn't surprised that when the rooms were later allocated, Dmitri only got the attic space. The rockers got the basement.

The plenary sittings or house assemblies were never ending. When Germans organise something, it happens with the most irritating pedantry, whether it be a party, culture or a squat. Well, during the daytime the students had their seminars, training courses, Marx exegeses, so maybe they needed the evenings to try to put what they'd learned into practice – hadn't Engels also said something about the allocation of detergents, or Mao something on the question of whether the KSV needed to occupy two tiled bathrooms? For us outsiders there was no point in trying to divide these Marxists. No matter how much of a lather they got into about the right path to the dictatorship of the proletariat and the question of whether AG Westend was or was not an agent of capitalism, when they had to defend their rights in the face of anarchist pests or lumpenproletarian Blanquists, the Marxist factions closed ranks at once and stuck together.

'Hands off our tiled bathroom!'

'A reading room for Red Student Action: German Language Studies Division!'

'Where's the KSV's ping-pong table supposed to go, then? Comrade Lin Biao said that ping-pong represented the defeat of capitalist heteronomy, social democratic lethargy and Russian hegemonic self-importance.'

'Who bought this crate of beer?'

'Alcoholism is the imperialism of the little people.'

'I thought you supported the little people.'

'Comrade, in China there are no little people any more.'

'Oh yes, a platform heel for everyone in China.'

If I'd been a strong character I'd have moved up to the attic with Dmitri, but I'd had enough of attics. Eventually I got a room with a balcony on the first floor, parquet flooring, stucco angels. Besides me on that floor lived the commis chef, a KSV student – Gertrud, a bitter blonde girl with man problems – Alf, the go-between for the rockers, the divisions of Red Student Action, other groupings that were remaining in the background for the time being, and representatives of the Italian squatting scene from Lotta Continua, a few Milanese with fanatical eyes and very stiff ways of behaving who soon decided to keep themselves to themselves with their spaghetti pots, their bottles of red wine and their arrogance.

Bernadette was a Trotskyite, but perhaps French Marxists weren't as orthodox as ours; at any rate I noticed that she responded to my looks in the evenings, when we sat in the assembly room on the ground floor, discussing all the problems associated with such a large house, from the heating costs to the distribution of flyers, as well as Lenin's ever-relevant question: 'What is to be done?'

I kept up valiantly; what did I have to lose? And I didn't want to become anything. In Red Student Action: Law Division there were a few more independent minds, in whose presence you could express deviationist, ironic or offbeat views, without immediately being reviled as an agent, a clown or a petit bourgeois. So I made a play for Bernadette, I rehearsed rebellion every day, I set off fireworks and, with the black flag on my balcony, visibly blended in with the ringleaders of the revolution which we mouthed like Tibetan monks do their prayer formulas. Nobody asked me what on earth I was doing amongst the would-be subversives, the state-subsidised Maoists and the lumpenproletariat in search of a warm little corner for winter. Every day I heard the thousands of linguistic variations of the political lie; I could have said: 'I may not be writing literature at the moment, but I am inuring myself to some of its modes of expression.'

Red Student Action: Law Division organised a party on their floor. I hadn't been to a party since my schooldays, and this one wasn't much different, only a bit louder, a bit more hardcore, a bit more debauched. You put something in your mouth, cavorted about for a while, then, fancying a bit of the other, you put something else in, this time down below. Bernadette was up for it, too. Mind you, no one had given me kisses like that at our class parties. With Bernadette, every kiss was a frenzied attack, a breathtaking insurgency, a coalescence with abandon. Somehow we found my room. The student next-door was playing Janis Joplin on her record player, Janis Joplin, Janis Joplin. We took the occasional gulp of wine. In the end we were lying beneath the duvet on my mattress. 'Busted flat in Baton Rouge, waitin' for a train.' Bernadette wrapped her legs around my back. In the moonlight her black hair was spread out like a banner. 'Freedom's just another word for nothin' left to lose.'

thirty

Bernadette moved in with me. I couldn't believe it. It was pure coincidence that I was allowed to be part of this, and now I had the most beautiful girl in the house. In the house? Beneath every red flag in the world. I had her every night. During the day Bernadette worked in a bookshop. That was fine by me. I needed the day to recover. I gave up the job at the Bundesbank straightaway. The head of personnel was not at all happy. He didn't understand me.

'You ought to think about this long and hard, young man! You'd have had a pay rise soon!'

'Yes,' I said, 'but do you know what? I really *would* like to make it as a freelance writer now.'

He shook his head.

'Freelance writer? What's the point of being free if you don't earn anything? You're twenty-seven. Just don't go thinking it'll be easy for you to get a job like this again.'

Later on I often thought about these words.

I told Bernadette. Our nights were quite long, but she didn't seem to need much sleep. And if we weren't making love, we talked.

'Forget your job,' she said. 'If they'd found out where

you were living they'd have thrown you out anyway.'

'Don't say that. The Bundesbank isn't any old branch of a savings bank. It's a job for life.'

'That sounds as if you regret it, *chéri*.'

'Nonsense. It's just that I've got to earn *something*.'

'There are always jobs.'

'Not for me. What can I do?'

'The bookshop is looking for a packer.'

'Me packing books?'

'What's wrong with that? They're paying six marks an hour.'

'No way. I'm a writer, not a bookshop dogsbody. I *write* books, not pack them.'

'That's reactionary. Socialism has removed the separation between manual and cerebral labour.'

'Maybe it has. And I've got nothing against factory work. I mean, if it has to be done. But I'm not going to pack books.'

'Hold on. You say you're a writer, but you never write anything.'

'Writers don't always have to be writing.'

'But if you're not writing you can't earn any money from it.'

'Bernadette, it's possible to live without packing books.'

'Oh *là*, I was just trying to help. Come, *chéri*.'

'Dmitri said his firm's looking for people.'

'What sort of work is it?'

'Oh, you know, it's sort of … well, Dmitri mainly sits somewhere in a factory and makes sure that nothing happens.'

'Is it a sort of policeman?'

'No, no. They call it night watchman, gatekeeper. He says he spends most of the time reading or sleeping.'

'Night watchman? You mean he works at night?'

'They don't need him during the day.'

'But at night,' Bernadette said, bringing the discussion to an end in her own way, 'at night *I* need you. Like now, you see, *chéri?*'

Dmitri was right. No sooner had the students moved in than an orderly, regulated life, managed by committees, panels and the Dietz edition of Marx and Engels, took its course. Obviously there were breaking points, but organisationally they were kept to a minimum. This was evident from the allocation of the living spaces. The rockers had already left the basement, which had now been heavily bolted up to keep out uninvited guests.

The common rooms were on the ground floor, as were the rooms allocated to some obscure groups which were committed to practical action. Then there was the mixed floor with the Italians and us, above that the quarters inhabited by the head honchos of the Red Student Action, the KSV and postgraduates. Finally there were the attic rooms, housing the unemployed, foreigners and anarchist splinter elements.

'I want to show you something,' Dmitri said. He opened the door to his room and crept in. 'When I shout "GO!" turn the light on.'

He shouted 'GO!' and I turned the light on. He'd stripped off the bedclothes. The mattress was full of bugs. 'The entire attic is ridden with bugs,' he said. 'It's often like that in these old houses.'

'Oh, fuck!' I said. I looked at him. 'Dmitri, I'll get you a room downstairs. You can't stay here.'

He cast me a coldly cynical look, a look which a man adopts for dealing with the political commissars amongst his troops.

'What about the others up here? Can you get rooms for them downstairs, too? On the best floor, perhaps?'

'The entire attic should be shut. Bugs!'

'But that would be a waste of living space,' Dmitri said. 'Come on, we can cope with a few bugs.'

He grinned and offered me some of the food he'd bought for his night shift: Greek sheep's cheese on special offer and black olives.

From my old room I'd brought only the mattress, my clothes, my books and a box with my manuscripts, the mountain of paper that gathered as soon as you wrote. If, of an evening, there was no house assembly, plenary sitting or internal anarchist discussion, and Bernadette wanted me home, sometimes I'd leaf through my old stuff. Candlelight, a bottle of red wine, my Trotskyite strumming on her guitar or playing records. Handel, Segovia, domestic bliss bang in the minefield of the social struggle. If you were broke, you couldn't complain. Bernadette washed her hair in the tiled bathroom, then sat by the radiator in her dressing gown, a towel wrapped round her head like a turban.

'Let me read what you wrote,' she said, filing away at a fingernail.

'Oh Bernadette, it's all rubbish. You know, old hat. The next time I write something it'll be very different.'

'But please show me the book that's meant to be coming out now; I'd love to read it.'

'*Stamboul Blues*? But it's hard to understand.'

'What are you saying? Do you think I'm too stupid?' She unleashed a torrent of French, then continued in German: 'A French person who's read nothing in their life apart from a sports newspaper has a greater understanding of literature and more feeling for the language than most students of German here, believe you me!'

I believed her. After all, she was French, and had come to Germany to learn German. She also worked in a bookshop and was a Trotskyite, and Trotsky had been quite proud of his appreciation of literature. And, not least, she was my lover, *mon petit ange*, *mon amour*. All the same, I doubted that *Stamboul Blues* was her sort of thing. I gave her the manuscript I'd revised for Gutowsky. The white plastic cover was worn and stained. Bernadette snuggled up in the bedclothes and read. She frowned all the while. Oh well, I thought, Trotskyite literary criticism is one thing, the judgement of a man like Lou Schneider quite another. When it came to literature, the Marxists had shown that they still had fairly reactionary tastes. The same was true of politics, ultimately. Eventually, Bernadette put the manuscript to one side and snuggled up to me. She sighed.

'You were right, *chéri*; it really is hard to understand.'

'Don't worry, Bernadette – it's hard for Germans, too.'

'But not because of the German, you idiot! It's hard to understand because it reads as if it's so literary, and yet it's completely unliterary – also, of course, because I don't know what you're writing about.'

'Oh, most of it's just verbiage.'

'Why do you say that? I can see your scars. If only I knew who'd hurt you so much, so that you hurt yourself so much.'

I cleared my throat. This was the sore point. The thing read as if I'd been subjected to some God-awful horror. OK, there had been a bit, but most of the time I'd felt that this sort of horror was actually quite comical. The comedy hadn't really found its way into the text, however; perhaps only people like Lou Schneider or Anatol Stern could detect it. If you wanted the comedy in there, you had to lay it on thicker.

'Just forget it,' I said. 'Nobody hurt me. Anyway, I've been thinking whether I shouldn't start working for Dmitri's firm. They're looking for casual employees, two or three nights a week. That would be an easy hundred and twenty marks.'

'*Ecoute, tu es complètement fou …*'

I knew that the *Stamboul Blues* discussion was now over. I was looking forward to these three nights in the week. Time to think in peace. Time to relax. Bernadette's demands as a woman were far more extensive than her political ones, and she wasted no opportunity in making that perfectly clear. Of course, Sarah had done that too, but ultimately with her, pure theory had vanquished love – to say nothing of literature.

thirty-one

The offices of Germania Security were near the university, in a new building from the final phase of post-war reconstruction. The anarchist commis chef had lost his job as a chip fryer in a fast-food shack – there had been some uncertainty over a delivery of chicken halves which had gone missing without trace – and so the two of us were interviewed for jobs in the security sector. The commis chef was all in black, from his hair to his horn-rimmed glasses, and his parka to his boots, which he'd greased specially. I was wearing a calf-length trench coat in a green military look with a black Basque cap and my well-worn Clark desert boots. Well, I'd never done military service.

We went down a corridor on the first floor. Germania Security was a hive of activity. There was the shrill ringing of telephones, men in uniform dashed here and there, sticking their heads in doorways and calling for coffee and papers; somewhere people were playing a game of skat, and a two-way radio crackled. It felt as if this corridor, with its shabby linoleum and roll-front cabinets, led to a whole new society with its own procedures, legalities and conflicts. A little world in itself, which blessed everyone who entered it with glory, followed by immediate punishment if necessary.

This was true of every job, of course. Employers always acted as if you were coming to them to save your soul, and afterwards they were offended if you complained about all the deductions. You had to be on guard as if you were in enemy territory. The three Turks in their salt-and-pepper coats, who sat at a round table and were supposed to be filling in forms, had already made their decision. One after another they stood up and left the office. A little man with a white mane of hair stuck his head through the door.

'Where's Kemal Atatürk?'

'If you mean the three Turks,' I said, 'they've just left.'

'Really?' He peered at me through his thick glasses. His head reminded me of Hegel. 'They'll come crawling back on their knees, just you wait! But it'll be too late; they've blown their chances with Germania! What about you? Are you planning on collecting for charity, or do you want a decent job?'

'We've heard you're looking for casual workers,' the commis chef said cautiously.

'You're dead right we are, gentlemen! Come in, come in! If you're looking to go to heaven, you'll have to try somewhere else, but here on earth you've come to the right place. Now, if you don't mind, look this way please, head up, say "cheese". Click ... OK, one more. Now you ... click ... and now fill the forms out, please. Do you have a criminal record? No, of course not. We'll discuss everything else once you've got your uniforms, OK? Yes, that's right, capital letters. I can see you're educated people, you can't imagine how I have to pore over these forms sometimes. Good, that's all done. Now, please wait and I'll call you one by one.'

He vanished into his room with his camera and forms.

The commis chef and I looked at each other and couldn't help smiling. I was sure we were thinking the same. Anarchists as auxiliary policemen. We smoked our cigarettes and watched the lively activity around us. Another bunch of people looking for work turned up. Some of them looked as if they'd come straight from the men's hostel or the train station, specks of blood on their cheeks after a hasty shave with cold water, dirty shirts, and plastic bags containing their worldly belongings. Bottles clanked. All of them resolutely filled out the forms. Then Hegel called me in.

'Congratulations! You're now employed as a temporary security guard. This is your ID badge, whatever you do please don't lose it. Any further questions, Herr Gelb?'

'Yes, I'd like to know the hourly pay ...'

He gave a figure that sounded extremely low.

'But on top of that, of course, you've got extras – night bonus, weekend bonus, overtime – it all adds up, young man, and in the end you'll be better off than if you spent eight hours a day sorting out empty packaging at Hertie ... and anyway, you can't begin to compare the two, not only is the work here full of variety and thus less of a chore, but you're also performing a service for society that no money can compensate for, it really is a position of responsibility, and I can see that someone like you, well, you're attracted by that ... and, Herr Gelb, as a student of human behaviour, the human personality in all its manifestations, you must admit this is the ideal job for you, prove your worth as a security guard and I guarantee that there'll be a position for life, a life's mission waiting for you ... oh yes, the uniform, come with me, what size are you?'

I was handed my coat, trousers, peaked cap, whistle, torch and ID badge, which gave me unrestricted access throughout the building I was assigned to and allowed me to detain suspicious people temporarily. I didn't ask Hegel how I was supposed to carry this out. I already felt like a prisoner.

Bernadette made some extraordinary noises when I took my new work gear from two plastic bags. Then she stood on tiptoes, threw her arms round me and gave me a kiss.

'*Tu es fou, chéri*,' she exclaimed in a pause for breath. 'You're completely crazy! Oh, you're so crazy! You're the craziest man I know! Oh, you're so sweet! You're crazy! I could eat you up! Mmmmmmm! *Tu es complètement fou!*'

She had to try on the uniform, of course, the baggy trousers, the coat with the Germania badge – an eagle being struck on the beak by lightning – the cap, also with a badge, everything made out of grey, scratchy material, bits of uniform from all the lost wars, maybe even looted from the police barracks of Lvov, Kiev and Bessarabia. Bernadette looked like she'd been miscast in a Jean Genet play performed by the amateur dramatics group of Offenbach District Adult Education Centre. The door to the adjoining room opened and Gertrud, the severe KSV girl, smiled. I hadn't seen her in ages. Her Nordic face radiated an unmistakable sexual satiation, rather than its customary hunger for men and disappointment in love. On her bed lay a black-haired young man with an Afro, dressed in an expensive leather jacket, creased trousers and fancy ankle boots. I heard a strange squeaking.

'What on earth is that?'

'It belongs to Fred.'

'Who's Fred?'

'My new boyfriend. Come on, Fiffi, look at this.'

Something hopped about on her shoulder. A tiny monkey, a baby chimpanzee wearing striped rompers. The monkey was tugging at her blonde hair. Oblivious to it all, the guy on the bed was smoking a cigarillo and skimming a magazine. He looked hopelessly out of place beneath the Mao poster, but who didn't? Having said that, I wouldn't have put the KSV blonde down as the type to fancy a pimp. Well, perhaps that was the Peking Central Committee's new watchword: seek allies where the class enemy least suspects you will find them.

The commis chef appeared. He was already wearing his uniform. Together with Dmitri we'd be able to start a Germania Security group in our house. What the Opel factory in Rüsselheim was to the Revolutionary Struggle and the academic staff to Red Student Action, the Frankfurt pimp scene was to the Maoists and the security industry to us temporary anarchists; and if, in the end, you didn't reach your goal, you could always say you'd taken some valiant steps along the way.

It was time for my first shift. Bernadette walked some of the way with me.

'During the war Simone de Beauvoir always took Sartre to the train when he had to go to the front,' she explained. Although I knew that Sartre had never been at the front and thought the comparison rather questionable in the first place, I was touched and gave Bernadette a hug. It was good to know there was at least one person who shared my view that work was also a form of war.

We kissed again at the corner and then went our separate ways. Bernadette hurried off to the socialist Christmas celebrations, and I strode to the security firm's offices. They had a Christmas tree, too, and Hegel was handing out coffee and biscuits. From the rosy cheeks you could tell what was being added to the coffee. I was handed something I didn't like the look of at all: a black truncheon about 50cm long.

'At Christmas time they think they can clean up to their hearts' content,' the chief of operations said. He left open the question of who *they* were. 'What that means for us is greater vigilance and, if necessary, to act without mercy. Right, men, before we go I'd like to wish you all a happy Christmas! And so, let's raise our mugs, even if they've only got coffee in them, ha ha ha!'

I looked around at the faces. Those with permanent jobs seemed elated, determined to do anything. And if this Christmas Eve came to a bloody end, then even better. The temps looked more pensive. I was certain that, given a different scenario, some of them would be on the side of those to whom the chief of operations was calling for no mercy to be shown, if necessary. Well, I was a student of the human personality in all its manifestations, as Hegel had put it. We lumbered down the stairs. It got increasingly colder. Candles were burning in the windows and we could hear Christmas carols, the potpourri of Hesse Radio. Culture was being deployed too.

I was the last to be driven to his premises. We did a long arc through the gloomy area around the Osthafen, then the chief of operations stopped outside a factory building. We got out. The ground was frozen. The sky seemed very high, with all those glittering things we called stars. Somewhere a freighter hooted. The chief of operations rang at the gate. Scraps of music skipped through the night. Footsteps crunched, a dark figure came closer. Shift change.

I was given my brief. Three times during the night you had to do a patrol of the compound, where key boxes were stationed at strategically important points. These keys had to be turned in the timer you brought with you, and a piece of paper inside the timer showed the times at which you'd arrived at each control box. The chief of operations showed me the compound. There was a factory hall, which looked more like an indoor junkyard, the grounds, then another factory hall, a hostel and an administrative block that led to the road. And those key boxes were everywhere. I asked him how I was supposed to find them all.

'There's a plan in the control room,' the chief of operations said. 'And anyway, it doesn't matter if you miss the odd box. After all, it's your first night here.'

And my last, if I've got any say in the matter, I thought. I felt as if I were over the border somewhere in East Germany.

'And keep a close eye on the hostel,' the chief of operations instructed me. 'It's not part of this compound, so if anyone comes over here and starts making merry then give him one with the truncheon, OK?'

'What sort of people are they?'

'Italians.'

The night ahead was looking a little brighter now. They left me alone in my control room. A desolate wooden shed.

Alone with a tiny electric fire, a wall calendar from the Metalworking Federation, a wobbly table and the logbook. In the logbook you had to write the patrol times, the name of the guard and any particular incidents. I made myself as comfortable as I could on the hard office chair, drank my first cup of Nescafé from my Thermos flask, and turned my attention to the logbook. It made for instructive reading. '23/11 04.56: Italians v. noisy. Got them quiet again. 26/11 02.12: Lorry damaged fence. Tried to get number plate, but driver drove off. Müller.' I pushed the logbook aside and took out my own book. I'd brought Dostoevsky with me, *Demons*. A judicious choice, I thought, burying myself in the chapter that opens the second part, 'Night': 'Now, when everything is over and I am writing my chronicle, we know what it was all about; but then we still knew nothing, and naturally various things seemed strange to us.' *Demons* was one of those books I read over and over again. I thought it more useful to know a few books really well than to have read a few thousand from which you retained only vague memories. It gradually warmed up. I went on reading.

All of a sudden I jumped. A dog had barked very close by. A burglar with a dog? Unlikely. Must belong to the Italians. But what sort of sound was that now? Somewhere there was a ticking. A soft, metallic ticking. Didn't sound very nice. I stood up carefully and grabbed my torch. What would Dostoevsky have done in this situation? Guard, watch out! I opened the door a fraction, switched on the torch and aimed the beam of light towards the factory entrance. Wasn't that a rat scurrying around the corner? No one had said a word about rats so I decided there weren't any. All the lights were on in the Italians' hostel, they were singing. That's how prisoners-of-war sing, I thought, in those Siberian nights, 'O sole mio', 'Heimat, deine Sterne'. One of them leaned out of the window and shouted something at me. Then he waved with a bottle. I waved back. I could still hear the ticking, although the sound was weaker. I closed the door again. Now the ticking was louder. I stared and stared at the wall of my shed until I worked out what was driving me mad. It was the timer, which was hanging on a clothes hook. I looked at the clock. Almost ten. Time for my first patrol. I had to smile. Maybe I was a born security man, my faithful timer ticking down in my mind the seconds to the next patrol, even when I was reading or asleep. Maybe when you left Germania Security after thirty-five years of service you were presented with an old timer which you could hang above the bed, and later, when it was time for your last big patrol, take with you to your maker, where now the watch-word was 'Guard, rest!' I put on my cap, drank another coffee and lit a cigarette. Two hours' work and I was gaga already. Next time it might be better to bring something by Sartre, something really rational. *Being and Nothingness*, the book which, like sleep, banishes time for the security guard.

It took me almost two hours to find at least a third of the control boxes. When I came back a white-haired man in full Germania Security uniform was sitting at the table, flicking through *Demons*.

'Good book,' he said, and introduced himself. 'I'm the duty supervisor tonight. And you're the new chap, right? Everything OK?'

'Yes, everything's OK.'

'Anything you need? You're sweating buckets.'

'Oh, that's nothing. I had a bit of trouble finding the control boxes.'

'Oh well, the first step is always the hardest. I've never agreed with the idea that every soldier carries a marshal's baton in his knapsack. Cigarette?'

He offered me a Roth-Händle. His hands were white and slender, and he was wearing a heavy gold signet ring. His face was narrow and red, and his eyelids twitched nervously.

'What we would have given for a cigarette back in Russia, my God,' the supervisor said, inhaling deeply. 'And the peasants over there, they'd smoke leaves and bark. Oh yes, the Russian winter. I was a major,' he added. 'Outside Stalingrad. And when it gets really cold here, the old chilblains start to itch as if they were saying, "Well, Jack Frost, remember Chernyshevsk and Dnipropetrovsk?" But here,' he added with a weak smile, 'here it never gets really cold.'

I nodded like fury; I was so cold. I saw that he'd moved the heater right next to his legs. I went over to the table to get some of the warmth too, and logged the details of my patrol. Particular incidents: None. In truth it should have said: Went wrong five times. Drunk half a bottle of Valpolicella with Italians. Using greater vigilance and acting without mercy, forestalled attempt to incapacitate me by emptying more bottles.

'Yes, that Christmas,' the supervisor said, entering the time of his check. 'You'll write me off as an old officer, but sometimes I wonder whether the only true Christmas we celebrated was that one in the war, even though the cannons fell silent for no more than an hour. He rapped his knuckles on my book. 'Great read, Dostoevsky. Understood the human soul. I don't read much these days – at my age the letters fade away – but when I do, I only read the Russians.'

I accompanied him to the gate, and as he was getting into his battered old Beetle, he turned round once more.

'Happy Christmas, young man!'

He threw something to me. I picked it up. It was his cigarette packet. At least I didn't need to smoke leaves and bark.

The night ticked on. When the Italians quietened down it was already two o'clock. Now it was proper night, ice-cold night. Dostoevsky just made me nervous, all those dark expressions, those fleeting glances, those heated disputes amongst 'our people', and then the teas with the highly respected Varvara Petrovna, where Stepan Trofimovich fell to his knees again and again. I plodded around the control room. Control room! Guard duty! Was I crazy too? Good mates with Jack Frost? I'd truly come a long way – from the roof in Istanbul, via the editorial team of *Zero* magazine, to this wooden shed at the Osthafen in Frankfurt am Main. From a writer to a temporary security guard. Was nothing ever going to become of me? I thought of Bernadette. A girl like that wouldn't go wasting her time with me if I didn't have anything. But what? After all, I wasn't suddenly going to be the greatest lover east of the Seine, *mon ange*, *mon amour* – how could I have been? What did she see in me? The revolutionary with the black flag, the future chief ideologue of the IVth International, or indeed the young Sartre, forever on the way to all the fronts in the world? Something was not right. I was struck by the feeling that she was in bed with somebody else. I knew these socialist

Christmases. It all went off there too, didn't it? Let me give you my consciousness. Those lefties were no better than the hippies, always hanging around to try and poach a fuck. I did my patrols, but in every corner of the factory hall I saw Bernadette shagging someone who looked like Trotsky, on every office desk she was doing it with Trotsky and Mao at the same time, a horror threesome. My cock rubbed itself raw on the hard material of my uniform trousers, a greeting from all the fronts in the world.

In the morning just after seven o'clock I carefully opened the door to our bedroom. My gaze made its way slowly up the bed to the pillows. The black flag of her hair was flawless. I quickly slipped out of my clothes and under the covers. She snuggled up to me, and before she grabbed my cock I thought, Tomorrow you can chuck in your job, Osthafen, Jack Frost, leaves and bark. But the following evening I did saunter over there with my plastic bag and ID badge which entitled me to detain people temporarily. In front of me went the commis chef, beside me Dmitri. The country could rest easy.

thirty-two

Intravenous veterans have a wise saying up their sleeves for each and every thing in this world, including for alcohol. Don't start on the bottle, they say, when you throw away the needle. All the opiates, all the pervitin, the nice little things you want nothing more to do with – what ingratitude! – they've knocked your body into such great shape that in the evenings it'll put away two bottles of schnapps as if it were mineral water. But, they say, unwrapping the silver foil on a marzipan ball, what your body can handle, your head is nowhere near up to dealing with, so keep well away from the booze – surely you don't want to end up a blathering old soak who chokes on his own vomit in a cell at five in the morning? They pop the marzipan ball in their mouth and keep sucking on it till they've sucked out their last hollow tooth, too, while their pupils slowly contract. You think they're after the next marzipan ball, but really they're staring into the loo at the train station, into the anonymous doss-house where one morning they'll be found by the cleaners, in the clammy dawn of the concrete city, with their final needle sticking out of their arm.

I liked booze. One of the places where left-wing drinkers

used to meet was Club Voltaire in Kleine Hochstrasse, in the city centre, surrounded by the opera house ruins, stock exchange, banks and the hash meadow. Although Club Voltaire was monopolised by proper left-wingers – the pacifist Easter Marchers, now slightly grey; the rest of the traditional SDS; the old moles from the shadier end of the spectrum, who were now burrowing down again through the rich soil of the SPD – squatters were certainly tolerated, and then the turnover was boosted, of course, by all the rockers and casual workers and their mates. Bernadette hated Club Voltaire. Her idea of a good evening was a delicious but not overly heavy dinner, followed by a stirring discussion, maybe a film, a book, a little reading and learning, and then a long, feverish night of passion. I could understand that; if you spent half your day selling books and also squeezed in a seminar, a training course or even just a language course, then the prospect of five or six hours in the smoky club, wedged between anarchist part-time security guards with the cider blues, bawling raiding parties from the antisocial estates, and seasoned old communist beer drinkers on a trip through their second youth, was hardly an enticing one. And yet I needed material for my writing.

'But you're not writing anything,' Bernadette exclaimed. We were standing in the kitchen, and she was trying to bring some order to the chaos. Sometimes I was reminded of the Berlin commune. Every day the Italians from Lotta Continua threatened to take drastic measures.

'You don't need to shout,' I said. I didn't like it when she mentioned my writing in public. 'You need to gather experiences before you sit down at the typewriter, you know.'

'In the pub?'

'Of course. I mean, those are people too, aren't they?'

She spread half a tin of scouring agent on the cooker and started working away at the encrusted grease. But rather than exhaust all her strength, it set free new energy.

'So, you want to write about all of that. Perhaps about me, too?'

This was tricky. I hesitated. But as a writer you have to tell the truth, even about your nights of passion if necessary.

'But of course, Bernadette. A writer exploits –'

Maybe my glasses were dirty again, but afterwards I doubted that I'd have been able to see her throw it even with clean lenses. After all, I'd heard what she'd learned in her communist women's groups. I expect Bernadette could have thrown me through the window with a flick of the wrist. At any rate, the tin with the scouring agent hit me right on the forehead and my glasses were spattered, too.

'You're not going to write anything, do you understand? Nothing! *Rien du tout!*' She planted herself in front of me and her eyes shot black daggers, but maybe that was just my imagination. My sight was still very blurred. 'That's bourgeois literature, bourgeois literature through and through, *compris*? And I'm not going to let you write about me like that.' Her tone changed. 'I didn't hurt you did I, *chéri?*'

'No, only literature.'

Even Bernadette smiled at that. She wanted to make up straightaway on the mattress, but it wasn't that simple for me. In any case, I was expected elsewhere. In the pub.

Drinking was considerably cheaper than all the opiates and

murderous paraphernalia. Although Club Voltaire wasn't for members only, the prices were lower than normal. Amongst comrades it was hard to imbibe enough. For ten marks they could get a nice buzz, but I couldn't. My tolerance was just too high. At any rate it could hardly be the handful of beers and schnapps which made me sing along with my cronies at one in the morning. At the bar in Club Voltaire they no longer asked for 'Mr Tambourine Man' or 'A Hard Day's Night', but rather got straight down to business, glasses in hand: 'They betrayed Karl Liebknecht, Rosa Luxemburg lay in her own blood …' As none of us knew the words, we'd improvise, and then you could feel how the Easter Marchers and the trade-union strategists itched inside when the names Baader or Meinhof suddenly cropped up. You could titillate them with the Red Army Faction. And if they remonstrated, then you were always the poor old drunkard – Marx, bless you – one of those antisocial buggers who'd fallen by the wayside on the long march through the institutions and sadly had to be left behind. They always reserved particularly penetrating looks for me, however. Whether they were publishers or editors, big cheeses or hangers-on, it was all the same society, the ruling cultural class, and whether I came to them as a zealous writing slave or a cut-up junkie, as a comrade or companion, for them I was nothing other than an agent provocateur, and agent of the dark forces from whom they had to defend their savings plan, their job and their wife.

At half past one we finally had to pay up. Outside, slushy, dirty snow, the last tram waiting at the opera house ruins, a tramp trying to crawl through the fence. There were three of us: me, the commis chef and Fritz, a failed student in his early thirties who'd drunk away his final semester with his last cheque before eventually being thrown out. But now it was the end of January, the cheque was history, as were most of his books, clothes, furniture and the toaster.

'Christ, I'm still thirsty.'

It didn't matter who uttered the sacred phrase. It was always as if a choir had spoken. Thirst was just a synonym for life. Perhaps a somewhat questionable synonym, but the only one that made sense at this time of night, and I found it an attractive change to what the needle always prescribed: a little death.

'I can think of somewhere,' Fritz said. His red nose protruded like a foreign body from his parchment-coloured face.

'Nutten-Louis must be closed by now too.'

'Yes, but maybe we can get a beer from those guys in the cellar. They've usually got beer.'

'What cellar?'

'Oh, the cons,' the commis chef said.

'Which cons?'

'You know, the scum they don't let into the houses. They've got the cellar at number 95.'

It was another block to number 95, which was being squatted by groups a little less fussy than ours. So that's where the rockers had ended up.

'Oh man,' Fritz said, 'you've got to take a look at this. It's like Dostoevsky.'

'But I'm thirsty,' the commis chef said. We'd crossed Opernplatz and turned into Bockenheimer Landstrasse.

There were a few shops on the corner. I pointed to a window full of wine bottles.

'There's enough here,' I said. The two of them stopped. A few steps further on there was a hole in the ground. Frankfurt was full of holes in the ground. Everywhere was an invitation to help yourself, full shop windows, full holes in the ground. The pane of glass was tinkling already. The few cars that were about just drove on, but somewhere a light went on and a voice shouted something into the night. The commis chef cursed. Blood was gushing from his hand. Fritz took the bottle of red wine off him and we skedaddled. Suddenly a siren wailed nearby. Police patrol. We fled down Kettenhofweg. The commis chef pressed his sleeve against his bleeding hand. Fritz vanished into the darkness of a brand-new building. Here, a bank branch was about to enter competition with the other one thousand seven hundred and ninety-nine bank branches. We ducked behind a cement mixer. A newspaper rustled. Someone was behind the pillar. A tramp, holding up the newspaper as protection. 'Shh! Stay absolutely silent!' The patrol car crept past. They'd turned off the siren and were now combing the streets. If his fucking blood drips onto the fucking snow then we're fucked, I thought. The patrol car disappeared round the next corner. Fritz already had the bottle open. We offered the tramp a swig, but he said no. Perhaps he was a teetotaller. In Frankfurt anything was possible.

The commis chef continued bleeding, so we took him home after making a temporary bandage. The Italians were just returning from their community work, reeking strongly of garlic and wearing the sort of faces that said they'd fixed that Sunday as the D-Day for world revolution. Maybe it was time for another osso bucco. We served them up some crazy story and left the commis chef with them. A grappa would do him the world of good, even if it came with a revolutionary talking-to on the side.

We managed the short distance to Schumannstrasse without difficulty, but then saw the patrol car crossing the junction of Bockenheimer Landstrasse and Zeppelinallee, and heading towards us. We continued on our way and turned into Schumannstrasse. It was only when you felt under surveillance that you noticed all the lights in the city at night, strange lights in office blocks and on the façades of institutes. Surely these can't *all* be colleagues of mine, I thought. That would make Germania a giant of the security industry.

'Is it following us?'

'Yes.'

'Just don't get nervous,' Fritz said. 'Thank God we look civilised.'

'Civilised?'

'You know, no long hair, no Mao insignia.'

'Well, if that's what you call civilised …'

The patrol car drove past with a scrunch. The driver peered over at us; Fritz raised his hand and gave a casual wave. The driver said something to the passenger, and then the latter looked at us, too. They had young faces, young and indistinct. They drove on.

'Alla,' Fritz said. He came from the Rhineland. We crossed Schumannstrasse. Here there was a rear courtyard which belonged to the squat. Overflowing dustbins and orange crates between tufts of grass and bushes. It stank of rubbish, petrol, wet paper, piss. A man was standing beside a rusty bike rack by the wall, emptying his bladder. We stopped and watched him respectfully. When the guy was finished he turned to us. A lanky chap with tatty jeans, boots and a leather jacket. His muscular arms were tattooed down to the wrists. Fritz seemed to know him. They gave each other a sober greeting. When Fritz explained we were thirsty he flashed his teeth.

'Come in to the parlour, then,' Lanky said. We negotiated the slippery steps to the cellar. The stench was more pungent down below but it was no longer possible to distinguish the different odours, it was a single, devastating smell, a smell that emanated from the very bowels of the city. A dim light illuminated what had once been a utility room. In every corner were mattresses and dark figures that looked like rag-bags. A cassette recorder was blasting out an old Stones number through the catacombs: 'Out of Time'. In one corridor a massive guy with long hair and mountains of flesh in place of shoulders was towering menacingly over a short, dark man wearing a waiter's jacket and long johns.

'Leave the Hungarian be,' Lanky commanded. The mountain of flesh grinned and backed off. Lanky seemed to belong to the inner circle here. Wherever you went there were inner and outer circles, and men like the Hungarian always belonged to those clutching for dear life onto the outermost circle. Lanky opened a door and we followed him.

It was one of the cellar rooms which the heating pipes

ran through, and the temperature was overwhelming. The first thing I saw was a wall, every square centimetre of which was pasted with cuttings: colourful breasts, thighs, arses, faces, bare arms, legs, feet, bellies, navels, toes, lips, noses, ears. Sticking them all together like this had brought them to life in a way, for the wall seemed to be pulsating, making waves, vibrating. I looked at the other walls and gulped. The entire room was decorated with magazine flesh. It was the most naked wallpaper you could possibly imagine. After I'd cleaned my glasses, Lanky introduced me to the artist. He was a skinny, blond chap, wearing a suede jacket with cowboy tassels, a Tyrolean hat with a feather, and glasses with thick lenses, which made his eyes look like a toad's. His face seemed to be assembled from pieces that didn't match, and when he laughed you could see that most of his teeth were missing. They called him Fuzzi, and his girl-friend's name was Trixi, an ugly duckling who was lying on a sofa salvaged from the dump, browsing well-thumbed magazines and out of boredom filing her filthy fingernails. The rest of the personnel consisted of tattooed muscles, crude sayings and beer breaths. Fritz and I tried to remain in the background, but Fuzzi had identified us as kindred spirits. He had to tell us the whole of his life story there and then, which – in contrast to his collages – consisted only of breaches, holes and patches of white, from the refugee camp, youth correction centre and borstal, to this cellar, where he now felt at home.

'My first real home,' he said, 'and I furnished it all myself.' He pointed proudly to the sofa, the armchairs, the bedside rug, the rusty fridge, the chest of drawers: 'That's where

we're going to put the children's things, aren't we, Trixi?'
But Trixi was staring at a split nail. 'And here, the bookshelf,
I mean I must have a bookshelf.' The bookshelf was from
the scrap heap, too, and now housed carefully piled volumes
of Kommissar X, Jerry Cotton, copies of Edgar Wallace and
Mister Dynamit that had passed through thousands of pairs
of hands – all stuff that high-and-mighty cultural critics had
consigned to the literary scrap heap. Well, one could hardly
expect that people who had consigned society to the scrap
heap in the first place would feast on Marcel Proust.

'Hey, man,' Fritz said quietly, 'did I promise too much?
Like Dostoevsky.' But I knew it wasn't like Dostoevsky, and
I knew that we didn't belong here, either. Did anybody? The
beer ran out.

'Off you go, Fuzzi,' commanded Lanky, who'd been
regaling us with tales from his colourful past as a car thief.
'Then I can finally bang Trixi – eh, Trixi? So she knows what
a real man is like.'

The assembled company laughed dutifully, including
Trixi, who didn't seem to have heard. Fuzzi put on his boots.
At home he wore slippers. I offered to accompany him. The
heat was bothering me, and Fritz was being shown by one
of the rockers how best to use a bicycle chain. As we made
our way through the cellar a groan shot out from one of the
partitioned-off areas, as if someone were being murdered. I
stopped, but Fuzzi tugged my sleeve.

'They're just cracking a nut,' he said.

'And what's the story with Trixi?' I asked when we were
outside.

'Oh, Lanky's just all talk,' Fuzzi assured. 'Besides,' he

continued, 'even if he did, I don't think Trixi would notice much. What do you reckon?'

I didn't know what to say. We crossed Senckenberganlage. In front of us was an all-night petrol station.

'They've got those nice eight-packs of Pils,' Fuzzi said.

'But I'm broke,' I said.

'Me too,' Fuzzi said. 'But that doesn't matter. Just make sure the attendant doesn't see.'

We stayed out of sight of the attendant, who was restocking a shelf.

'Look,' Fuzzi whispered. 'The eight-packs are beside the entrance; they've just been delivered. The moment a car comes to fill up and the attendant's outside, I'll sneak in, grab the packs, and if he catches me you've got to distract him so I can get the beer home. If we come back without beer it won't be so great.'

'How am I going to do it, distract him?'

'You'll think of something. I mean, you're thirsty too, aren't you?'

That was true. After an eternity, a car approached the pumps, a fat BMW. The attendant came outside and the driver got out to tell him something. In the cold light their breath formed fleeces of cloud. Crouched, Fuzzi crept behind the backs of the two men. I held my breath. He was already at the door and I could see him grab two eight-packs, then scurry away immediately, still crouched, towards Senckenberganlage. Fuzzi hadn't spent hours gawping at Westerns and Vietnam TV in vain. I waited till he'd already crossed the road and was walking upright again before running away. I attracted attention immediately.

'Hey, what are you doing skulking around here?'

But I was already too far away. When we got back we met the Hungarian in his waiter's jacket. He had been on the receiving end of something. His cheeks were full of blood. Fuzzi gave him a beer, which was very generous of Fuzzi, for in his digs the atmosphere was already below zero, given that there were no supplies. And a quarter of an hour later the other fifteen bottles were empty. When I crawled into bed soon afterwards it took me a whole minute to realise that Bernadette was sleeping elsewhere that night.

thirty-three

I lay on the floor of my room, playing with the revolver that I'd filched from Bärbel back in Hamburg and had carried around with me ever since, together with an old Röhm gas pistol, also unloaded. It was a good thing that Bernadette hadn't discovered the weapons yet. There's no doubt she would have been capable of finding ammunition and staging a drama of jealousy, complete with shot to the stomach and headline in the *Nachtausgabe*: 'Revolutionaries Revolt – Shots in the Squat!' And as she was one-quarter Corsican, she'd feel she was in the right. I was actually working on a bit on the side. A seventeen-year-old from Club Voltaire who seemed to idolise me. A sweet little thing. I was just waiting for the right opportunity to show her I was a man, too.

The door opened and I hid the weapon under the mattress. It was two guys from the upper floors. I could tell from their dark expressions that they hadn't come to solicit my opinion on the employment ban. The campaign had just been launched. Another mountain of overtime. But the subject they first broached could not have been the only reason for this VIP visit. In any case, there wasn't much to say about it.

'I'm not going to discuss this,' I told the delegation. 'Nor will anyone else on this floor. These Italians may be the most genuine avant-garde of the proletariat, but for us they're nothing but upstarts.'

'Yes, but day and night they're busy with political work,' the riposte came. 'And what are the rest of you doing?'

'We're busy with political work day and night, too,' I assured them. 'It just looks a little different. As you know, the revolution has many fathers, and if it's got many fathers then it must have many children. *Molti bambini, capito?*'

'Who said that about many fathers?'

Typical academic, they think only in terms of quotes.

'Trotsky, of course; who do you think I'm living with?'

'How are you getting on with Bernadette?'

'Better than Bakunin would like, but what's that got to do with you?'

'Well, she's now got involved with this women's group.'

'I don't have a problem with that,' I lied, 'but why *are* you here, in fact?'

Finally they came out with it. It was my neighbour Gertrud, the blonde girl from the Communist Student Union. Her liaison with Fred the pimp (my visitors resorted to a euphemism for the word 'pimp') may have caused her Germanic acerbity to flourish, but the comrades were no longer prepared to accept the situation. KSV and pimps didn't go together. Not that they had anything against the chap personally – he did everything in style; the sparkling wine had flowed on occasion – and they were able to differentiate between the system and its victims, but here the circumstances were different. If he were a safe-breaker then of course, no problem. But a pimp? Especially now that women were playing such a key role in the political struggle. The women's groups were already grumbling and the KSV leadership complaining about people breaking away; here in the house the mood was decisively against this young love affair. Just imagine she were to go touting for business on the streets one day and the press got wind of it. The consequences would be unthinkable.

'OK, so what do you want me to do?'

'You've got to talk to her. She'll listen to you.'

'Me? Are you mad? She only listens to me when I pound at her door to get her to turn her music down. And vice-versa sometimes too.'

'But you've got, how shall we say, a certain rapport with this scene; I mean you're somehow, I suppose, connected to it …'

'Oh, that's what you mean.' I stood up. I'd squatted, laughed, drunk and argued with these people, and also in a certain sense fought with them – and now they were revealing themselves as exactly what their parents were supposed to be: dreadfully bourgeois and narrow-minded individuals, who feared nothing more than dealings with those they had declassed. 'I'm sorry,' I said. 'You'll have to do your own dirty work.' I took out the gun from under the mattress. 'And as I presume that I'll soon be the next on your list, let me make it quite clear that anarchists won't be chucked out on the streets without a fight.' I put the gun in my waistband and looked around the room, as if I were saying goodbye to a much-loved but, alas, defiled thing. 'Although perhaps I'll soon find it utterly nauseating to live here.'

Their expressions as they left told me that this would shortly be the case – one way or the other. Of course, Gertrud didn't move out. She chose instead to chuck Fred with his sleek sports coupé, his expensive clothes and miniature monkey. I never exchanged another word with her, and when she turned up her music too loud I turned up Bernadette's record player even louder. Soon afterwards she left the KSV and joined Bernadette's women's group.

My thirst became ever greater. I was on guard three nights a week, and the other four days I spent largely in pubs. But it wasn't the beer I found most appealing. These sorts of pubs were new to me, the cheap pubs of Bockenheim, where during the day you could sit in the gloom amongst the old brewery pennants and football posters, with pensioners and housewives and jobbers and tarts and cripples in this delightful haze of beer and schnapps and piss and beef sausages and mustard and smoke; and in the evenings, when the workers and tradesmen came to drink with their spouses dolled-up to the nines, and the students with their crowd doing some moves and spinning their philosophy, there was scarcely a seat to be had. My favourite was Nutten-Louis on Bockenheimer Warte, opposite the tram depot, a place where every evening the classless company of drinkers from all walks of life discovered their soul in the head of their beers, and forgot it again at closing time.

I could spend whole days sitting and watching and chatting and slurping and smoking. For years I had only ever listened to the whining of junkies, that sing-song which was always the same, proclaiming one sole purpose on earth: the

Nirvana of the needle. And now the revolutionaries with the revolution, another Nirvana, even though it purported to be worldly and could prove this with millions of corpses. But I no longer had any interest in death; I wanted beer and laughter, and most of all I wanted girls. I'd never sought them out so keenly as now, in these pubs and dives, in snack bars and student cellars. Sales assistants from cut-price department stores with stunning black lines around their eyes, tired librarians with a weakness for black cigarettes and oral sex, draughtswomen with blue fingernails who dreamed of journeys to the South Pacific and were bringing up three children – only occasionally would one of them go to bed with me, but all I needed was to see them, to know that they existed and took two sugars and licked the juice from beef sausages off their fingers like millions of others, to put me in a state of deep satisfaction and great expectation. They intoxicated me. Ultimately it was not about love, I was shot of love and consciousness too, it was quite simple, you could drink them away and extinguish them, everything in one night, in one intoxication, with a wild, wicked shag. If you needed three or four women, then you'd get them, and love only got in the way like the fatuous search for the meaning of history. There was no meaning, there was only blood and thunder and the upwards and downwards movements from below and above. Women could lie on top, too; the important thing was that I was what they were lying on. I was crazy, I thought I'd finally found the way out of the labyrinth, and I wasn't bothered about writing any more, either.

It was more difficult with Anita, however. She perhaps looked a couple of years older, but had actually only just

turned seventeen and was in her first year of an apprenticeship at Kaufhof. Shining, long, chestnut-brown hair, dark
eyes, a cheeky nose, a full mouth, always slightly open. Her
well-developed breasts swelled beneath a tight pullover. And
even at a distance you could guess what was beneath her tight
black trousers. This guessing made me weak at the knees, but
guessing was as close as it had got so far. At any rate, 'so far'
was what Anita's mouth was saying. Her hands took a while
to communicate anything at all, and then I didn't know
what they were saying. They probably didn't know themselves. We lay on my bed and kissed. The kiss lasted almost
half an hour, and any minute Bernadette could have come
back from the university, from the women's group, from
the central committee of history and the politburo of love,
where at this very moment they were discussing the appli-
cation pursuant to my expulsion. Finally I had my hands
under Anita's pullover. I felt something silky, and above that
were the two mounds, the manna, but well wrapped in a
bra. I thought I could feel her nipples. Moments from the
onset of madness, and then Anita closed her eyes, let down
the curtain of her thickly mascaraed eyelashes, as she sucked
my tongue into her mouth, harder, deeper into this hollow,
while the trams leaped off the rails and the wind had its
wicked way with the black flag. My hands had spent an age
opening Anita's trousers, my head somewhere in her hair
which smelled as good as the advertisement promised, and
suddenly I felt her teeth in my neck. I caught my breath,
then screamed, but it wasn't this that suddenly caused Anita
to stop biting. We were kneeling on the bed, entwined, and
she was staring at the door. Her lips were twitching. OK, I

thought, this is it, now comes the expulsion order, the sack, a blessing that they can't yet put me up against the wall, not that there was any lack of walls.

'By all means, carry on,' I heard Fritz say. 'I thought we might go out for a beer. I've just pawned my confirmation suit.'

'Oh yeah, I'd love a beer now,' Anita said with a sweet smile, kissing the bite wound on my neck.

Fritz lived in a partly furnished mansard in Grüneburgpark. He was three months behind on his rent and the landlady had already taken away his key to the communal bathroom. Astonishingly, however, she'd accepted Speedy as a tenant in the next-door room. Speedy was the product of a marriage which had ended in the alcohol rehabilitation clinic and the usual career as a petty thief, with lengthy spells in Höchst, Rockenberg and Butzbach. In 1969–70, when the Baader–Meinhof lot were intent on lighting the beacon of social revolution in the minds of the lumpenproletariat, Andreas Baader had once given him a beer, and Speedy had been waiting for a sign from the underground ever since: 'If you need me, I'm ready.' As it hadn't been worth his while seeking out a regular job in the meantime – and anyway, he knew from experience that he'd never have got one – he lived off the crumbs that were swept from the tables of political groups, stolen eggs, and the hope that next week someone would lend him some money.

'Here,' he said, winking knowingly at me as he put a stamp on an envelope, 'this is going straight off to Essen. It's a brand-new thing: "Loans delivered free to your door". The cash postman arrives with ten big ones.'

'What are you thinking of getting, Speedy?'

'Well those prats think I'm buying a fitted kitchen because I want to get married. But I'm going to invest it in Uzis, this Israeli machine gun, the best on the market. I've got contacts, you see.'

'Why do you need Uzis?'

'Listen, Harry, I can't stand there with nail scissors when it all kicks off, when Andreas gives me the nod!'

He shook his head at my complete lack of worldliness, stuck the envelope down, and looked at it once more. He seemed to be satisfied with his work. Another day well spent.

'Do you really think they're going to deliver you ten thousand marks that easily?' asked Fritz, who was sick and tired of all this. 'For God's sake Speedy, you haven't got the slightest security for a loan!'

'What do you mean? After the revolution they'll get it all back, every last pfennig. Besides, money will be abolished so they won't need it anyway.'

Speedy didn't get an answer from this credit company, either, so he had to give up his room and move in with Fritz, without the landlady getting wind of it.

'It's only till I get the call from Andreas.'

But Andreas took his time, and the two of them had increasing difficulty in scraping together sufficient dough even to get enough beer each evening. At the social security office in the Dominican monastery there were food vouchers which you had to lie left, right and centre to get your hands on, but the supermarkets were under strict instructions not to exchange them for alcohol. Until you'd hawked your herring chunks and tinned sausages to wary Turks and even warier female students, you could always plunder the fridges in the halls of residence. The fact that the future educators, leaders and freeloaders of the German people held Lambrusco in such high regard was not a good sign. By now I was so exhausted that I had cut my security work from three to two nights, and even that was still a struggle.

'But it's a good job,' I said to Fritz and Speedy. 'Better, at any rate, than making merry with those vouchers from social security.'

Fritz said he'd rather kill himself, but Speedy immediately trotted off. What would life be without Romantics? He returned two hours later swearing like a trooper. Hegel had even threatened to call the pigs.

'What did you do wrong, Speedy? They'll take anybody.'

'Nothing! I did nothing wrong. They're fuckers! I even said I'd happily do overtime, and I'd guard the most dangerous things they had, IG Farben, the Yanks, all that nuclear shit, everything! It was going fairly well – of course I didn't let on that I'm on probation – but then the guy gave me the uniform and the torch, and I said I'd like a weapon, too; I mean I wasn't going to go and defend the electric power station without an Uzi!'

And then yet another evening with candles, red wine, Janis Joplin and Bernadette, her long, black hair, which she generally wore under a headscarf these days, flowing freely again.

'What's wrong, *chéri*? Why are you so depressed?'

'I'm not depressed; I'm just having new experiences.'

'But you could have different experiences.'

'You can't always choose them.'

'Of course you can choose them, *chéri*; you can decide. You do have a consciousness, after all.'

There it was again.

'I don't know what consciousness is.'

'Well, you certainly had a political consciousness when you came to squat this house.'

'You really think so? Perhaps I just wanted somewhere to live for nothing. Perhaps I just moved in here because of you. Perhaps I didn't have a better offer.'

'You talk yourself down, *chéri*.'

'How is that talking myself down when I say I'm not sure why we're doing this or the complete opposite?'

'Marxism …'

'Screw Marxism, Bernadette. Why don't the two of us go away from here together? Anywhere, France if you like, I don't care, just somewhere I can start writing again and where we'd have time to find out what life really is.'

'And what do you suppose we'd live off? That's assuming I can be ordered around as you wish.'

'Look, there's always something to live off. People need security guards everywhere. And one day I'll be able to live off my writing.'

'I still love you, you know, *chéri*. But I can't live with someone who drifts like you do, whose feet are never on the ground, who doesn't want to gain awareness, but just live like this, without responsibility. Of course life is pointless and idiotic if you don't try to understand it and shape it yourself.'

They were all the same – communists, Nazis, parents, Church, book reviews, features section, editorial, revolutionary struggle, Baader–Meinhof, capital, television, Club

Voltaire, pacifism, guerrillas, Mao, Trotsky, Red Student Action: Law Division, the underground scene and Germania Security. They were all part of the same idea, they knew how things ought to be, they had a monopoly on consciousness, love, human happiness.

'And do you lot know what you're up against? Just Nutten-Louis, nothing else.'

'Yes,' Bernadette said. 'You've got to decide between Nutten-Louis and me.'

That night I made the decision, but I thought how unfortunate we were that we couldn't have both. Janis Joplin knew: 'Oh Lord, won't you buy me a Mercedes Benz?'

thirty-four

Every Saturday evening there was a knees-up in the hall of residence on Beethovenplatz. Walter Kolb Hall was named after the mayor of the post-war reconstruction period, and the old socialist would be permanently turning in his grave if the worms whispered to him what slogans were now plastered over the walls and corridors of the building. A group of hall honchos used to organise these Saturday evenings in the cellar, the records, the beer, the lemonade, the schnapps. Apart from that there was little trace of organisation. It was a seething cauldron down there.

Around midnight it was a real bunfight to get downstairs, as the German intellectual elite of the future was huddled together with anyone seeking the whiff of an insurrection or those on a direct route for the gutter. The ladies of the left-wing glitterati came here to find their antisocials for the night, and the men, who in their robes or pinstripes fought the system by day by not being able to get enough of it, came to Kolb Hall on Saturday nights to get their adrenaline rush by stridently endorsing Mao's dictum that power grows out of the barrel of a gun, and beguiling with their longing looks Palestinians, Vietnamese girls or runaways from care homes. Action for everyone. Everything quite open. 'I Can't Get No Satisfaction' nine times in succession until the plaster started flaking, two Asbach and Cokes down the hatch, Speedy there too, of course, with his blond locks, his astonished eyes, half a bottle of beer already tipped down his trousers, and the inevitable remark: 'Andreas knows where to find me.'

In the dim light the dancers jerked about like robots. They were in a circle, and an ever-growing wall of non-dancers formed around the perimeter – the onlookers, the passive, the drinkers, the anxious, the muscle mountains, the ironics, the wallflowers, the aggressors, the refuseniks, the aesthetes, the wankers. A bit later the first blood flowed, just being friendly you understand, he came on to me, the fucking queer, this social fascist spilled my beer and is still complaining, drooling all over my missus, what do you mean by woman? I bet you think you're better than the rest of us. Just wait till we've got our hands on the Uzis, the Kalashnikovs, you'll all be slaughtered. Action for everyone. 'Jumpin' Jack Flash' nine times in succession. If you still know who you are then you're 'out of time', because nobody in this age knows who they are. And sometimes at seven in the morning still discussing the armed struggle, guerrilla strategy in the big cities, 'propaganda by the deed', Fidel Castro, fathers, sisters, everything that's missing, and when the last joint was smoked and the last sip drunk and the last bottle smashed against a wall and the last phrase spat out, the journey home under an indifferent sky, with flowing traffic, beneath trees whose boughs were soaking up the rain.

One lunchtime I was in the filthy kitchen, trying to rustle up something edible, when Dmitri showed up. I hadn't seen him for a while. He had many more grey hairs and the wrinkles had burrowed deeper into his face. He was wearing his only suit, a white shirt and the coat he'd bought with his loan.

'Off somewhere, Dmitri?'

He handed me a plastic bag.

'Here's some bread and cheese. I'm going.'

I lowered the bag. 'What do you mean, you're going?'

'I'm going to Berlin. I might have a job in a film lab. I'm done here, it's over, finished.'

I didn't know what to say, but then asked, 'Is the film-lab job definite?'

He laughed. 'Definite? What's definite? What is definite is that here it's all over.'

'But what if it comes to nothing?'

'My wife wrote to me. Then I might go back to Greece. I'd spend some time in prison, we'll see. But I think that prison in Greece might be better than here.'

We stood there for a while in silence. In the background we could hear the excited voices of the Italians.

'Why didn't you tell me earlier, Dmitri?' I said finally. 'I might have come with you to Berlin.'

'Oh come on! What would you do in Berlin? Just make sure you don't fall apart here. You're drinking too much. Are you still writing?'

'Send me your address, Dmitri, and I'll write to you.'

He laughed, but his eyes weren't laughing with him. I shook his hand and he patted me on the shoulder. Long after he'd left I was still standing there, holding the plastic bag. The Italians sounded like lunatics. Perhaps we'd all been lunatics for ages and only Dmitri had noticed. Eventually I made myself a cheese sandwich. There were a couple of onions in the bag too.

I'd shown the revolver to Alf, the go-between for the rockers and pimps, and one day he brought me a box of bullets.

'Do you think they'll fit?'

'No I don't,' Alf said. 'But I'll try all the same. Looks like twenty-two calibre.'

The bullets didn't fit exactly, but Alf carefully filed around the edges and in the end he got them into the chamber.

'Where are we going to try it out?'

'I know a good place down at the sewage works in Griesheim …'

'Down by the Main? But that's far too far away. We'll try it here, now.'

Alf gave me a doubtful look. 'Here?'

'Sure,' I said. 'The room next to Gertrud's is empty at the moment; we can spray bullets around to our hearts' content.'

'That's all well and good, my friend, but this thing's not a water pistol you know.'

'Look, the Italians aren't there at the moment and the others will just think I'm having an argument with Bernadette. Let them think what they want.'

We got hold of an old vase and locked the door behind us.

'Who's going to shoot first?'

'Well, Alf …'

'OK, I will.'

I put my hands over my ears. The bang really was rather loud, but Alf's hand was still in one piece. He'd just missed the vase. Two minutes later we'd broken it.

'I need to take the thing to an expert. The kick is way too big.'

I never saw the revolver again, of course. But somehow word spread around that we'd been organising target practice in the house. My time went slowly. Fritz lay in my room with hallucinations and Speedy pawned everything that wasn't screwed to the floor. There had been no word from Baader, and he'd given up on the loan companies.

If you wanted to go to Fritz's room, you had to climb the stairs as silently as possible so that you weren't accosted by the landlady, and once at the top give a particular knocking signal, otherwise neither of them would open the door. Then Speedy was standing there in a pair of flowery pants, and before I got fully into the room he was back in his sleeping bag on the foam-rubber mattress, his nose in a crime novel. It was such a dark day that they had the light on. The room was beginning to smell like a men's hostel. Fritz was lying on his folding bed, buried in blankets and snoring. Bit by bit the furniture was vanishing from the room, but the pile of thrillers and dime novels kept growing.

'How do you cope with this snoring, Speedy?'

'The snoring's not so bad, man. Have you ever heard him talking to his grandmother? In Rhineland dialect? In the middle of the night? Or when he thinks there's a string quartet playing in the water pipe? The snoring's fine. The only thing that bothers me is the *hujas*. If he goes three days without a beer it's like a horror film.'

Huja meant hallucination and was an ingenious neologism coined by the translator of an Australian crime novel which featured a periodic drinker. It was Fritz and Speedy's cult book.

'Wake him up. I've cadged fifty marks and I want to go to Nutten-Louis and have a few draught beers …'

'Oh, OK then. If you want.'

'What do you mean "OK then"? Since when is freshly pulled draught beer just "OK"?'

'You see I've only got another forty or fifty pages … but you know what? I'll save them for tonight; at least I'll have something left.'

Speedy was a real bookworm. I was suddenly struck by the desire that one day he should want to read my books, too, and if some guy or girl came along with a beer, a job or French kiss, Speedy would say, 'But I've got to finish the page first.' While he got dressed and convinced Fritz that this time it wasn't a *huja*, I stared through the window at the mist above the trees. The mist reminded me of Göttingen. A man and woman were walking hand in hand down the street alongside the park. I'd done the same with Sarah. Followed by a tight embrace, a cup of tea and back to the manuscript. *Stamboul Blues*. Cabbage roulade at Uncle Just's. The long path to the post office. Dear Sir or Madam. Please find … And then the train back to Istanbul, clouds of smoke in the Balkan ravines. Maybe everything was a *huja* after all.

The first person we saw when we entered the cellar was Fuzzi. He had a fresh wound on his cheek and a black eye, and his glasses were held together with a plaster. He didn't want to say anything at first, but in the end we discovered that Lanky had taken over Fuzzi's cellar flat.

'I wouldn't mind,' Fuzzi stammered. 'It's just Trixi. She's a bit slow on the uptake. I know that Lanky's going to beat her up and then he'll let the others at her.'

'Why don't you just take her away?'

'Where to? This is our home.'

'Fuzzi, the house is going to be pulled down soon anyway.'

But he didn't want to listen. For now, this was his abode, and while his room was being occupied he was camping with the others in the coal cellar and checking to hear whether Trixi was screaming. If that happened, he didn't care about anything else, he'd put himself between them and Trixi, they'd have to stab him, he'd got it into his head that he was responsible for her.

'And, has she screamed yet?' Fritz asked, eyeing Fuzzi's wound.

'No,' Fuzzy said uncertainly. 'I got that from the pigs when they chased me from the Zeil. I'm well known as a pavement artist.'

'Look,' Fritz said. 'Most women dig that sort of thing. Don't get so upset about it, it'll pass.'

'You're mad,' Fuzzi said, pushing past us to get outside.

'Like Dostoevsky,' I said to Fritz. I didn't like him very much at that moment.

'Oh come on, we're all arseholes, every single one of us. Shall we drop in?'

'I've got an appointment,' Speedy said.
So we left.

In Club Voltaire the atmosphere was becoming increasingly antagonistic. The rockers were being left to their own devices. They'd been buttered up, used, worked up, then revolution had been declared, but nothing happened, so once again it had all been a heap of bullshit. Now they were sitting around, getting plastered and threatening brutal violence when asked to pay. Of course, the seasoned leftists had always known this was going to happen; it was never going to end well, once a thug, always a thug, they were the new SA, now it was time to pull up the collars of your raincoats and demonstrate the solidarity of the progressive forces. I'd had it up to here with them all, the studded jackets and rollneck jumpers, the slobbering of one lot and the views of the other, Sodom and Gomorrah or Marxism–Leninism, coats and trousers, but when they looked to see where I would sit I always opted to put myself beside those who had no savings plan, no party mandate and no political illusions to lose, only their back teeth.

Next to me sat the draughtswoman with blue fingernails, and I suggested we clear off before the next riot broke out and glasses were smashed, maybe some skulls too. We left. Another Saturday night in Frankfurt am Main. The neon city in the drizzle. Ambulance outside Onkel Max's. Pakistanis with the last copies of the *Nachtausgabe*, Africans lugging their ivory trinkets from pub to pub, the Hauptwache full of tramps with two-litre bottles of red wine, hippies with Berlin Tincture, policemen with indistinct faces and radios.

Up to the top of the Zeil, past the display windows of the shopping palaces, where at this time of night the mannequins with their bizarre contortions and French lingerie attracted only exhibitionists, voyeurs and masturbators. The snack bars full of men in checked coats who, as the beer frothed slowly down the sides of their glasses, recounted once more their life's victories, all of which led inexplicably to Stalingrad and to this avenue of a fast buck, in which their only stake was the hours spent standing by the sausage grill, the beer tap and the promotional calendar with its bikini-clad beauties: 'Up, up and away!' Past the cinemas, the dance halls, the construction trenches and brothels, where the Zeil suddenly became narrower and shabbier and made do with far less light for the antiquarian booksellers, the jeans shops, the bargain-price stores, the carpet dealers, up to the drinks kiosk at Friedberger Anlage, which marked the end of the boulevard, the last few metres of the city centre. Although beer and schnapps could be had a hundred metres away, this drinks kiosk was always surrounded like a national monument or first-aid station.

Hilde had a flat near Friedberger Landstrasse in old Nordend. Three children, cats, the smell of fresh paint and soiled nappies, candles, half a bottle of Amselfelder, a tentative kiss, the impression of sandy softness and fuzziness, her brown locks over a face that appeared to see a lot and express little, an earring with a stone, turquoise. Then one of the children started wailing.

'Go and lie down,' Hilde whispered. 'This might take a while.' I went to her bed and fell asleep immediately: all that beer. Then she woke me, perhaps much later, and I sank into her almost at once, into that soft, feminine fleece, into that fertile womb which smelled of honey and bath foam and children. We'd barely exchanged half a dozen sentences; I'd never slept with a woman who said so little, it was almost worrying – was I doing something wrong? Should she not have been telling me about her last boyfriend, problems at school, that holiday on the Costa Brava, her first love, the paternal friend at work, her star sign, what she liked for breakfast, the Caribbean? And what about questions? But she didn't ask a single one, she just lay there, her blue fingernails guiding me this way and that, then I saw her eyes glisten in the dark, and again it was time, but another child was now wailing, and before I could finish the glass of Amselfelder, I'd fallen asleep again, without explaining where I'd got my scars from, where I'd like to live, or with what means.

Around midday I took a tram to Westend. I had four ciga-rettes and four marks forty left, and a shift that evening. Only the wealthy could afford to work as a security guard. I'd been doing it for months now and I owed money eve-rywhere, not large sums, but it all added up. I was almost twenty-eight, and I couldn't even scrape together five hundred marks. The West German economy was rumbling and grinding incessantly, day and night – so, now, was the East German economy – with culture at the forefront, naturally, ever since Heinrich Böll had declared the end of modesty. I, meanwhile, was living off the crumbs of friendly women as though I were a pigeon or a swan. It couldn't go on like this. After all, my plumage was anything but white.

'It can't go on like this,' Bernadette said with a piercing look. I'd hoped she would be out – even with her women's group – so that I could just sleep off my depression, but, of course, there she was, her turban wrapped round her washed hair, delicate and dangerous, amidst half-packed suitcases, and her lower lip was quivering.

'That's exactly what I've been thinking,' I said nervously. 'I feel I ought to look around for another job. You were right, this night-time security stuff is absurd, we hardly ever see each other …'

'Where were you last night?'

'Hey, are you going somewhere?'

'I asked you a question.'

'You don't have to shout; I'm not deaf yet.'

'And you're not drunk either. Where have you come from?'

'Oh, you know, there was a party in Sachsenhausen, a guy from Club Voltaire. I actually dozed off there. I tell you, this stupid job isn't worth it for the handful of marks I get.'

I lit a cigarette. We were still standing there as if we were on stage. I noticed that she'd packed her record player. So that was it, then. Sometimes the man left; sometimes the woman. *C'est la vie.* Bernadette stared at me. She'd always wanted me to make something of my life. Maybe that was true love, rather than the folk dance around dubious consciousness and for brief moments of ecstasy at three in the morning.

'It's a shame you don't have the courage to tell me the truth,' Bernadette said. She uttered it like one of those marbled lines from a Corneille or Racine play. I felt quite queasy. 'You slept with another woman, *je le sais*. I feel sympathy her.'

'For her? Why not for me?'

Bernadette gave a bitter laugh. She was good at that. 'So you admit it, *voilà*. Sympathy for men? Never, *chéri*.'

'Yes,' I said, raising my voice. 'That's obviously straight from your women's group. You wean yourselves off everything there, and in the end you wonder where all the men have gone. But before that you were happily waving the flag and praising love ...'

'Love?' Her voice became shriller. 'Who was it who praised love? It was you when you couldn't think of anything else, and then you went to see your friends and drink beer with them and laugh about it, didn't you? I never said a word about love, instead I tried to achieve solidarity with you, intellectual, emotional solidarity, but that never entered your beer brain, your bourgeois, literary beer brain ...'

She stood there like a female prosecutor at a tribunal before the welfare committee in 1793, with that turban and her long, black skirt, and the bright red belt around her narrow waist. Just like a Delacroix painting, even the bread knife – which all of a sudden was in her hand – fitted perfectly.

'I've had it up to here with all that stuff about bourgeois literature,' I told her. 'The fact that it hasn't worked out between us hurts me just as much as it hurts you, but don't start blaming it on bourgeois literature. You see, it's like this with literature: there are good books and bad books, and a whole heap of the bad ones are written by people who were under contract to your firm.'

She looked at the knife as if for the first time, then she knelt to pack it into the suitcase. I was not worth it. She looked at me and her eyes were gleaming. I had a lump in my throat. Not only from the sublime to the ridiculous was it just a single step.

'I'd like you to go now,' Bernadette said. 'In an hour I'll be gone from here, then you can invite all your drinking chums and girlfriends over for a party, but now I want you to go, and if we bump into each other in the street, you don't know me. *Adieu*, darling.'

'But Bernadette …'

'*Adieu*.'

'But we don't have to –'

'Go!'

I went. No sooner had I closed the door than the bread knife was hammering against it. I stubbed out my cigarette. Now I had three left. I decided to do something for the lump in my throat, so I walked through the city on that endless Sunday afternoon. There was always someone in the club who'd hand out a schnapps, or a woman who had something left over from her weekend money. When I opened the door they were all standing there with their meaningful expressions, the functionaries of sociability. They told me I was barred from the premises, me and my sort, and half of humanity to boot. The night before the rockers had gone on the rampage and ripped out all the telephone wires and power supply lines, and wrecked all the machines. Typical, I thought as I shuffled back to Bockenheim, an unfinished job. Why didn't you burn the whole city down while you were at it? I lumbered past our house. It was a while since the black flag had hung from the balcony. Maybe the guys in the cellar would have something left to drink. In fact, after the previous night they definitely would. I met Fuzzi on the steps. He was wearing a familiar-looking cap. Germania Security. Wild caterwauling coming from the cellar. One of them had the torch, another the coat, and Lanky had the whistle around his neck. Perhaps they'd all signed up for Germania. There was plenty to drink at any rate. Hello, friends. Fritz was already legless, spittle around his mouth, eyes flickering; hello, Gorki. The commis chef was lying in the corner, snoring, his sandwich and monthly statement still in his plastic bag. I was certain to forget Bernadette that night.

thirty-five

At the Westbahnhof in Vienna I talked to an elderly lady in a traditional Austrian coat. From what she was saying I understood that she was offering me cheap accommodation in a private house. Although I was unsure why she thought I'd opt for a cheap private room over a hotel – I was wearing a jacket, tie, ironed shirt and had a hundred marks on me – out of curiosity I followed her. She looked as if she urgently needed the money, perhaps for an operation. And as they said, the Balkans began in Vienna. We took a train, then walked for a while. A mild, sunny April day. Occasionally the light flashed like gold between the new shoots on the trees. So this was Vienna, there lay Schönbrunn Palace. As I stood in the musty flat with its mail-order furniture I understood why the lady was renting it so cheaply. The lorries thundered endlessly up and down Schönbrunner Schlossstrasse. The windows shook.

I went into the city centre and sat in a café. So this was the Viennese coffee-house atmosphere. They only had bottled beer, and what flowed out of the bottles tasted more like lemonade. Still, I was in Vienna. Yet another city. And I'd arranged to meet Sarah. We'd written the occasional letter to each other over winter. She was now living in the country, near

Zwettl in Lower Austria. Why and by what means remained a mystery, but apparently there was a doctor who had a little house there. Sarah extolled the rural life. She'd always had a weakness for it. 'I've dyed my hair henna red, and the old women think I'm a witch.' They must be strange women, but then again, Sarah's letters were always a good example of the old adage that you can say everything and nothing with words. Oh well. I hadn't been to the country for a long while.

I strolled through Vienna and found the famous Café Hawelka. Everyone talked about Hawelka, even in Istanbul the Viennese would always say, 'I saw Pepi in Hawelka recently,' or, 'If you come to Vienna you'll find me in Hawelka.' Aha. In Hawelka I found the international hippy brigade, enriched with locals, the artist crowd. It was fairly loud, everyone thought themselves very important, and the waiters were from Berlin and fed up with it all. The beer was bad. Perhaps the Viennese didn't have a flair for beer. I drank a slivovitz. The slivovitz was bad, too, but when drunk in tandem with the bad beer it was almost good again. So Vienna, farewell, Joseph Roth! Roth hadn't particularly liked Vienna, only the idea of Vienna, the Viennese ideal, the Habsburg ideal. It had all turned out differently. Politics was an outrageous nonsense, but on the other hand it existed, it was fashioned, it was necessary. Two people together, that was politics in itself. A hippy cadged a cigarette off me. I drank another slivovitz. After all, in my bag I had the firm commitment from a publisher who wanted to bring out *Stamboul Blues* in autumn. Anatol Stern had brokered the deal. He may have been an unknown publisher in deepest Bavaria – actually a young man from the printing business who for some inexplicable reason had moved into publishing – but he had already done one book. And if *Stamboul Blues* was ever going to see the blazing light of day, then I probably had no other choice. After all, Ede had exhibited his paintings in the Pudding Shop, and there was a long literary tradition of small publishers, 'little mags', groundbreaking editions away from the razzmatazz of the big firms. And *Stamboul Blues* was going to continue this long literary tradition. To celebrate, I allowed myself another slivovitz. Strictly speaking, it was this young publisher who was continuing the long literary tradition. I'd have preferred a juicy advance, even if that was a rather profane literary tradition. Oh well, you can't have everything. You couldn't have everything in Vienna, either. You sat in Hawelka, you sat alone, but you were an author, the beer was bad, as was the slivovitz, but together they were good. A woman with red hair shrieked at what her bearded companion had whispered to her. I paid.

In Schönbrunn there were cheap *Beisels*, where I felt more comfortable. The beer was better, too. You couldn't serve up that pissy lemonade to workers. On the other hand the workers were served up everything else, particularly the idea that they had to change the world. That's to say, they didn't have to change it themselves, but help those who planned to by acting as killers and cannon fodder. The lies of the revolutionaries sounded different from those of the reactionaries, but they were lies too. Revolutions were a hoax. One ruling class was replaced by another, and the cultural apparatus spat out the pertinent editorials, the witty observations, the feature articles, the propaganda, the aperçus. I ate some goulash and drank more beer. If you saw through the lies, you could live in spite of them. What madness, that Frankfurt winter! Sometimes all you needed was a little distance to realise how ridiculous these contortions were that people gloated over. I liked the *Beisel*. I drank some more slivovitz, then struggled up the road, lay down on the mail-order bed, listened to the lorries, and marvelled at the fact that I was alive.

Sarah's hair did in fact have a touch of henna, but it wouldn't have made me think she was a witch. Her face, however, had lost its thousand-and-one-nights beauty; the rustic inheritance of Ukrainian Jewry showed through quite clearly. We drove towards Zwettl with friends of hers who also seemed to have a house out there. I wasn't given any details; that was probably regarded as typically German. Everything articulated in that nasal style which made each word sound like a sigh. There was music, too, on cassettes, Austrian pop, not Alpine yodellers, but proper rock and roll. Sarah talked about Hofer, did I know Hofer? What, you don't know Hofer? I only knew Andreas Hofer, by name, surely she didn't mean him? Hofer – the guy with the hit, that song, the number one. I listened to Hofer, didn't understand a word and told her that too. Sarah was quite put out. She thought I was against it in principle. Not much had changed. She spoke with an Austrian accent, however. And I was fine with that. I'd have been happy if she'd spoken with a Chinese accent. I still loved her, but there was nothing I could do about that now. We drove through Austria.

From Zwettl we went into the mountains, mountains with forests, all rather sinister. Beyond the mountains were more mountains, mountains as far as the eye could see, and then Czechoslovakia, even more mountains. A barren region. What do you mean barren, they said, everything that man needs will grow here, even vines. Sarah's face shone in the sun like bronze. Rural life was certainly good for her complexion. We went through the village – it wasn't particularly big – and then the final stretch was a path through a field to a hillside where there were two houses, or cottages, stone huts. Well, this was all very bucolic, and everyone was immediately given a job; I had to chop wood. After the wood-chopping there was tea – the water in this region was renowned – and home-made bread. Not as rock hard as the stuff Sarah had baked in the past. The doctor wasn't there, the doctor was in the hospital in Zwettl, but there was lots of talk about him. He was a big traveller, he got around the whole world, yes, that was something which Sarah was impressed by, expeditions to the inner and outer worlds. I didn't have much to offer on that score.

'You've got fat,' Sarah said.

'It's the beer.'

'You should spend some time living in the country, dealing with simple things, feeling the earth in your hands, growth, decay …'

'Look, Sarah, I get growth and decay in the city too, you know? Have you got a beer by any chance?'

There wasn't any beer, there was tea and then there was the water, of course. And there was the panoramic view across the forests. And later, alone in a narrow, hard bed, there was the cold. I wondered what they were up to in the cellar at this moment, Fuzzi, Fritz, Lanky. One thing was certain: they had beer.

I stayed a few days. There was a pub in the village, Die Post, where they sold a strong bottled beer, a good schnapps and schnitzel with fried potatoes. There were also the villagers, the cemetery gardener, the gravedigger, the forester, the fool, as well as the Viennese who had their houses here, their hunting, the cultural industry.

I drank them all under the table, then staggered out into the night. Where was that bloody house? Where was Sarah? Why wasn't I in her bed, as was the way things should be ever since Adam first saw Eve? Total darkness. Suspicious noises from the forest. These stars were utterly useless, they were so far away. Well, those villagers might have their Viennese money, but it wasn't enough for a lantern – avarice came first. Alpine dumplings, that's what Joseph Roth had called them, dumpling brains. Up ahead was a tiny light. I teetered towards it. It leaped away. Deer. Maybe wild boar, too, and it was common knowledge that they attacked people who walked alone in the forest. What was I looking for in this godforsaken corner of the earth? A tree could be a friend too. I embraced a spruce. It scratched me, but smelled good. I rubbed up against the spruce, I told it a few funny tales from my life, I held it close to me. The spruce comforted me. We all die, it said, but we all return again, as humans, spruces, worms, rainbows. That's good, if it's true, I said. And what about Sarah? Should I just leave her, or come and live here too, chopping wood, baking bread? You mustn't look at it so narrowly, the spruce said. The earth is everywhere, but only trees know the forest.

'Camera!' the director called.

'Camera running!' the cameraman said.

'Action!' the director said.

At that moment one of the junkies drifted in front of the camera and said to me, 'Hey, don't I know you? What are you doing here?'

'You can see what we're doing,' I said. 'We're making a film.'

'Oh shit, man. I thought you'd have a fix for me.'

The other junkies and dopeheads in the amusement arcade on the hash meadow were not that keen, either, but despite my misgivings Niko had insisted on using this location, and even though I'd written the screenplay for the film, he was the director, the man in charge. Besides, supposedly he understood something about film. I'd met Niko some time back through Dmitri. He was from Athens, was my age and worked as a camera assistant at Hesse Television, from where he'd borrowed the equipment. The camera was operated by a Yugoslav colleague who was also doing the lighting. Niko's girlfriend, Anette, was supposed to be doing the mike, but we'd chosen to film without sound in the amusement arcade. Having a camera there was bad enough, but the extras we needed for the scene wouldn't have cooperated if we'd been recording their voices too. Half of them were being sought by the cops, and the only reason why the other half weren't was because the cops knew where they could find them. Pop. A bulb had blown. No matter. Hesse Television had enough of them. The junkie still hadn't realised that he was standing in our way. He had red hair, blue glasses and smiled like a rat.

'Hey, what kind of scam is this? You're working in films now? Like Charles Bronson?'

'Just get out of the way of the camera, would you?'

'Come on, man, get us a coffee. I always gave you clean shit, didn't I? So what's it going to be when it's finished?'

'Two coffees,' I said to the woman who ran the café. 'With lots of sugar. You know, we're just trying to get something off the ground. If it works, we'll do a feature film.'

'Oh really? So what are you doing? Grip, or something like that?'

'I wrote the screenplay. I write, you know.'

'Oh, I didn't know that. Listen, I didn't want to say, but you've got fat, you're really bloated. You haven't quit, have you?'

'Yes, I have.'

'Of course, it shows. But it won't do any good. You look seriously unwell. Hey, do you think there might be a job for me, too? I could get you some Berlin Tincture, you know, the really good stuff. Get you back in shape, man …'

'I've told you, I'm done with all that shit.'

I left him standing there with his rat-smile and Dracula teeth. It wasn't the junk but the sugar which messed them up. Now several bulbs went. Short circuit. The Yugoslav pulled a face. He wasn't enjoying himself at all, and at most he was getting a beer and a schnitzel out of it. But he was Niko's friend and perhaps it was a change from the village halls, the opening of stretches of motorway and the drunken local politicians they filmed for Hesse News.

'I think we could do without this scene,' I told Niko.

'It's your script,' he said, fondling his beard. 'I think it's important that the viewer sees from the start the milieu the hero lives in, without us having to explain it at length.'

'Yeah, but look – this here is nothing. These guys are just getting on our nerves. I can easily think of something else to replace this scene.'

Niko shook his head solemnly with its mass of hair and large eyes.

'We're professionals. Nobody gets on our nerves that easily. But you're the one who knows. If you want to do it differently ...'

'Just look, Niko,' Anette said. 'Our two actors are really nervous, too.'

The two 'actors' were Bramstein, my colleague at *Zero* magazine, and a friend who looked even more of a mess.

'Please don't interfere,' Niko snapped at his girlfriend. 'What on earth do you know about actors? Actors are always nervous, they have to act and otherwise keep their traps shut. Don't you know what Hitchcock said about actors? Right then, let's do that scene again, please. Camera!'

I tried to remain inconspicuous in the background, but I knew that the junkie was whispering. It did happen that people who took shit might stop for a while. But to go straight back to the place and start filming where only yesterday they'd been begging for a fix, well that took cockiness to new extremes.

Our short film was to be a homage to the gangster movies of Melville, a highly stylised sequence of scenes that hung together very loosely, a collage of rituals – the hangout, the handover, the secret woman, the fatal shot – a harmless play on light and shadow and dreams, or so I'd thought. A nice bit of fun. Writing it had been fun. And it wasn't difficult either. I'd provided a little atmosphere and Niko would see to the rest.

But Niko initiated a flurry of activity; suddenly everything had to be 'professional'. I suspected that he wanted to show himself and his acquaintances in television that he was a proper film-maker. And also show those reviled young German film-makers, that Wenders, Wyborny or whatever they were called. And he didn't care what screenplay he had; I even got the impression that he would have filmed without a screenplay altogether. At any rate, almost all of my subtle, meaningful dialogue seemed to have gone by the board, as had any hope of payment of any kind. These people all had jobs or were studying, with the prospect of a house or a doctorate; it was only me who had nothing, not even a temporary job. I'd handed in my notice at Germania. At twenty-eight you couldn't gift your nights away. And even the publisher of *Stamboul Blues* wasn't assuming that in autumn it would make the literary world sit up and take notice. He'd fixed on a print run of five hundred and was planning on doing the typesetting and printing himself. I was back living with my parents.

The situation was tense. I'd never been keen on going to school, but at least back then things had looked decidedly rosier.

'Action!' Niko called. Bramstein's girlfriend, who was positioned on the street, raised her arms and waved, and we heard Bramstein's old banger rattle off. Then it came round the corner, turned into the yard, and at that moment the boys who were playing football next-door kicked the ball over the fence. It bobbled in front of the car, which Bramstein stopped abruptly.

'Cut!' Niko cried, grabbing the ball and throwing it back to the boys. He laughed. This was now the fifteenth time that this sequence had been filmed, but as long as he had film left Niko would go on shooting.

'You've got to take the bend with far more precision,' he told Bramstein, who was dressed as a gangster – dark hat, dark coat, dark glasses – and showed him. 'Look, this is the camera angle, and if you go one metre out you'll vanish from the shot, like that. But if I sway that way I've got that silly backdrop with the children's playground. No way …'

'What do you mean?' Bramstein, too, fancied himself as a film-maker. 'The children's playground as a backdrop is actually rather symbolic, it gives the scene a new ambivalence, don't you think?'

Anette was making rather urgent signs at me, but Niko couldn't be stopped now. He clenched his fists.

'I see. So are you going to do it as we discussed, or what? Are you taking over as director of the film? Wrote the screenplay, did you? Am I right in thinking it's your film?'

He looked as if he'd launch himself at Bramstein at any

moment, but the latter, coming from the Palatinate, was not so easily cowed.

'That's not what I'm saying at all, Niko,' he said. 'But I do think that in this sort of film it must be possible for everyone to pitch in their ideas. I mean, you don't have to put on some sort of authoritarian performance like in, I don't know, a major production company, or Hitchcock, Melville. I mean, we're all friends here, aren't we?'

'Friends? I see.' This didn't go down well with Niko. 'Let me tell you something. You don't have the faintest idea about film –'

'Just stop it now, Niko,' Anette shouted. 'Let's push on, it's about to rain.'

'You can shut up!' Niko thundered. 'When you're filming it doesn't matter whether it takes five minutes or five hours, there's one name and that's the director, and he's the one with the responsibility. That means he's the one to decide what each second of the film is going to look like, do you understand? Every centimetre belongs to him and him alone, can you get your head round that?'

'But Niko,' said Bramstein, who could be as tough as a dry Palatinate salami, 'Buñuel and Dalí ...'

'Are you crazy? Why are you talking about Buñuel?' Niko was gradually losing his rag. 'Buñuel is a god, why are you talking about God now? Who do you think you are that you can even utter that name? You're playing a part in this film, you're here as an actor, I'd rather say performer; you're not going to mention the name Buñuel and start a discussion. Either you obey my instructions or you can get out of here!'

'Come on, Niko,' I said. 'It doesn't have to be like this.

It's ridiculous to start picking a fight now. Buñuel, Dalí –
for Christ's sake, we're just making an amateur film here; if
we're lucky it might get shown at some short film festival at
half one in the morning ...'

'Oh really? If that's what you think then go ahead and
make the film yourself.' Niko spat out these words with
some tiny flakes of tobacco and cast the two of us a look
which excommunicated us from the holy halls of the cin-
ematic art for all time. Essentially I thought he was right.
Bramstein could quite easily have kept his mouth shut. The
thing had now fallen through. It was also high time that I
finished with this nonsense and got myself a job. Maybe
there was a tiny opening in the cultural world I could still
crawl through. Something in some third or fourth channel;
there were people who'd been doing local radio for twenty-
five years, church radio, didn't they need someone, perhaps,
who could write them a few neat sentences on this year's
turnip harvest, or female applicants for the mission in
Melanesia? Niko was already dismantling the camera. The
Yugoslav was on the road with Hesse News, doing a feature
on church bells in the Vogelsberg Mountains. Suddenly
a window was thrown open somewhere at the rear of the
house, and a voice called out: 'They've caught Baader.'

thirty-seven

Nothing became of the film, but I did find a job. The airport was urgently in need of staff. Their new computer-operated baggage handling machine had broken down, so good old manual labour was the order of the day, casual work. As I couldn't pass as a student any longer, I had to register as a full-time baggage handler. For a fortnight I sat in training classes with the other aspiring public-sector workers: thick-set Portuguese for whom refuse collection was too strenuous; silent Turks saving up for a hotel on the Black Sea; elderly technicians from the pharmaceutical sector with half-corroded lungs, who grumbled about being retrained for a job which only brought them half the money; and shady figures from the main train station and below platform level, who arrived every morning with the plastic bags that contained their worldly possessions, and sat tenaciously and silently through the classes, until the exasperated training manager gave them two hundred marks part payment. There were specialists who rode this scam throughout the Federal Republic, from Kiel to Friedrichshafen, wherever the public service was hiring people. Only one of them remained after the fortnight, and he only stayed until the first lot of wages were paid. When they opened his locker, dozens of packed lunches tumbled out that he had fished from dustbins. Evidently the tramps from the B-levels had high gastronomic standards.

At the end of the course there was a written exam in which I got the best mark. That wasn't saying much; I'd always had a good head for numbers and figures, and this was mostly about the international codes for airports: LAX = Los Angeles. They couldn't outsmart me on this one. No one had got a mark as high as mine for three years. I'd barely been there a week, sullenly examining the calluses I was getting from the luggage trolleys, when I was summoned before the boss. He couldn't believe it, and fired one at me straightaway.

'BGK?'

'Bangkok.'

'Well,' he said, 'I see you've got your school-leaver's certificate. It's rather unusual that now you should be here working as a baggage handler ...'

He looked at me. I straightened my glasses and said nothing. The underarms of my grey Frankfurt Airport shirt were bathed in sweat.

'Oh well,' he said. 'We all have to start somewhere, and here at Frankfurt Airport there are huge opportunities for promotion, if you want to improve your situation.'

'What would those be?'

'Well, I can imagine that in a year you'd take the skilled worker exam, if you want to stay in this field. Then you can be a foreman, and there are some vacancies all the way up to head of department. Baggage check-in is becoming increasingly important from the innovation side too. Or you could change to the technical sphere. As I'm sure you know, Frankfurt Airport is directly responsible for ramp service, operations on the apron and piloting, so technical developments are of interest there as well …'

'Hmm,' I said, 'I think I'll stick to baggage handling for the time being.'

'Fine,' he said, standing up. 'Make yourself familiar with everything and then we'll see. By the way, are you in the transport union?'

'No.'

'Have a think about it, Herr Gelb.'

I returned to Hall C and loaded charter passengers' luggage onto the trolleys. Tenerife. Palma de Mallorca, Dubrovnik, Crete, Mombasa. Strange how little difference there was between luggage. There were brown artificial leather suitcases and grey Samsonite ones, plastic ruck-sacks, battered hogskin travel bags, there were standard cosmetic bags, occasionally something metal, there were special cases for gentlemen's suits and heavy, black beasts on fixed wheels. But in fact all of it was uniform, and so they'd swarm off to their uniform hotels and uniform menus beneath the uniform palms on uniform beaches. A pretty boring world. I finished loading the final trolley then fetched a cola and my book. This was another job that gave you time to read.

One day I was in town with Niko and met Anita as she was coming out of Kaufhof. Only a few months had passed since our tempestuous but rudely interrupted venture on my mattress, but both of us had changed a great deal. With schnitzel and chips washed down with cans of beer in the airport staff canteen, I'd put on a number of kilos, while Anita had really blossomed. Her eyes glowed with heat, her hair stood in flames, and her mouth burned bright red without the need for any lipstick. You only had to glance at her to know what was up. It was a miracle that the air around her was not sending out sparks.

'Niko,' I said, 'you're spending the weekend with Anette, aren't you?' He understood and gave me his second key.

Niko had Dmitri's old mansard. It felt strange to be back up in that attic, with the familiar smell of dust, unaired beds and mouse droppings, which Niko enhanced with his black cigarettes and the kit he developed photos with. I prised open the slanting window hatch, but outside the air wasn't circulating either; a muggy Saturday evening and everything that went with it: fires, games of football, knees-ups, punch-ups, piss-ups, all hell let loose. A police helicopter was rattling above Westend.

Anita needed no preamble, no Pink Floyd, no glass of rosé, no crisps, no persuasive looks, no witty comments nor sentimental ones, no anecdotes, no cigarette, no hand caressing her knee as if by accident, no kiss breathed into her hair, no recollection. All she needed was a place to put what there was of her clothes, a shoulder to bite into and all that. Anita needed sex.

'Look,' I said a while later, gasping for air, 'I'm on early shift tomorrow; I've got to leave at five.'

'And?'

'Well, I need a few hours' sleep, Anita.'

'You can sleep at work,' she whispered, throwing her arm around me.

It went on like this for a few weeks, then I started to lose my ability to function properly. The early shift, which ran from six in the morning to two in the afternoon, caused me serious problems. I'd sit amongst the conveyor belts with swollen eyes, barely able to pick up a rucksack. After they'd noticed the bite marks on my shoulder while I was getting changed, my colleagues didn't hold back with their emphatic comments when I started sweating buckets as the first trolley was loaded. I could see that the Turks, in particular, thought I was a right prick, someone who'd completely abandoned himself to the dervishes of sexual desire.

'What did you say, Anita?'

We were sitting in Traube, drinking cider and eating rissoles. That's to say, Anita smoked and I ate the rissoles. I needed the calories. Traube was packed, as it was every night, with drinkers, whores, junkies, car thieves, artists, sex maniacs and public service employees who were all these things as well, but with a full salary and pension.

'What do you mean, darling?'

'I mean, what did you say?'

'I didn't say anything.'

And she was right, all she'd done was kick my leg under the table. That was another demonstration of Anita's tenderness, just like her juicy bite.

'I know I'm rushing this,' I said with my mouth full, 'but I really need it. That shift was utter hell.'

'Stop lying. I know all you do is sit around drinking beer.'

'Quite apart from the fact that you're wrong, sometimes that can be utter hell too.'

But I couldn't fool Anita. She looked at me with her dewy and velvety eighteen-year-old eyes, and in the dead corner of my soul she found a tired man who, with his double life as a writing baggage handler, would rather spend his evenings sitting in the pub, bragging to female teachers and deputy leaders of the local branch of the young socialist movement, but never showing anybody what he was writing.

'I'd love to read something of yours,' Anita said, tenderly pinching my jugular.

'Oh, it's all rubbish, really,' I said, removing her hand. 'I'm sure I'll be able to make a career in baggage handling, then I won't need this literary world any more.'

Anita's eyes flashed with irony. 'What sort of career can you pursue in baggage handling, darling?'

I ordered another bottle of cider and a lemon schnapps to go with it. The rissoles had been rather fatty.

'Look, Anita, first I'll be a foreman at the airport, but only so I can learn everything from the bottom up. Then I'll go to Lufthansa – I've already made enquiries – to their ground staff. They give you first-rate training, all you've got to do is get through the course, but seeing as I'm a practical person I'll sail through. And when I've sailed through I'll get myself a transfer abroad, what do you think of that? Head of Lufthansa baggage check-in in Bangkok, boss in Kuala Lumpur. Or do you want to spend the rest of your life at Kaufhof?'

'What do you mean? What have I got to do with it?'

'You know, in case we stay together.'

'Oh I see, so we're together, are we?'

'You're at your most beautiful when you're being ironic, Anita.'

That comment earned me another kick in the shin, and yet sometimes I could see it all clearly before me: done up in a white linen suit and panama hat, sitting in my austere office in an airport block overgrown with creepers somewhere on the edge of the Asian jungle, drinking a pink gin with a one-armed reporter from *Newsweek*, while assuring him that the rumours of a revival of the local guerrillas are absolutely false. The ceiling fan rattles away rheumatically, the three hippies from Hannoversch Münden are still camped out in the arrivals hall in the vague hope that their rucksacks will be found, and when I clamber out of my jeep in the evenings, shattered, Anita is waiting in our bungalow in a shabby part of the European quarter, wearing a silk kimono from Shanghai, holding in one hand a large jug of Campari, and in the other the eight-day-old literary supplement of the *Frankfurter Allgemeine Zeitung*, and as she gently massages my shoulders I mutter, 'Don't wait up for me tonight, darling, you know the freight plane's coming from Frankfurt, perhaps your mixer will finally arrive …' and at some point in the early hours, after I've dropped off at his hotel the pilot of the freight plane, Anatol Stern, and daybreak is already brushing the jungle with its rosy shadows, I'm sitting on the veranda, hammering out another page on my old Olympia Splendid, these raw, rough-hewn, lugubrious phrases, which long after my premature death from malaria will cause a furore in the German literary supplements.

'What?' I sat bolt upright. 'Did you say something?'

'You're daydreaming,' Anita said. 'Come on, I'd rather you talked to me.'

I talked to her.

Anita lived with her parents in my old area of Westend, and when her parents were away in their camper van, I'd sometimes spend the night there. There were even tins of beer in the fridge and the milk I needed in the mornings on an empty stomach, and when I was on early shift on Sunday mornings, Anita would make me fried eggs with ham. In the evenings we'd watch a crime series on television, go down to the pub, come back again, a shower with Anita, fresh bedclothes in her girl's room with its scent of laundry, deodorant spray and lily of the valley, and her flawless sunburned body that smelled of coffee cream and tasted like every hot dream. It was lovely, this youthful scratching and biting and kissing and testing and tasting and groaning, and the eyes shining in the moonlight, and on top of it another can of beer. It was homely, too, maybe that's what you ought to have at last, I thought in the mornings as I plodded towards the train station after one last kiss, to the airport, past yawning whores and helpless drunks, past election placards announcing that we could be proud of our country, maybe you should move in with Anita, three rooms, kitchen, bathroom, up in Nordend, cosy, baggage handling and Kaufhof, a kid perhaps, find peace, let the scars heal, take what comes, transport union, Palma de Mallorca, why not? You can still write, and if not, who's going to care? What would you be missing? Who'd be missing you? The little toe of a good woman is better than a good novel. Literature – what good is it anyway? Sure, there are good books, you can still read them when there's nothing decent on the box in the evening and your wife's at the theatre. I knew, however, that it wasn't this homeliness I was looking for or missing, but new surroundings, for surroundings meant home, and home was what I found when I discovered the Schmale Handtuch.

1 Raw Material Raw Material Raw Material Raw 1
terial Raw Material Raw Material Raw Material
1 Raw Material Raw Material Raw Material Raw 1
aterial Raw Material Raw Material Raw Material

thirty-eight

I had a furnished room in Wiesenstrasse in Bornheim. It was a stone's throw from Bergerstrasse. I took a deep breath of the autumn air, the lovely combination of damp leaves, wet asphalt, fresh platters of meat on sauerkraut, beer, dog's piss on concrete, the partially fermented cider they were already drinking in the pubs, the wind that blew over from the Ostpark. The smell made me hungry and very thirsty. The weather was affecting my bronchial tubes. My cough didn't sound good. Which wasn't surprising, given my work in the large cargo halls over by the forest. It was that time of year when you'd rather be doing an office job, easy work in a space heated to the right temperature, with pot plants to stop the air being too dry, and the sing-song of secretaries, the balsam of indigenous Frankfurt babble.

From Bergerstrasse it was a little way further down Saal-burgallee. It was still afternoon, not yet clocking-off time, but a slight fog hung over the streetlamps, and the trams had already switched on their lights. Past the post office, where, of course, they were standing in long queues, the winners of the smallest prize, three correct numbers in the lottery, now wondering whether it was really worth waiting half an hour for three marks sixty. I queued up too. Three marks sixty – in the Schmale Handtuch that was precisely three bottles of beer.

The Schmale Handtuch stood opposite, on the corner of Wittelsbacherallee. Yes, the yellow Binding Brewery sign was already illuminated and I quickened my pace. You had to be careful – they said that many a thirsty drinker, their eyes focused squarely on the glowing sign, had been struck by a tram when crossing the tracks in the autumn fog. Well, then it was time for your wreath, and at Bornheim Cemetery the priest had had a few words to say to mourners in the past. But that couldn't happen to me; it's common knowledge that this sort of thing only happened to other people. I was already on the other side, I'd already crossed the small front garden where the last flowers were giving up the ghost, fading away. Two children were standing by the sliding window, and Walter was bending down with his head of grey hair, looking affectionately at the little urchins: 'Well, what would you like for your twenty-five pfennigs? Sweets, liquorice, gummi bears?' I opened the door and for one absurd moment I felt my throat constrict at the noise, the heat and the vapour of beer. I was home.

The bar stools were all taken. At this time of day pensioners were feeding the two fruit machines with their marks and groschens, especially Karle and Maria, two veterans of the Bornheim drinking halls and bars, in the pub every day, pissed every day, broke every day, but the pensions arrived promptly, so basically these were dependable customers, even with their undone flies, dribble-stained coats and dentures that always slid into the beer glasses. Karle had just missed the jackpot yet again and started hammering on the machine with his gouty fists until one of the reps who'd also gathered at the front of the pub – travelling salesmen of obscure varieties of sausage and joke items for the big funfair in Frankfurt – put his coffee with kirsch on the bar and, wearing an expression of disgust, let Erich know that this pub was going to the dogs. Erich was Walter's twin brother, and even regulars weren't always able to tell the two landlords of the Schmale Handtuch apart. I stood there and inserted a couple of groschen into the fruit machine. I needed this dialogue sometimes just as other people needed their dose of Marx Brothers' films.

'Give me the bill, Walter,' the rep said, straightening a tie printed with parrots that was the width of a hand. 'It's getting too loud; I can't hear myself speak.'

'I'm not Walter,' Erich said. 'I'm Erich. What did you have?'

'It doesn't matter,' the rep said.

'It does matter what you had.'

'No, I meant it doesn't matter what your name is, Walter or Erich.'

'Oh, you think so, do you? Why don't you ask Walter, he's already had his heart attack. So, what did you have?'

'Walter!' Karle suddenly bawled. 'Where's my beer?'

Walter was unmoved; he was dealing with the two children who were now after gobstoppers. He forgot the pub.

'Coming,' Erich barked back to Karle. 'And don't shout so loudly, this isn't a playground!'

'You are Walter, after all,' the rep now laughed. 'The two of you could go on television, you know, on Kuli's game show, step dancing with the Kessler twins! What about that, eh?'

'I am not Walter,' Erich said impassively. 'I am Erich and if you're too drunk to know what you ordered from my brother, then show me your beer mat, young man.'

The rep, around fifty years old, turned red, and there was only one way out: 'Oh, go on then, give me another bottle of Beck's, Herr Woite, the day's finished anyway.'

'I'm sure you can allow yourself another,' Erich said, putting a glass into Karle's bony hand, which trembled until the beer had found its way to his stomach. I moved to the back of the room. My two groschen had not been in vain.

At the back was a seating area with a round table by the window, a colour television set, which had pride of place high up on the wall, and a few more stools and high tables on which to put the beer and perhaps hot sausages or chops that the Woites or Frau Bergmann had prepared in the tiny kitchen beside the toilets. This makeshift arrangement had never been approved by the health authorities or hygiene inspectors or planning authorities or whoever else was responsible, and would be forbidden on the spot if there was ever an inspection of the premises. One was long overdue. The Woite brothers were over seventy and very relaxed about this possible but rather unlikely development. In the meantime they carried out a daily dusting of the glass sign on the wall which read in gothic letters: *Never forget the homeland / Where once you were born. / If you forget your homeland, / Then you are forlorn!* The Woites were from Silesia, and the sign was the only thing which got a daily dusting in their pub.

The doctor wasn't there yet, but Heinz, the roofer, and Horch, who was a teletypist at the *Rundschau*, were standing by the swing door, and in the narrow space between their beer bellies stood the thin Greek, Archimedes, who was a head taller than either of them. Looks like they're all taking the day off today, I thought. Today sees yet another meeting of the shirkers club. But Archimedes had a valid reason for drinking. The barber's where he worked had closed.

'The man gambled everything away,' he said. 'He's mad – horses, roulette, the lottery, poker. But totally manic, I tell you. Once he sent me to London with a suitcase full of money to put on the horses. Then a partner lost the lot on a poor tip – madness, sheer madness.'

'So what are you going to do for work now?'

'Oh, I'll find something, something always turns up, barbers are always in demand. I'm going to take a week's holiday first, you know, go to Salonika and have some good food. You can't eat well here, it's always the same pork chop. Erich, where do you get these chops from? Come on, give us four schnapps.'

That's how it always began, you just popped in for some cigarettes, a read of the paper, to speak to someone you wouldn't catch anywhere else, and each time one of them would be there with something to drink to, a new job or one that had gone down the drain, a final separation or something that was just beginning, a pension adjustment, the first crocus of the year, the annual fair, FSV Frankfurt's rise up the table, the new suite of furniture or the fact that the old one had finally gone, all of it, the loss of a driving licence, a new prosthesis, a small inheritance, the motor-bike that had turned up again – and exactly where I'd left it, the hottest day of the year, how can anyone insist that I work, or the first snow, hey do you remember when we were young and everything seemed different? If there were fifteen people in the Schmale Handtuch it was effectively full, but sometimes we all needed it at the same time, and then there was room for us all.

We drank our bottles of Binding, which we felt was safer than the draught beer that sometimes had a hint of Vim. Besides, the bottles were colder and cheaper. We drank the schnapps; there were days like this when you simply had to drink whether you wanted to or not. Heinz, the roofer, was an expert in such days. Fat beads of sweat would emerge from beneath his checked cap and meander down his rosy, Hessian baby face.

'Hey, Walter,' he said to Erich, 'four more beers and turn the heating up, too. Do you want to make us all sick?'

'You're throwing a sickie anyway,' I said.

'Me? Sick? Are you joking? They just failed to pick me up this morning, the wankers, and don't think for a minute that I'm going to let them get away without paying me.'

'Come on, admit it, you overslept. It's no wonder, given how pissed you were last night.'

'Me? Pissed? You can't be serious. The last time I was pissed was when the pigs took away my driving licence. That's a year ago now, and the reading was only 0.24 per cent. Where I come from in Frankenberg that's still sober.'

'Here's the doctor,' Horch exclaimed.

'At last,' I said.

Dr Müller-Salzmann guided his one metre ninety-five through the Schmale Handtuch, unmindful of the chaos and vermin below him, and reached our group. His hands were shaking and scattering cigarette ash. His eyes were not looking anywhere in particular. Dr Müller-Salzmann did not need to place an order. Eric was already passing him a bottle of beer and schnapps was on hand, too. It was sobering to watch a doctor drink. Then he focused his gaze on us. What he saw did not seem particularly to impress him – four of his patients for whom there was clearly one prescription only, the same prescription that should have been given to him long ago: stop.

'So, gents, any fractures at the moment? With your spine, young man, you're not going to make it to forty-five, but I wouldn't worry about it, after forty-five life is nothing but a meaningless shambles.'

He knocked back the second of the three schnapps that Erich had brought him. I knew that now it was time for me to speak up.

'Doctor,' I said, 'this cough I've got isn't getting any better, and with the work I'm doing at the airport there's no …'

He gave me no more than a fleeting glance. 'Cough, then, for God's sake.'

I coughed until I was practically choking. Archimedes slapped me on the back and poured a lemon schnapps down my throat. Sarcastically, Horch blew a cloud of smoke into my face.

'Morning surgery,' Dr Müller-Salzmann commanded, turning to the roofer who was getting worked up about FSV Frankfurt. Dr Müller-Salzmann also worked as a team doctor, but only in periods of sobriety, which were becoming ever more seldom. All the same he was an authority in the field of sports injuries; his methods for healing complicated bone fractures were internationally renowned.

'The team's got no fighting spirit,' Heinz said agitatedly. 'They're a bunch of amateurs. You've got to dope them, Doctor, nothing else is going to work!'

'I'd like to see you in my surgery again, too,' the doctor said. 'I don't like the look of your neck.'

'My neck?'

'It's completely crooked,' the doctor said. 'I need to straighten it again,' he added, downing his third schnapps.

'But then you'd have to sign me off work for a week,' Heinz said, his face crimson. 'I'd need to brace myself for it mentally first, Doctor. Last time it took me three days to get over the shock.'

'Morning surgery,' Dr Müller-Salzmann commanded, loudly knocking three times on the table before he left the Schmale Handtuch with a spring in his step, touching nothing but the ground beneath his feet.

It became one of those days you wished you were any-where apart from in the Schmale Handtuch, and for this reason you stood even more obstinately by the swing door, shovelling in your chop and fried potatoes, washing these down with beer, then decomposing and acidifying the lot with schnapps, these mouthfuls, this existence. After five or six hours everything became jellyfish-like, philosophi-cal fluff, existential froth, and there all of us stood and sat, roofers, teletypists, barbers, baggage handlers, former detec-tive superintendents, managers, tramps, students, pension-ers, commis chefs, pickpockets, mariners, prostitutes, rent boys, jugglers, Alsatians, and Frau Bergmann with the last of the fried potatoes, staring at the box and there's Egon Bahr, a supernatural apparition, no doubt about it, light years away from the Schmale Handtuch, so remote that even the most diehard CDU voter could only shout, 'Hey, Frau Bergmann, just your kind of man, isn't it?' at which Frau Bergmann started from her reverie, fished a cigarette from her breast pocket, lit up, stroked her white hair beneath the hairnet and smiled serenely: 'Yes, well, he's a far more decent prospect than you at any rate.'

All of a sudden I had another vision. Standing there with a glass in one hand and a bottle in the other, half-listening to Horch, who was telling me about some complicated internal matter from the *Rundschau*, I caught sight of Ede coming through the door; Ede, just as I'd last seen him four years previously, with unkempt hair, scruffy beard, pale face, flaring eyes, only now he was wearing a sheepskin coat rather than paint-spattered T-shirt. Strange, these hallucinations, I thought, and only after beer and lemon schnapps too. I must have a fever, ah well, doctor's tomorrow, I'd surely be advised to stay in bed for a week, which is what I needed. Hopefully it wasn't pneumonia, I mean you were always prepared for minor crises, but you weren't so keen on major setbacks.

'Well, well, Harry, I managed to track you down after all,' somebody close by said in a Swabian accent. I looked up. It really was Ede. Suddenly it went very quiet. I could hardly even hear the football broadcast. Ede moved nearer.

'Long time, no see,' I said to Ede, and to Horch I said, 'A friend of mine,' and to Ede I said, 'Would you like a beer?'

'I don't have time,' Ede said. 'I need to talk to you. Come with me, I've got people waiting.'

He was on speed, as always at this time of day, early

evening, and now he wanted to go out and score something, but what had given him the idea that this was Tophane? We made our way out of the pub. The air was bitterly cold. A car was by the roadside, its engine running, shadowy faces.

'So, how did you find me, Ede?'

He laughed. His laugh sounded somewhat hollower than in the past.

'Oh, junkies always find one another.'

'Yeah, but I'm not a junkie any more.'

'I can see that, Harry. But you must have contacts. I'm passing through, you see, on my way to Sweden. I've got a wife there, a fantastic girl, but I need a fix, right now, or I won't get any further.'

I carefully poured the rest of the beer into my glass. The head looked good. Someone in the car hooted the horn.

'I don't know anybody any more, Ede,' I said. 'I'm completely out of the scene. But if you give it a day or two, I'm sure I can turn up something ...'

But Ede didn't have a day. You never did when you needed something. He was gone again in a flash and I stood there in the front garden with an empty bottle and a glass, until another customer arrived and snapped me out of my daydream. This was someone who needed something too, but he could find it inside, inside the Schmale Handtuch, and if you opted for the bottle you got it immediately.

thirty-nine

The black-and-blues chased the visitors' lead for almost an hour, and when the equaliser finally came in the eighty-first minute the FSV players and the last five hundred fans were too exhausted to savour the goal properly. The atmosphere had long been as sombre as that Sunday afternoon over the Bornheim stadium, a sky that froze the heart, a Sunday-of-the-Dead light.

'Watch, they're going to get another,' Heinz said scornfully as an FSV player took a foul throw-in.

'You're optimism personified,' I said. 'And anyway, you're only sulking because Müller-Salzmann didn't give you more time off work.'

'If I were in the public sector, I wouldn't be mouthing off so much about working. Oh look at that – see how they're playing!'

They were playing crap. Five more minutes. It was getting colder. Soon it would be December, which meant I'd have been at the airport for six months. I wondered what I ought to do. I'd long abandoned the dream of a foreign posting with Lufthansa, the jungle job in the tropics, just as the FSV players had abandoned their dream of promotion. Anita had also taken her leave; she'd probably written me off as a hopeless case. As had Ede. I was a no-hoper, both as a former junkie and a future husband, but I did feel that this might advance me as a writer. The only difficulty was that I made little time to write, and in the meantime people of my age were bringing books out every year, their novels, their poems, their essays, their recollections. Supposedly, literature had died three years ago; now it was flourishing again. Well, at least I was flourishing with it, even weeds were allowed to flourish. *Stamboul Blues* had actually been published, the typescript was riddled with errors. If the man was as bad at publishing as he was at typesetting then I could forget the book. But maybe the literary world was no different from football – time and again the favourites were toppled, and by nobodies who then spent a week in the spotlight. In the eighty-ninth minute an FSV defender lost the ball on the edge of the box, the centre-forward of the nobodies from Fulda took a blind swipe, and the ball smacked the inside of the crossbar, where it stayed fleetingly as if on the tip of an invisible pointer, before taking a mischievous half turn and being heaved into the net by a gust of wind. After the restart the referee blew the full-time whistle. As the players staggered off the pitch they were met by a hail of paper cups, bread rolls, smouldering cigars and rude insults. This is how they were hounded out of stadiums all over the world, league leaders who'd plummeted down the table, the matadors of yesteryear, the favourites who were not worth the entrance money. I peered more closely. One of the abused players was sticking up a finger at his detractors. He immediately got another paper cup on his head. Bad losers. But suppressing anger supposedly gave you cancer.

The Schmale Handtuch was closed on Sundays. Well, the brothers were old – they wouldn't carry on for that much longer anyway – but the fact that they chose to take their day off on a Sunday turned this day into a punishment. You'd occasionally see one or two of the regulars drinking at the kiosks, but that sort of thing was slightly beneath them, and from November onwards it was dangerous: if you didn't snap out of it in the evenings you'd soon be a goner. There were pubs aplenty in Bornheim, of course. You had Old Bornheim, the Riederwald, Ostend, then Sandweg on the way into town, the area from Breite Gasse down to Vilbeler Strasse, the fluid transitions from the working class to the criminal class and from the petit bourgeoisie to the bohemian world, but when you'd been in the Schmale Handtuch all week, you only went to those places reluctantly; it was a little like being on holiday, quaffing warm stuff in some establishment called Casa Henninger on a filthy beach, just waiting for the moment when you could down a well cared-for beer in your local again. Besides, the Schmale Handtuch was more than just a watering hole, a bar, the little pub whose praises were sung in ballads. The Schmale Handtuch was the refuge which some people needed in the heart of their homeland, the free port where they could deal in their dreams, a home for which they needed no mortgage and no rental agreement and no suite of furniture, no bedclothes and no little honey-bunny, just an insatiable thirst and the feeling that their neighbour, whoever they might be and whatever they looked like, could be a friend for the evening, so long as they were thirsty enough too.

You couldn't deliver the same eulogy to the Fass in

Bornheim. There, everyone sat at separate tables, the Eintracht fans and the FSV fans, the petit bourgeoisie and the petty criminals, the regulars and those that usually drank at the Schmale Handtuch, that rabble. Nonetheless, people would still go to the Fass on Sundays after the match and drink their beer there, even though it tasted insipid.

'How much dough have you got left?' Heinz asked on his second beer.

'Twenty marks.'

'Christ! How's that going to get us through the whole of Sunday?'

'I didn't know we were going to spend the whole of Sunday here. I was about to go home.'

'What are you going to do at home?'

'Just relax, Heinz. It's another hard day tomorrow.'

'Listening to you, you'd think you have nothing but hard days. What do you earn? What do you take home?'

'With overtime, nine hundred marks a month.'

'Exactly, Harry: peanuts. Come and work for us, even Ali earns fifteen marks an hour, and all he does is shovel cement.'

'It's too exhausting, Heinz, and I don't mean the work, but the drinking. You're pissed the whole time.'

'Pissed? What do you mean, pissed? You don't climb the scaffolding without six or eight beers inside you, that's obvious. So what are you talking about being pissed? It's the basis on which we work, fully acknowledged by our professional association. So, when are you going to start?'

'Thanks, but I've already got a job.'

'Bollocks to that!'

He stared gloomily into his glass. It was clear he only wanted the best for me, but I couldn't understand why. I was wary of asking him. These people's sympathy was not in their brains but in their bellies, where beer flowed in before coming out again, and even if it was sometimes babbled out, the meaning was perfectly evident. Asking for the reasons behind it was like asking why beer contained hops rather than oats.

'Shall we go to my place, then?'

'What are we going to do at yours?'

'Look, all I've got on me is ten marks. Do you think because FSV lost we'll get free beer today?'

I could see that protest was futile. Something was preying on Heinz's mind and he needed either a piss-up or a punch-up to be shot of it. A good fuck would have been the best solution, I thought, a night with a woman who allowed you to forget everything. I couldn't complain. I'd had nights like that. And what if these nights were all there was, I wondered as I trudged down the street beside Heinz.

After his military service Heinz had come to the city to make money. Now he was twenty-five, married, one child, and had a three-room flat in Wittelsbacherallee, complete with fitted kitchen, nineteenth-century-style bedroom, television cabinet, washing machine, hi-fi, upholstered three-piece suite. The monthly payments swallowed almost everything he brought home, and in a long week that was often two thousand, minus what he deposited in the Schmale Handtuch.

'Come on, offer our guest a vodka,' Heinz said to his

wife. We were standing in the kitchen, on the table were the coffee cups and the remains of a cake after a visit from family. The baby was whining. Margit was a genuine Frankfurt girl, fourth generation from Riederwald, with a sharp eye and malicious tongue. She was a few years younger than her husband, but only according to birth certificate. 'I've got to look after the kid, can't you hear?' she said, darting me a look of disdain. 'The two of you look as if you're deaf to the world. Have fun.'

She closed the door. When Margit closed a door, it stayed closed. Heinz sighed and fetched the vodka from the freezer. There wasn't much left in the bottle, just enough for half a tumbler each.

'Take a seat,' Heinz said. We sat at the coffee table. They'd been eating cherry tart with cream, and you had to watch out your sleeve didn't dangle in it. 'That's life,' Heinz said. 'First it's love and all the trimmings, then you're sitting there with wife and kid, wondering if you'll be able to cover the bills next month.'

'Everything has its price,' I said. 'But you do have a woman in bed when you come home every evening.'

'Indeed, and it's always the same one.'

'Love is supposed to mature every year like wine.'

'I know nothing about wine and maybe nothing about women either, but there is one thing I do know: I'd be better off if I hadn't got married.'

'Responsibility makes the real man.'

'There I am thinking you're some kind of anarchist, and you write books too, and then you start talking like my granddad in Frankenberg.'

'Now you see how one can misjudge one's grandfather.'

That made Heinz laugh, and when he'd finished laughing we drank up, but he stayed sitting there, listening to Margit talk to the baby. His fat, rosy face would have loved to exhibit pride, but all it was good for now was cluelessness.

'You've no idea the grief Margit gives me when I've had one too many. And yet, since we've been married she hasn't had to do a stroke of work, while I just keep on grafting.'

'Maybe she's missing it.'

'What, her? The whole family's work-shy, the father permanently on benefits, their only income is from the social security office, it's become a habit. Look, they're an antisocial bunch, back home they're just one rung above gypsies, because they're German. Whenever I see them I feel primitive hatred welling up inside me; it makes me want to vote CDU tomorrow.'

What was I to say to that? Instead of getting pissed up with part-time anarchists I should have done an agitprop course with Red Student Action, but the problem was that I found every opinion equally valid.

'Come on, let's go,' I said instead.

'No way. There must be some whisky around here somewhere. We'll polish that off first.'

Heinz disappeared into the bedroom to look for the whisky. I could hear the married couple arguing. The argument quickly escalated. If Margit went on like that she'd get a slap. I was hungry. The tart didn't look bad. I ate a piece and started hypothesising. If FSV had won, if Schmale Handtuch had been open. If men had the women and women the men they needed. There was the first slap. I took the copy of *Stamboul Blues*, already stained, out of my coat pocket and leafed through it. The text was basically a long poem, a prose poem. Maybe I ought to start writing poetry again, short, clear statements that went straight to the point, like a sip of vodka, like a slap.

l Raw Material Raw Material Raw Material Raw I
terial Raw Material Raw Material Raw Material
l Raw Material Raw Material Raw Material Raw I
aterial Raw Material Raw Material Raw Material

forty

Things had been happening in the world of small magazines, publishing, counterculture and underground literature, and a number of threads were coming together at Anatol Stern's. I kept well away from the meetings and the little groups that were forming; I was the outsider who also sat on the outside of the outsiders. With increasing boredom I read through the pamphlets that Stern was sent, the things which Aldo Moll in Bottrop pasted together for his info sheets, this German obsession with belonging to associations with numbers and distributors and copiers, or maybe it wasn't purely German but global, yes, the whole of humanity with subscription cards and a permanent three-line whip. But the Germans do these sorts of things with extreme thoroughness, and thus we had a German Communist Party faction, a Muslim faction, a Shiva faction with a Hare-Krishna department, the spontaneous leftists and those who resolutely banned spontaneity. There was organic farming, too, of course, and the rock-hard avant-gardists, mainly in small villages in the west of the country, near France, who thus smoked Gitanes, but didn't fit in with those who only drove fast bikes and wanted to be high and free – and then there were the women. The hurly-burly was ignored by the cut-up brigade with its American perspective, even though I never seriously believed that Bornheim was in America. In any case, I'd stopped doing cut-up.

Once Horch was at my place, skimming one of these texts which put you in Alexandria in the first sentence, Alphaville in the second, and by the end of the first paragraph you were in Alpha Centauri, in space. Like my friend Bramstein from the Palatinate, Horch was a big beer drinker, a friendly individual, an Asterix fan and a sci-fi authority.

'Hey,' he said, 'what's that supposed to be? You were never in Alexandria.'

'My dear Horch, that's just a cipher. As a sci-fi fan, you –'

'Here it says: "Danse Macabre in the Spitfire Bar. Pock-marked Masai from the shanty towns of Alexandria dance up close with the delegates of the World Church Council." And so on and so on. Come on, Harry, that's nonsense. And then these space travel fantasies, you ought to leave that to the science-fiction writers, they do it far better.'

'That,' I said, 'may well be true. But this isn't science fiction, it's new literature.'

'Let's go to the Schmale Handtuch,' Horch said in an attempt to close the discussion, but, of course, the discussion was far from closed, for later on, right in the middle of the evening chaos, before the Woites finally closed, when Karle's head was in a puddle of beer and Archimedes was dancing the sirtaki with Maria and Heinz was slurring some drivel about buggering off to Brazil, Horch and I looked at each other briefly and thought the same thing at exactly the same moment: Why have the Danse Macabre in Alexandria when the stuff was going on here before our very eyes?

But for that I first needed to reassemble the sentences which the cut-up technique – a quick skim and check, followed by a fragmentation of the linear, one-way prose – had chopped to pieces. That was like the sentences written by Bukowski, the American, but more particularly by those authors who were virtually ignored by the literary critics because they wrote crime novels. It was a distinction they shared with many authors who meant something to me. I devoured Ambler, Ross Thomas, Deighton, I read a story by Hammett before breakfast and with my last beer a chapter by Chandler, and, of course, I read Graham Greene. His new book was called *The Honorary Consul*, that was storytelling, no one here did anything like that; what long-winded bores German novelists were by comparison, and those endless missed opportunities which they explained away as passion or drive.

Anatol Stern excoriated these circumstances. America, he'd say, why aren't we in America? Sometimes it all got a bit too much for his wife.

'Just shut up with your bloody America!' she'd shout. 'America this, America that! You put on a record: Of course, you'd only get that in America! You read a book: An American obviously, they can do that sort of thing! What about politics, then? Can they do it all in politics too? Vietnam? Cambodia? Kissinger? Nixon? Watergate? Is that so great too?'

I was the only one who'd never been to America, nor was I so keen on America; how could you be if you took seriously the American books I read? But that wasn't the issue here. What bothered us was this German mush, this sticky sauce they served with their cultural products, and the sauce tasted so bad because it was made from the residue of political maladies, from the twentieth century's out-of-date doctrines, and spiced with the fashionable political ideas of the season. It made us sick, sometimes it drove us to despair, the sight of these gluttons, the fawning and slobbering at tables which still groaned under bowls full of dead theories and aesthetic principles, and then the vomit in the culture sections and the traces of blood as far as the high-security wings. Anatol Stern tried to explain all this to his wife. It was all right for him – all he had to do was get into his uniform and float up through the air to America, Africa, Asia, while back down in the airport I hauled the luggage from the conveyor belts and then had to face the merciless literary criticism of my drinking pal, Horch. I was sure of just one thing: either you go on writing, then you have to wade through it, through all this crap, or you stop for good, for ever, and then for a year at most you've got the chance to find a middle-class job before you end up in the gutter.

'Tough it out,' said Lou Schneider, who was driving me home. He'd come over from Mannheim to discuss our new magazine project. 'Start by doing that for a few years. You've no idea the shit they often have to struggle through in America before they get an opportunity. When I think of some of those characters in the East Village – my God! The scene here is a picnic by comparison. Take Carl Solomon, who Ginsberg dedicated *Howl* to. He's now sixty, no hair, no teeth, he exists only with hernia trusses and compression socks and enemas and prostheses, five hundred electric shocks behind him, yet he still has an unshakeable belief in literature and is single-minded in his endeavours to fine-tune his poetry. Now that's what I call control!'

'Lou, this is great encouragement you're giving me. You can drop me off on the corner here.'

'My pleasure,' Lou said. 'By the way, I think your idea about the poetry is a good one. Stay on the ball and make sure you put a bit of flesh on the bones. We don't want any slimming.'

'Do I look like that to you, Lou?'

Both of us laughed and Lou dropped me off at the corner of Wittelsbacherallee. The Schmale Handtuch was pretty empty; it was approaching the end of the month. The Finnish woman was enthroned right by the entrance. She worked as a beautician, and her ninety kilos were always well honed, apart from when she'd guzzled a few too many Mosels and crossed the path of her paranoid husband who was devoured by jealousy. Paranoiacs were always right. That evening, the Finnish woman was almost sober and rather pensive. No wonder that there was still a free seat beside her. I sat down and ordered a bottle of Beck's.

'Oh, the gentleman can still afford a bottle of Beck's,' Nellie said.

'This evening I can pretty much afford anything I like.'

'Have you won the lottery, darling?'

'No, I've just found out that I've got to tough it out for just thirty more years, with a hernia truss, periodontitis, compression socks, beer-warmers, sciatica and enemas, then when I kick the bucket I'll get a wreath from the chief of culture and five lines in the miscellaneous cultural news.'

'That's better than nothing,' Nellie said. We drank in

silence for a while and thought about death. The radio orchestra was playing something mournful by Gershwin. When the mood in the Schmale Handtuch was muted you could sometimes hear the angels brushing their wings.

'You've got no reason to be bitter, Harry,' the Finnish woman said. 'Look, you can still afford to drink Beck's and sit here cosily, while outside there are millions of people wandering about with no home, let alone beer. So what's your problem? That you haven't been discovered as a poet? Don't make me laugh.'

'That's not my problem, Nellie,' I said. 'My problem's that I don't know what the point of it is.'

'What's the point of it? It allows you to kid yourself about life; everyone would love to be able to do that.'

'Well, I don't think you can kid yourself about much through writing.'

'Really? Whenever I look at a book it's very rare that I find one where either I'm not being deceived, or I notice that the author is kidding themselves about something. Do you know what happened today, darling?'

'Did he beat you up again?'

'No, no. He left me.'

'But that's not the first time, and he's always come back in the past.'

'You've got a nice way of comforting people, Harry.'

She may have been right. I wasn't particularly sensitive to the hidden vibrations in the female soul. I wondered whether she fancied slipping off with me. If she had trouble with her husband, well, you never know, but then I decided not to pose the question. For some reason I couldn't get Carl

Solomon and his hernia trusses out of my head, nor what Lou Schneider had said: 'Make sure you put a bit of flesh on the bones.' He'd read a few of the poems that I'd recently written, mostly at night when the DJs on American Forces Network broadcast their hare-brained patter, and the last cans of beer danced on my desk to the rhythm my fingers were hammering onto the typewriter. I could feel my fingers already tingling. Hmm, I thought to myself a minute later, as I was striding home through the drizzle and sludge, it's not often that you've left half a bottle of Beck's and a lonely woman in the pub just to work on a poem. If this becomes a habit you'll soon have a whole volume. Another book. Lou Schneider was bloody well right. You had to tough it out.

l Raw Material Raw Material Raw Material Raw l
terial Raw Material Raw Material Raw Material
l Raw Material Raw Material Raw Material Raw l
aterial Raw Material Raw Material Raw Material

forty-one

Niko, the camera assistant, was living with his new girlfriend in a house in Wittelsbacherallee, and when their
friend moved out of the mansard I got the digs with all its
contents. The loo was in the anteroom and there was no
heating, not even a stove, but there were two rooms, one
looking out onto the rear courtyard and one onto the street
which the trams jerked along. I didn't have a bath or shower,
either, but that didn't bother me, and up here was only one
other tenant, a nutter who lived with a canary and would
often go for days without leaving his room, after which he'd
make a noise as if he'd acquired a harem. Perhaps he was a
day patient at the loony bin. Perhaps he was just a perfectly
normal crackpot like the rest of us. At any rate, when you
looked around you suspected that the sane ones were probably all sitting in the asylum and discussing the Battle of
Austerlitz, Picasso's cubist phase or the development of the
post-nuclear world, while the rest of humanity was gaping
at television advertisements and getting all excited about the
sixth number in the lottery or the Russian invasion.

The landlord still came by personally to collect the rent.
If you weren't in he'd come back another time, he wasn't in a
hurry. He lived in Niederrad, near the race track, where his

own horses would compete, too, and if I didn't have enough to pay the rent, I said, 'Herr Niebergall, what was wrong with your horse last Sunday?'

'Oh, were you there?' he replied.

'Of course, Herr Niebergall, I must have looked a right idiot when Vanity Fair only came in eighth. That was my rent I put on the horse, fifty each way, all down the tubes!'

'Oh, I'm very sorry, Herr Gelb,' he said. 'You can pay it with next month's rent. But let me give you a piece of advice: don't put any more money on my horses for the time being; they're not up to scratch yet this year!'

'And I thought you were going to try to discourage me from betting altogether.'

He laughed and put on his hat that he always removed when he came to the door. 'My dear Herr Gelb,' he said, 'that would be rather hypocritical of me, don't you think?'

I'd bid farewell to the airport job, but I hadn't registered myself as unemployed; I wanted to get out of this whole temporary and assistant nonsense. What was the cultural world there for? Hadn't I spent years writing for radio, women's radio? Wasn't I the expert in half-hour essays? Wasn't the head of women's radio forever praising my sensitive programmes about the life and work of famous women? Maybe I wasn't so sensitive when they were there in flesh and blood and I had to deal with their feelings, but when the goal was to give the listeners of Hesse Radio a better insight into one of these personalities, no one was more sensitive than me. I got into the skin of Clara Zetkin and Colette, of Angela Davis or Else Lasker-Schüler, I made no distinction, it was professional work which was paid professionally. As soon as I took out a sheet of paper the thing almost wrote itself, another little comment here, an impressionistic detour there, season well with ironic criticism, finish with a spray of arty pretentiousness and I'll have my fee, please, cash.

I could have expanded into school radio, features, but you're better off leaving that to others, I thought. After all, I'd already been an editor-in-chief, desert boots on the table, grabbing the phone: 'Yes, Herr Enzensberger, great work once again, but I think the text has more panache if we simply leave out the penultimate paragraph. Don't you agree?' It certainly seemed to be the superior occupation, on this side of the desk, rather than peddling manuscripts around the place, a three-part piece about Alcoholics Anonymous, a poetic radio report about the River Main from Würzburg to Hanau, or adapting the recollections of Freiherr von der Trenck for middle school. I applied, therefore, for a traineeship. I might not have a doctorate, and my interrupted studies certainly weren't going to impress any personnel department, but ultimately I was a practical, hands-on person, or more accurately, I had the nerve to become one.

I needed to hold forth, document my existence, leave an impression; I just didn't know which one. I brushed down my Trevira trousers, I cleaned my desert boots, I went to the barber's; I didn't have long hair anyway, so I had it cut very short. I stared into the mirror above the basin. What did I actually look like? Maybe you'd be better off approaching the city council, I thought, scratching away the dried blood from a razor cut on my chin, they've got a cultural department, too – but without union or party membership you haven't got a chance. And surely the people at Hesse Radio, too, need someone who can play the class clown on work outings, our secret poet, Harry Gelb, he used to be an anarchist as well, now he's doing farming radio. I ate a soft-boiled egg. Some of the yolk dripped onto my tie. I began by wiping it, then hurled the thing in the corner in disgust. If they really wanted me they'd take me even without a tie. They didn't want me.

The Bundesbank had moved into a high-rise building on Miquelallee. The tower stood there like a fortress in this desolate area. I felt queasy straightaway. Inside the air was so sterile that I could barely breathe. The tie was choking me. There certainly wouldn't be index cards here any more, with handwritten lists, poker sessions amongst the flowerbeds. The head of personnel didn't seem to recognise me.

'You say you've worked for us in the past?'

'Yes, it must be on file somewhere … two and a half years ago, and eighteen months ago …'

'It's not in the system yet,' he said, peering at me from above his glasses. 'So what do you want to do now?'

'I was working as a trainee then,' I said. I had to clear my throat. I'd never experienced such a feeling of emptiness, at least not when going for a job. 'So I thought that now – no, I'm determined …'

'Oh you are, are you?' he said, taking off his glasses. He'd aged ten years in this short period. So had I, by at least twenty. 'Herr Gelb, yes I do remember. You terminated your contract without notice, didn't you? Artistic career, wasn't it? And now you want to return to us? Well, I'll see what I can do. You'll find the way out.'

I did. But I heard no more from the Bundesbank.

If you can't get a job, it's only because those others are up and out early, I thought as I sat opposite the publisher of the satirical magazine at nine in the morning. How could you be so level-headed at nine in the morning? I was a night owl, never got up before eleven if I didn't have to, gradually found my form in the afternoon, after five beers I was ready to take on the world, and by two in the morning I could have uprooted trees with my bare hands. The publisher of the satirical magazine looked as if he'd had two brilliant ideas and written a scintillating editorial even before his boiled egg arrived on the breakfast table. He'd probably done twenty press-ups and sprinted five times around the desk.

'What have you done in the past, Herr Gelb?'

'Well, I produced *Zero* magazine, surely you must know it, even though it was forced to close, for political reasons …'

'Oh really? Never heard of it.'

'That's strange. Anyway, I write, but obviously you can't live off books, so recently I've been working at the airport, although for health reasons …'

'At the airport? How interesting. What did you do there?'

'Oh, mainly loading suitcases, baggage handler.'

He put down his coffee cup.

'Fantastic! Undertaking a thorough examination of working life, like Wallraff, eh? Why don't you do us a little reportage, something satirical? That's exactly what we're looking for: "I was a baggage slave at Frankfurt Airport".'

'Oh no,' I protested. 'It wasn't like that at all. It was a very normal job, you know, public service, there's nothing to uncover.'

'A normal job. There's no such thing. Herr Gelb, what is a normal job in your opinion?'

'Well, I don't know, I suppose the sort of thing you do to pay the rent, all the other stuff ...'

'I'm not interested in that,' the publisher of the satirical magazine said. 'You're a creative person, aren't you? What do you want with a normal job?'

'Hmm, writing satire, I don't know ... I was thinking more of the practical side of the profession, it's something I know a bit about, as I said I've already been an editor-in-chief ...'

Our conversation was beginning to bore the publisher. He wanted a Wallraff rather than somebody who spent his days learning how to be an editor, and evenings sitting at home, maybe writing a novel. There were enough of those people around. He needed exposés.

'As I said, there are no normal jobs here. Perhaps you should try calling Herr Cloppenburg. We've got a small shipping department; it's possible they need a packer, if that's normal enough for you. You know the way out.'

I'd never had any trouble with my stomach, but now it started to revolt. I couldn't blame it. These mad, early-morning rushes, all for nothing, and then at lunchtime sitting in the slowly atrophying kitchen, looking at the job advertisements. There was not as much on offer as there had been two, three years previously. In the evenings an arduous session in the Handtuch, and when the alarm clock rang at seven, my stomach was already starting to flutter. Now I understood why so many men needed a beer in the morning and some schnapps to follow. I forced down two eggs and a cup of tea, but this failed to rob the day of any of its horror.

Horch had told me that the *Rundschau* was looking for a co-worker in its archives. Co-worker – a newfangled expression. Everyone was looking for co-workers, co-workers for the warehouse, co-workers for the registry, co-workers for the product line, co-workers for the cleaning, co-workers for the archive. So, once again it was tie, jacket and Trevira trousers. The evening before I'd run up a hefty tab at the Greek place. Sweat was running from every pore by the time I'd got as far as the porter. A senior co-worker from the archive came to fetch me. I could feel palpably that he was eyeing me with mistrust. That's the thing with aniseed schnapps, the next day it flows out of your pores with the sweat. The man showed me the archive. Shelves full of newspapers, newspaper cuttings, dust. The smell of paper, mothballs, paste and floor wax. The other co-workers stared at me in silence. The mere thought of sitting in this crypt and gutting newspapers scared the shit out of me.

At Hauptwache I felt the eggs coming back up. I just managed to get out of the tram and make it to a dustbin. Yolk, egg white, nothing had been digested. It was followed by a torrent of bile.

'Just look at him, already legless in the morning,' a woman said to her husband.

'Come on, Erna, don't watch,' the man said, pulling her away. Maybe he knew what it was like.

The telecommunications firm Telefonbau und Normalzeit was on Mainzer Landstrasse. I walked the last bit of the way to get myself some fresh air. It reeked of exhaust fumes, petrol and smoke, but it was air all the same. It started to rain. I didn't have a coat. When I got to the personnel office I was wet through. The secretary didn't offer me a seat.

'Show me your papers.' She glanced at my tax card. 'Where are you currently employed?'

'Well, the thing is,' I said, 'I'm freelance at the moment, my last employer was Frankfurt Airport …'

'I'll see if Herr Kaiser is free.'

Herr Kaiser looked like an out-of-shape heavyweight fighter and he filled the room with cigar smoke.

'Do you have any experience working in a warehouse, Herr Gelb?'

'I've got all sorts of experience, Herr Kaiser.'

'I can see that, young man. OK, you'll hear from us.'

The rain was getting heavier. This time I took the tram to the next stop. It was Line 12 and it stopped on the corner of Wittelsbacherallee and Saalburgallee. From there it was only a short stroll to the Schmale Handtuch.

'If you're looking for work,' Walter said, 'we need an assistant. Rudi is plastered the whole time, and with my heart I can't work all day long any more.'

'What would you pay?'

'Well, you're untrained, but you'd pick it up quickly. Rudi got four hundred a week, but then again his main job is as a waiter. So, if you pass muster you can have four hundred, too.'

'What about the working hours?'

'You know full well. We open at six and close at ten in the evening.'

'But that's sixteen hours!'

'You can take four hours off around lunchtime.'

I put down my empty bottle in front of him.

'Walter, I think I'd rather stay this side of the bar. Time definitely passes more quickly that way.'

The warehouse was in a rear courtyard in Nordend, where small artisans still flourished: carpenters, plumbers, undertakers. Old bicycles, geraniums in the windows, noisy children. Fleischwurst, briquettes, female students with badges on their parkas bearing feminist slogans. I entered one of these workshops where in the past a cobbler may have sat making shoes. Now almost the entire room was filled by a packing table, together with shelves where the goods to be shipped were piled up: records, comics, books. The two women and the old man, who were working at the packing table, shot me penetrating looks without interrupting their tasks. A few tugs on the packing string, snip, snip, and another package was ready. Then Herr Cloppenburg appeared, a sporty-looking businessman in a tailor-made suit. His eyes looked less sporty. They looked like eyes that love to see figures.

'So, you're our new man, eh? Excellent! Half days, is that right? Let me introduce you at once …'

'But, Herr Cloppenburg, I should tell you before I start that I've got absolutely no experience, I mean as far as packing is concerned …'

'Did you hear that, Frau Schmittinger? Herr Gelb has no experience! Well, how many days do you think it'll take before Herr Gelb knows everything there is to know about packing?'

Frau Schmittinger put a few records into a packing box. She didn't need to look at me any more. Her judgement was already settled.

'He won't find it easy seeing as how quick that student was we had till now.'

'That is all well and good, Frau Schmittinger, but we don't have the student any more and, let's face it, he was an exception. And you weren't so delighted that he smoked like a chimney, were you, Frau Schmittinger? Do you smoke, Herr Gelb?'

'On occasion, Herr Cloppenburg.'

'On occasion – excellent! Our Herr Gelb is a diplomat. Right, Frau Schmittinger, we are going to train Herr Gelb to become a pillar of our business, that shouldn't be too hard! So, hang your coat in the wardrobe here and then get yourself acclimatised, Herr Gelb, we're like a family here, and if the revenue keeps growing then one day we'll be a really big family. May I introduce you? This is Herr Anders, my partner and our head of planning; and this is Herr Gelb, our new co-worker. OK?'

I shook Herr Anders's hand. Beside Cloppenburg he looked like an absent-minded primary school teacher who can never remember where he's put his glasses. A truly successful partnership, each in his own little cubbyhole, one with his culture, the other with his slide rule. But they paid seven marks fifty an hour, and if I did that for four hours a day I'd make six hundred marks a month, which I could live off. I started to pack.

'That's not how you do it,' Frau Schmittinger said, after she'd watched me struggling with the string for a while. 'Have you never wrapped up a Christmas present?'

'No.'

'Show him, Frau Heppel, this is holding us up dreadfully.'

Frau Heppel showed me. The old man silently smoked a cigarette, and whenever the two women's gossip became particularly obtrusive, he'd raise his bushy eyebrows half a centimetre and hold them there for a full minute. He never said anything apart from 'Goodbye' and 'Please pass me the parcel tape, Herr Gelb.'

Although I knew how to pack up the packages, my output was very modest. Whereas Frau Schmittinger could get thirty packages ready in an hour, and Frau Heppel and the old man two fewer, if that. I managed a measly ten. The record orders were all right – straight into the cardboard box, tape over the top, done – but unfortunately the mixed packages piled up: records and books, or left-wing kitsch which they still flogged, buttons, T-shirts, posters. They did me in. I thought of Bernadette; what was it I'd said to her? Me packing books? Never! And now here I was, standing in this shed, packing books and progressive junk for deepest provincial Germany. One *Red Star over China* to 6411 Kohlhaus, two copies of the handbook of the Communist International – separate bills – to 7321 Wäschenbeuren, and then the handy Suhrkamp packet for 8581 Oberwarmensteinach, they'd have a whole year's worth of critical theory. From time to time Cloppenburg stuck his head round the door and announced, 'In February sales increased by 7.957 per cent! We're on the up, folks!' The pensioner raised his eyebrows.

On the fourth day I didn't go in. I rang.

'Herr Cloppenburg, I'm not the right man for the job.'

'If you say so, Herr Gelb.'

'Send me the cheque by post.'

'Well, you must know what you're doing.'

'I do know.'

I wandered up and down the corridors of the labour exchange. It seemed as if more people were looking for work than in the past, and all of them had something they could do, they had their Class II driving licences and experience in dusting and vacuuming or the art of waffle-making or cleaning ice-cream machines. I passed the department for security personnel. There wasn't such a crush here. I thought of Hegel, Hegel and Germania Security, those long hours at the Osthafen, and up at the electric power station in the Taunus – it had, in fact, been an interesting time. I opened the door. A man glanced up from his index boxes.

'Are you looking for someone?'

'Yes, a job.'

'Well, if that's all.'

I entered and closed the door behind me.

'Take a seat. What sort of job are you looking for?'

'Well, seeing as I've got a certain amount of experience in the security business, I thought I'd give it another try.'

'What do you mean by "try"?'

'You know, a regular job.'

'Where did you last work?'

I gave him my tax card. He scanned it and then looked at me more closely.

'What have you been doing from January to now?'

'I work as a freelance journalist. I was travelling.'

'I see. Let's take a look.' He flicked through his index cards. 'As a journalist I'm sure you're also interested in unusual jobs.'

'What do you mean by unusual?'

'I've got something for you here. Do you know the area around the station? Kaiserstrasse, Elbestrasse, Weserstrasse? Of course you do, you're a freelance journalist. Here, the Kokett Bar is looking for a doorman, what do you think?'

'Hmm, actually I was looking for something a little more respectable …'

'Oh, but this is perfect for you, I mean, you did say you wanted to try something out. You'll get a nice uniform and bundles of insight for your journalistic work. And just think about the tips.'

'Yes, but …'

He pushed a card over to me. 'Or do you want to register as unemployed, perhaps? Go on, get a move on!'

The Kokett Bar was a rundown dive in a rundown corner of town. The display case with photos of the girls had been smashed by a disappointed punter. And no wonder – the photos were at least ten years old. Back then the beehive hairdo had been all the rage, I was in my penultimate year at school and had started writing poetry. I peered into the bar. The girls had not moved on much.

'Looking for someone, son?'

'Me no understand.'

'Piss off, Dago.'

On the next corner was a telephone booth with a telephone, just for once. Germania, I thought, they're not going to take you back. No way. So all that's left is factory work or construction, shovelling cement with Ali and stumbling rat-arsed into the Handtuch every afternoon. I put a couple of groschen into the slot. I remembered the number.

'Germania Security.'

'Gelb. I had a temporary job with you until a year ago, and now I'm looking for work again …'

'Gelb, yes, I remember,' Hegel said. 'But we don't need temporary workers at the moment.'

'I was rather thinking of a permanent post.'

'Permanent? Let me have a think. You were a student, is that right? Yes, I believe we do have something for you, Herr Gelb, a rather appealing job. We're looking for someone with the right level of sensitivity, you know how it is, I mean, I couldn't put an employee with bad breath in a chemist's, could I?'

'What do you have for me?'

'The university, Herr Gelb.'

forty-two

There were four of us: Mustafa, the Turk; Schlappner, the temp, who could never remember the keys; Herr Kleinschmidt, who'd been doing the job for fifteen years; and me. Around eight o'clock the last Nobel Prize candidates and their disciples left the main building. At eight everything was locked up. Anyone wanting to study after that hour had to wait until a security guard opened up for them.

'I'll do circuit one tonight,' I said to Kleinschmidt. 'Then Mustafa can do number two with Schlappner. You'll manage that together, won't you, Mustafa?'

'Have to, Harry. Give me a cigarette.'

That was settled then. Circuit one was the longest – twice two hours – but it went through the entire surrounding area as far as Myliusstrasse, and if it was a beautiful night it was the best circuit. It was the beginning of May. Mustafa was the circuit one specialist; it was the only one he knew by heart, he could doze every step of the way, he'd been doing it for years. Every month he sent half his eight hundred and sixty or eight hundred and ninety marks back to his family in Konya. With a compatriot who worked for the rubbish collection service he shared a place to sleep in a six-man room, lived off bread, sheep's cheese, tinned sauerkraut and cigarettes, was thirty-six years old, and the only man at Germania I trusted further than the next control box.

Around ten I did my first patrol, returning at midnight, and entered into the logbook: 'Particular incidents: Window smashed in basement of Senckenberganlage 48.'

'That's the second time in the last few weeks,' Kleinschmidt remarked. 'I've told the caretaker a number of times that they ought to put grilles over the windows, but they don't listen to us, do they? And you know what the management think of the university building?'

'What?'

'They want to get rid of it.'

'Such a prestigious building?'

Kleinschmidt bent over the table. There were certain things he would only whisper. He was an elderly, painstakingly meticulous gentleman, who would have loved to reach the position of premises security chief or shift leader, although neither of these actually existed. Nor would Kleinschmidt ever make supervisor now; he was too old, too fearful, broken by a wife who sat in a wheelchair at home and was dying from the legs up.

'They never tell us anything,' he said, 'but sometimes I hear things when I take part in target practice. They want to get rid of the university because the insurance company won't cover them any more. Too many acts of violence, you understand? One day the whole thing will blow sky-high. It's too big a risk. When the time comes, keep in mind what I've said tonight.'

'Pretty major stuff,' I said, staring at him. 'I've never

looked at it from that perspective, but it does sort of make sense. Terror, eh?'

'And they're using us as cannon fodder! It starts with the windows. What do you imagine is going on in the physics department? Smashed windows every day, acids poured all over the place, soon we'll be needing gas masks. And if I say anything, all I hear is, "Oh, Herr Kleinschmidt, they're students, who gets worked up about students?" Mark my words, Herr Gelb, it always starts with broken windows.'

'Like in 1933, you mean?'

But Kleinschmidt was at great pains to avoid this subject. His life could be divided into two periods, before 1951 and after 1951. In 1951 he'd returned from prisoner-of-war camp in Russia; before that everything was taboo. After 1951 he had two sub-periods, pre-Germania and after he joined Germania, and then there were two further sub-periods, without his wife's illness and with his wife's illness. The only period of his life that Herr Kleinschmidt liked to talk about was the first sub-period of the second main period, before he joined Germania. He'd worked for Hoechst, bought himself a Volkswagen, saved up for their little house, and believed in Adenauer. Now all he believed was that the world would keep going downhill for as long as he lived. And he'd been forced to give up his car to hold on to the house at the very least. It took him two hours to get to work, two hours to get home, we only had one day off each week, and each shift lasted ten hours, twelve at weekends. I wondered why Kleinschmidt was at Germania, but never asked him the question. That sort of thing was taboo. And the answer was as clear as daylight. We all had something to hide. There we sat, failures, guarding other people's property, but unable to guard our own selves.

Mustafa and Schlappner returned from circuit two. Schlappner was already green in the face. The air in the chemistry department was not ideal for an alcoholic. He felt eagerly in his plastic bag for the bottle of cider. Kleinschmidt strongly disapproved.

'Alcohol at work,' he said. 'If the supervisor catches you, you'll be out on your ear, Herr Schlappner.'

Schlappner guzzled half the bottle then put the bag back in the cupboard and sat down.

'If you keep your mouth shut, no one will find out that I need the odd sip. Anyway, cider isn't alcohol.'

'I expect you put schnapps in it too.'

'Care to try some, Kleinschmidt?'

'Come on,' I said. 'Let's play a round of rummy.'

'I'm busy,' said Schlappner, who was looking distinctly better and brought out a folded newspaper. He unfolded it. It was the racing paper. He spent all his money in betting shops.

'Alcohol and horse racing,' Kleinschmidt said. 'And they put someone like that to guard the university.'

'You're behaving like you *own* the university.'

'I have been working here for fifteen years, you know.'

'For someone who's been with this firm for fifteen years,' said Schlappner, glancing up from his paper, 'you have to admit you haven't got very far, eh Kleinschmidt?'

For a second Kleinschmidt looked as if he were going to pounce on Schlappner. Schlappner may have been a few years younger, but he wouldn't have stood a chance against

Kleinschmidt. And Mustafa sat beside them impassively, spooning sauce onto his sauerkraut, then dipping into it with bread, and pretending he didn't understand a word.

'I hope you know circuit two inside out now, Schlappner,' I said quickly. 'We can't have someone going with you every time.'

'Exactly,' Kleinschmidt said with a cold smile. 'I suggest you do the last patrol on your own, and Mustafa will come with me on three. After all, we need to see whether you can finally do a patrol alone. Otherwise the firm will have to post you somewhere else.'

He picked up his radio and tuned it to *With You Till Two*, the post-midnight music featuring the Hesse Radio dance orchestra, conducted by Willy Berking. I left them sitting there: the Turk, who was eating his supper slowly and with great focus; the piss-artist, who was acting as if he were scanning the paper for the big winner, while shaking with fear that he might lose this job, too; and the thwarted premises security chief, who listened to the dance music with his eyes closed, as if these sounds could provide a soothing ointment for everything, for the second sub-period of the second main period of a pointless life, for the imminent end of the world. Outside the lecture theatres at the end of the long corridor in the main building was a coffee machine. I drank two cups, then turned off my inspection lamp and looked through the glass doors at Gräfstrasse. Two students were sticking up posters, another was keeping lookout. In the darkness I couldn't work out what it was about, but it must be some initiative which gave all of those involved a good conscience.

Around three o'clock I started my second patrol. The night honoured the evening's promise. The air was soft and tasted good. Satellites were shimmering in the sky and a few stars were out as well. Most lights were off by now, a pair of lovers, a last drunkard teetering home. Sitting by the bank on Bockenheimer Warte were two dossers, nattering away with a bottle. When they saw me appear they fell silent and looked uncertain; I was wearing a uniform, after all. I waved at them, but they didn't continue their conversation until my back was turned. Even night security guards represented the menacing powers of the state.

I slowly made my way through the institutes on Senckenberganlage, Kettenhofweg, Beethovenplatz. To begin with I cast an eye at the flyers, the activities of philosophers and sociologists, noticeboards, placards, events. My interest soon waned. If you wanted to know what students were up to you just had to look in their lavatories. I remembered the uproar when someone from Commune One had said 'What do I care about Vietnam when I'm having problems reaching orgasm?' These days there was barely a single exotic country that German students had not taken under their wings, but a brief inspection of the urinals showed you that their sexual problems made Commune One's difficulties in reaching orgasm look like child's play. I once showed Schlappner the ladies' loos in the main building; he turned red and marched out, then looked at me as if I'd written those disgusting comments myself. These days I only entered them if I couldn't avoid it, but when I saw the fiery slogans on the placards I sometimes wondered whether these, too, didn't reflect varieties of sexual obsession.

When I crossed Bockenheimer Landstrasse on the corner of Siemayerstrasse, I noticed a familiar figure in the light of the streetlamp. It was Fritz. I hadn't seen him since the previous summer when I was still working at the airport. We stared at each other for a while, then the two of us grinned simultaneously.

'What are you doing here?' Fritz asked.

'I could ask you the same thing.'

'I'm having a walk. Fresh air.'

'Me too.'

'You're not working for Germania again, are you?'

'You still in the same old room?'

'Yup.'

'There you go, Fritz. Nothing ever changes.'

'It does,' Fritz said as we walked up Siemayerstrasse. 'Something has changed. I'm not drinking any more. Not a drop.'

'It must have been pretty bad, then.'

He stopped. His face was somewhat thinner and harder, but now with a grimness around the mouth that hadn't been there before.

'Bad?' Fritz said. 'It was sheer hell, man. Do you know what made it so much worse?'

'No idea. Wait a sec, I've just got to go in here and stick this into the clock.'

'You recommended me that book,' Fritz said when I came back. His voice sounded impatient, as if he desperately needed to get something off his chest. 'Malcolm Lowry, *Under the Volcano*.'

'It's the perfect reading for someone who likes a drink.'

'The perfect reading? You're crazy, Harry. It was only after I read the book that I *really* started drinking. I drank like I'd never drunk in my life before. I was that consul – do you understand? – I had the *hujas*, I heard voices, I even started up a relationship immediately just so that I could wallow in the filth when the woman gave me the shove.'

'Don't you think you're exaggerating a little, Fritz?'

But Fritz didn't think so, quite the opposite in fact. The way he described it, *Under the Volcano* had seized hold of something in him like the Sermon on the Mount might a remorseful sinner. *Under the Volcano* had become Fritz's Bible, Mexico the Promised Land. And one day Fritz had made the discovery that he only had to read the book rather than drink. From then on he was converted.

'I don't touch a drop any more, man,' he said solemnly. 'I mean, Lowry wrote the book when he was sober. But he must have gone through hell first.'

'Are you trying to say that he went through hell for you?'

'For me?' Fritz looked at me as if I still hadn't understood a thing. 'Look man, I just want to say one thing. A few months ago I suddenly came to, in a field near Wiesbaden. I'd rented a car and was intending to pay one last visit to this woman, a big scene, final farewell, you know. I was plastered and came off the Landstrasse, boom, landed up in the field, woke up ages later, just left the car there, staggered back to Frankfurt, look, the scars are still new, I tell you, you don't have those kinds of experiences for nothing.'

'Sure,' I said. 'I believe you.'

'Three days later I suddenly knew what I had to do, and yesterday I bought the ticket.'

'Ticket?'

'I'm flying to Mexico, Harry.'

'Fantastic!' I uttered.

'I'm flying to Mexico, I'm going to go everywhere Lowry was, Cuernavaca, Oaxaca, I'll scramble up the volcano, I'll go into the cantinas.'

'Sober?'

'For one last time I'll drink everything they put in front of me and then I'll be cured for good.'

He gazed at me as if he were expecting that I'd fall to my knees on the spot and beg him to take me with him. Instead I turned into Myliusstrasse, where there was another institute. After all, I had a job to do. It took me a quarter of an hour and I thought Fritz would have vanished – maybe the whole thing had been a *huja* – but when I came out of the institute and locked up he was still standing there. We meandered slowly back to the university. The keys were jangling.

'Well, Fritz,' I said, 'that's quite some news. What's happened to the others? Speedy, Fuzzi, the gang in the cellar?'

'That's another story,' Fritz said. 'I was off the scene for half a year, out of town, and when I got back I didn't see any of them apart from Lanky. One afternoon they hauled him out of the snack bar on Bockenheimer Landstrasse, in handcuffs, his head covered in blood.'

'Shit.'

'It was bound to happen.'

'You could see it that way.'

Fritz stopped at the corner of Senckenberganlage.

'This is where I'll say goodbye,' he announced. 'What's

going to become of you, Harry? Are you still writing, or have you given that up?'

'Writing is different,' I said. 'You can't give it up like alcohol or the needle. The most that can happen is that writing gives *you* up. And it hasn't properly started with me yet.'

'Maybe you need a Mexico too,' Fritz said. 'Maybe not the Mexico I'm going to, but a different Mexico. We all need a Mexico.'

And with that he left me standing there. It was starting to get light and I watched him for a while longer, a small man in black clothing whose life had changed so radically because I'd recommended a book to him. But life changed continually anyway, and yet always stayed the same, whether you read novels or the racing paper, whether you wrote books or did your nightly patrols. I crossed Senckenberganlage and went to the high-rise law faculty, which was also on circuit one. There was a control box up on the roof. I went up in the lift. The view was impressive. In the twilight, with the slim silhouettes of the tower blocks against the reddish horizon and the smoking factory chimneys by the River Main, the city offered a view which compensated for many a bitter hour. Pigeons cooed affectionately. And beneath every roof stories were being lived that were waiting to be written.

When I rang, Mustafa opened the door. Kleinschmidt was doing his patrol alone. Schlappner was sitting on a chair utterly exhausted, tears running down his face, hair sticking out wildly from his head. It smelled of cider.

'What's wrong, Mustafa?'

'Schlappner finished,' he said, rolling a cigarette.

'What do you mean? Schlappner, what did you do?'

'I fell down the stairs,' Schlappner exclaimed at last. 'That's because we're not allowed to use the lift, but I've got a bad knee, and then I had a drink, I needed it after the shock, I injured myself, and then, of course, the supervisor came and now they've asked me to collect my papers.' He reached under the table and pulled out the bottle, but it was empty. He threw it in the bin. 'I've got just enough for the tram,' Schlappner sighed, wiping his face with the sleeve of his jacket.

'Me have rumpy-pumpy today,' Mustafa announced, drawing on his cigarette with relish. Once a month two old whores would do the rounds of his hostel. 'Schlappner, rumpy-pumpy too? Better than cider.'

'Leave me alone,' Schlappner whined. 'I'd just found two horses that were guaranteed to win me something and now I can't put any money on them.'

'When you go to get your papers you'll get your money too.'

'Yes, and what if I lose that? Then I might as well end it all.'

'I thought the horses were *guaranteed* to win.'

Schlappner put his head in his hands and cried silently. Mustafa smoked and smiled dreamily. Then Kleinschmidt came back, and when he found out what had happened to Schlappner he, too, smiled. Fritz was right: we all needed our Mexico. But the way there was further than to Cuernavaca, and no one knew where to get the tickets.

forty-three

I got off the train at Koblenz. A cloudless sky over the Deutsche Eck. West German army reservists with straw hats and beer breath. And the Rhine, too, and steamers and the MS *Vaterland* on its way to Bonn, with on-board band, German wine and day-trippers. But I wasn't a day-tripper. I was on my way to my first reading.

She met me at the barrier. A rather timid young creature with mousy hair and glasses and a bilious green jumper that accentuated her thin arms, and a body which could have done with a little flesh and muscle. Jeans. The voice, however, was just as erotic as the one that had wrenched me from my sleep a few afternoons previously.

'Am I speaking to Harry Gelb, the author of *Stamboul Blues*?'

'That's who I was last night. What's this about?'

'I got your number from your publisher; he said you'd definitely do a reading for us.'

'And where is that?'

'In Montabaur, we've got a little club where we do events. It's not so easy to organise cultural activities in the country, but we've had good people here in the past …'

She reeled off a few names, I knew them all from Aldo

Moll's info sheets. Well, they probably knew me from those sheets, too: Harry Gelb, author of *Ice Box* and *Stamboul Blues*. The voice was full of such promise that I agreed straightaway; I had another day off in any case. Montabaur, somewhere up in the Westerwald, fresh air and eager girls, and at some point you had to stand up in front of readers, the test of the public, have the raw heart of your poetry torn from your body, for travel expenses and a fee.

There she stood with a copy of *Stamboul Blues* and she still had an erotic voice. Her name was Gerda and she worked at the post office in Koblenz.

'We need to get a bus now,' said Gerda, who didn't seem to be too taken by me, either. And I'd put on my best white nylon shirt, my Trevira trousers were freshly ironed, and after my shift I'd been a good boy and gone home for a few hours' kip. But Gerda had probably been expecting a curly-haired hippie with an earring, filthy fingernails and patched jeans, who'd immediately offer her a joint and rave about the Paradiso in Amsterdam.

'I'd really love a beer,' I said.

She gave me a wary look, but then led us across the square in front of the station to the café inside Hertie. She ate an ice-cream, I drank a half litre. Obviously the sweat started to appear on my forehead at once, and my shirt went damp around the chest. Gerda looked as if she were already wondering how she could best get rid of me. I offered her a Camel, but she didn't smoke either. I paid. We left. It was only four o'clock. The reading had been scheduled for eight.

The bus was jammed. Commuters, farmers, market traders, housewives, army, and in the middle of all these an employee from the security industry on his way to a poetry reading. I'd wandered around this area as an adolescent, since when it had become substantially populated – entire desert-red estates of plain, prefabricated houses, then the bungalows on the hillsides, the access roads, marked-out motorway routes, hypermarkets, shopping centres, furniture warehouses, and the army had expanded, too, with all its related apparatus, from rocket stations to ten-pin bowling alley. I observed it all for half an hour, then asked Gerda what sort of club it was that had organised the reading.

'Oh, we're a sort of youth education club,' she said. 'We've got a number of groups, literature, film, theatre, sport … it's very progressive for Montabaur.'

'So who's behind it?'

Another wary look. 'No one's behind it, we organise it all ourselves. We had more than a hundred people at our recent reading, and he read exceptionally well, too. Do you know him? He's with the same publisher as you.'

I knew who she was talking about. He was a load of bollocks. If something like that could be a success, then the municipal hall would be too small for me.

'Yes,' I said. 'I know Montabaur is Catholic, but it's not the Church or CDU that manages it, is it?'

'Not directly,' Gerda said. 'Do you actually live off your writing?'

I desperately needed a beer, a beer and something stronger. So, I was going to be reading at the young conservatives. From part-time anarchist to Catholic cut-up. We were getting closer to Montabaur. The town looked positively wary, too.

'Not directly,' I said. 'I've got another source of income.'

For the first time her face assumed an expression of curiosity. 'So what do you do?'

'I work in the security industry,' I replied, looking out at the road, the tower blocks, the terraced houses, the half-timbered houses, downtown Montabaur.

It was ages till eight o'clock. I suggested a meeting-point so I could fit in a pub crawl beforehand. 'I mean, I'd like to take a look around Montabaur,' I said. But Gerda wasn't having any of it. She suspected that I'd take the first bus back if she let me out of her sight for a second. Instead we went to visit some other people from this dubious group, there was tea and liver-sausage sandwiches, and they played records, Lou Reed's junkie sound was popular in Montabaur too, the electro industry had everywhere in its clutch, whether on Lexington Avenue or Koblenzer Strasse. These young people could be in the young conservatives, the local folklore society, the transport union or Red Student Action – what would be the difference? They were part of it. I was part of it too. The age of reproduction spared nobody.

The event was held at the community centre next to a church. Oh yes, the Church looked after its sheep; everything was there, from a cinema and table-tennis tables to a bierkeller, with beer at one mark per bottle, though artists giving talks could sup for free. I got going straightaway and took a glimpse at the audience, the audience for my first ever reading. My predecessor had drawn in a hundred people, there were definitely fewer for me; I wasn't a big hit yet in Montabaur. On average they were around eighteen years old, mostly charming young rural types who'd grown up in houses their families owned and so were keen on increasing their inherited advantages, sturdy and jovial, you could already see the fat necks and double chins of future master craftsmen and majors in the reserve, candidates for the regional parliament and provincial brothel madams, but even here in Montabaur there were a few faces in which you could detect something different: the restless eyes of those who'd soon be out of here.

'Right, Herr Gelb,' said the youth pastor, who was wearing a black scarf and a blue roll-neck pullover. 'If you don't mind, we'll attend to a few internal matters first. OK, children, quiet please, what is there to discuss this evening? Our film week. Horst, over to you!'

It took them three-quarters of an hour to chew through their internal matters. The culture of associations and clubs was blossoming, and it was also blossoming in Montabaur Catholic Youth Club. Here, too, there was constraint, dissent, a cash-flow situation, shrinking membership, public relations work, the technical side of things, practice for future tasks, democracy, Church, state. And to ensure that procreation was not forgotten, the girls were already allowed to wear skimpy bras, stretch jeans, blonde locks and red lips, to get the boys horny for their wedding day, to make them aware that they had to hold on if the Russians invaded. A cultural event like this, therefore, was not a bad thing; they could clearly see where things might lead if they didn't stick at it. Antisocial behaviour made people think and perhaps convinced one or two waverers to join in with the cultural work of the young conservatives rather than leave the herd and become a heroin-fuelled poet.

Eventually they'd settled or deferred all the points on their agenda. I read. I'd had a few beers by this stage; for their fifty-mark fee – 'Herr Gelb, we are only a youth club, you know,' the pastor had explained – they were going to get a good show. I read a chapter from *Stamboul Blues*, I read about Tophane, the foghorns over the Golden Horn, the opium dens, the needles that snapped off in arms, the addicts, the paranoia and the corpses, the staccato sentences from Düstere Strasse, from Schmargendorf City. Nobody had ever talked about these things in Montabaur before, and nobody would in the near future, either. I read like there was no tomorrow. Then I took a short break and drank another beer. My nylon shirt was drenched in sweat, scrunched-up paper tissues formed wet lumps in my trouser pockets. My audience seemed slightly baffled, as baffled as the editors who had once written me off: 'We're unable to …', 'A little beyond reality …' 'Right,' I said, wiping my mouth, 'now a few poems.' When I looked at the clock I saw I'd been reading for more than an hour. I folded up my pieces of paper. 'Thank you,' I said. 'I've had my fill. I hope you have too.'

Some laughed. But I hadn't yet earned my fifty marks. The pastor opened the discussion.

'Well,' he said, 'what we've just heard is somewhat different from the usual fare at our literary events. I'm thinking of the young man from the literature working group or the recent satirical reading. I don't suppose that was satire, was it, Herr Gelb?' He got more laughs than me. 'If we want to classify that, then the models that come to mind are American, taking Jack Kerouac as a prime example.'

I stuck to my beer. I hadn't counted on a discussion. The goal of the discussion appeared to be to humiliate the author, it was the moment in which those with B grades in German opened their mouths and set about criticising the language of others. Was it good German, these chopped-up sentences? Could you expect the reader to follow it all? And was that poetry or was it actually prose, and indeed a rather crude prose, I have to say, not even everyday language, but tarted-up language, and the sexual content, does it have to be spelled out so blatantly, it was misogynistic somehow, and then all the social references were missing in the text. That's entertainment, I thought, that's literature; for fifty marks you have to fall to your knees and say, I'm a total idiot, a good-for-nothing, an antisocial misogynist, a danger to public order. It's your own fault, I thought, for falling for an anonymous erotic voice on the telephone. That was it: you let your heart be torn apart, but all the willing girls were already taken by the committee of the local young conservatives and the smart bookshop apprentices. And the fresh air in the countryside wasn't all it was cracked up to be.

Then they took me back to Koblenz to catch the last train. Gerda didn't show her face again. The pastor drove an old VW, and two boys who'd liked my work came with us, two boys with long hair and well-worn leather jackets, who probably had the local drug scene under control and now were unsure whether they should offer me some of their home-grown grass. I imagine I'd sucked at the beer bottle with excess abandon.

'Where can we meet you in Frankfurt?'

'Usually at the Schmale Handtuch.'

'Oh, is that where the scene is now?'

'Well, you could say that.'

I told them where the Schmale Handtuch was.

'Great, we'll drop by some day.'

'You write such sharp-edged stuff,' the other one said. 'But you're not so active any more.'

'It's OK,' I said.

'Don't you think,' the youth pastor said, 'that literature has a social function too, especially seeing the ruptures that are taking place in the countryside, the changes that have occurred so quickly where nothing had changed in decades before?'

'Hmm,' I said. 'With literature, everyone thinks they know what it's good for. The ones who write often have quite different problems.'

'I was in a mainstream job once too,' the pastor said. 'I worked in the furniture business in Frankfurt, then I moved to social work; in my job now you definitely need that sort of experience. I believe that literature – art – needs to integrate itself better into social processes ...'

At last we arrived at the station in Koblenz.

'There's still the matter of my fee,' I said.

'Oh yes,' the youth pastor said. 'It would have been quite something if we'd forgotten that, I mean you really earned that money, didn't you, judging by the sweat on your brow?'

He paid me the fifty marks. I bid them goodbye. It was still half an hour till my train, but the only pub in the area was a Wienerwald, and I didn't feel I should have to put up with that as well. I sat in the station concourse. It was still very busy, particularly around the gentlemen's toilet. Guys with pinned-up hair, platform shoes and crocodile hand-bags; the station loo was Koblenz's pick-up joint. When the train arrived, some of the rent boys got on. Business in Wiesbaden, business in Frankfurt. The night was still young.

Frankfurt am Main central station. I stood by the window, watching the city piece itself together again. Half a day in the country and you were already craving the railway tracks, the signal boxes, the Togal sign above the trains in sidings, the soot, the noise, the seagulls, the howling, the face of the masses into which you could disappear to preserve your own face.

On the platform I took a deep breath; I knew no smell that meant more to me than that of the city. Feeling hungry, I gobbled down a beef sausage. That smelled good too. I slowly wandered through the concourse, I took in the noises, I gathered snapshots. Uniformed Negroes were dancing to the music of their transistor radios, an old tramp was having a quarrel with station police, electric trolleys were bringing the mail sacks to the trains, at the beer stall Yugoslavs were shouting out for one final glass. A beau circling a rent boy, whores in heels twisting their ankles, pickpockets outside the bank counter, elegant women with stand-offish expressions on the arms of men in the no-parking zone, Indian families with squadrons of children and luggage trolleys, and outside the night with the tempest of sirens.

It was already half past midnight, I was still thirsty; that sort of reading, that literary activity made you thirstier than writing. At this hour the Schmale Handtuch didn't let anyone in. I could still make it to the Greek place, the

Traube, the Fass, but they'd soon be closed too. I had the feeling that if I went home too early I'd get the willies, I'd start throwing cans of beer or books out of the window. I took a tram to the Zeil and turned into Hasengasse. On the corner were pubs with night-time concessions until three, and if you needed to keep going after that the Salzhaus wasn't far, and then the station district, wipeout. Tönges-gasse, I could already see a sign. I thought of Fritz, maybe he too was on his way to a cantina to drink mescal, the last glass before sobriety, a glass which hopefully never empties.

'A Pils and a double Scotch,' I said when I sat down at the bar. The guy at the beer tap eyed me up, but I passed muster, even here where the drinking was more cultivated, there were crown glass windows and muted light, and food still available: spare ribs and rissoles, fleischwurst and cabbage. Animated dancing and the jukebox playing Satchmo, the old Jambalaya – the sort of nigger everyone wanted. The double Scotch was a hearty draught.

'Another double Scotch,' I ordered, gradually taking notice of the other customers at the bar and in the alcoves – this was more like Frankfurt night life, all show and no substance, but the woman who was coming closer to me had pretty blue eyes and a cleavage which could even distract a man who'd long drunk his last glass. Harry, stay on the Scotch, I told myself.

'Hey, don't I know you?'

I recognised the voice. I put down my beer glass and took a closer look at the woman. Blonde, blue eyes, slightly rugged face, those cheekbones … I felt myself starting to smile.

'Communist Student Union? Squat?'

'Well,' she said, 'you really *have* changed.'

So Gertrud hadn't stuck it out with the Maoists; the easy life had triumphed. I looked over her shoulder at the people behind her, but Fred and his monkey weren't there.

'Those are friends of mine,' she said. 'We go bowling together on Wednesdays.'

'I see. And what are you doing? I mean ...'

'I've got a boutique in Sandweg, children's stuff mainly ...'

'Unbelievable. And Fred? I mean, you remember that guy you had the trouble with ...'

'Oh, Fred,' she said dismissively. 'He's been inside for ages. He really bit off far more than he could chew; he lacked any business savviness.'

'And what about politics? I don't mean to offend you, but you were quite firmly committed ...'

She lit a cigarette. Smoking was something she'd always done. A diamond was sparkling on one of her fingers. Nothing large, a diamond you could wear out bowling.

'What do you mean?' she said. 'I'm still committed, if you want to put it that way. It's just that now I'm rather more committed to myself than to the Chinese.'

'Another double Scotch,' I said, and we clinked glasses. She was drinking sekt.

'So what are you doing now?'

'Well,' I said, 'I'm writing.'

'So what are you writing?'

'I've published a novel, and there's a volume of poetry coming out in autumn.'

'And you can live off that?'

'Oh, it all adds up. I'm sure you earn more with a boutique. But I always wanted to write. And if you gradually get a hold on it then you know why you're doing it.'

'Oh, right. Talking of literature, do you know who I bumped into in town recently when I was shopping? Bernadette.'

'While shopping?'

'Yes, she was just paying a brief visit from Paris. She got married.'

'To whom? Sartre?'

'No, but he is researching Goethe – isn't that funny?'

'Yes, it is funny.'

She stayed a while longer, but I wasn't really listening any more, then she vanished with her companions, and I started drinking in earnest, to life in general and to Goethe research in particular, especially French Goethe research. Well, I was a researcher too, and now the focus of my research was where I was going to get the money from to pay my bill; I'd had enough of this night.

'That's ninety-six marks, mate,' I heard him say, 'and here you've only got sixty plus a bit of shrapnel; what am I meant to make of that?'

'Well, you can see how badly poetry readings are paid,' I said. 'But it doesn't matter, I'll come past tomorrow and pay the rest; I've got a good job, you know, I work for Germania, OK?'

'You're not going to show your face here ever again,' someone said, before laying into me with fists and feet. Just make sure you don't fall on the ground, I thought. I held on to my glasses and got another kick to the stomach, then I was lying outside. So this was the pavement. I'd tasted plenty worse, but I didn't want to get used to it either. I looked for my glasses until I realised that I was holding them. I put them back on. Close up, this pavement looked interesting, there was even a crack running through the asphalt, and through the crack a blade of grass was growing. If that's the case, I told myself, you can get up too.